HAUNTED

AWAKENING BOOK THREE

JACQUELINE BROWN

Cover art designed by Aero Gallerie

Also by Jacqueline Brown

The Light, Book One of The Light Series
Through the Ashes, Book Two of The Light Series
From the Shadows, Book Three of The Light Series
Into the Embers, Book Four of The Light Series
Out of the Darkness, Book Five of The Light Series
"Before the Silence," a Light Series Short Story

Awakening, Book One
Gifted, Book Two of the Awakening Series

Altered, Book One

To receive your free copy of "Before the Silence," please
join the mailing list or visit
www.Jacqueline-Brown.com.

For the Church Triumphant

~ pray for us.

My ragged breath broke the stillness of the night. Across the room, golden embers crackled against the ashen bricks of the fireplace. Golden like the flecks in *her* green eyes.

My breathing was fast, too fast.

I inhaled, forcing the air deep into my lungs. I needed to calm down. I pushed my hair back—it was soaked ... I was soaked.

Why did I keep having this dream? She was so close and yet so far ... I couldn't reach her ... couldn't get to her in time. *He* reached her first, every time. The man with the dark eyes that held only evil. His skin was white like mine, his hair black and straight. Her skin was as brown as Luca's. And those eyes, the memory of her eyes ... eyes just like mine and Luca's.

Terror was all I felt ... all she felt.

Footsteps echoed off the floor and my bedroom door swung open.

"Are you okay?" Luca said, his voice higher pitched from fear.

He crossed the space between the door and my bed in three long strides. He sat beside me, and I clung to him. He was my lifeline—the tether that kept me from losing my mind to the world of my dreams.

He asked, "Was it the same as before?"

I could feel his heart beating almost as fast as mine. "Wh-why do I keep dreaming of her … of *him*?" I shuddered, trying to force the girl's ragged breaths from my memory.

"I don't know," Luca said. His arms wrapped protectively around me.

But he couldn't protect me from my dreams, no one could. They came without permission, forcing their way into my consciousness, terrifying me when I slept and haunting me while I was awake.

It had been a week now and every night ended the same way: me shivering, Luca holding me, the little girl from my dreams …. I whimpered.

"You're safe now," Luca said.

"She's not." I gripped him. "She's not safe. Whoever she is, he's hunting her and she can't escape." My tears were soaking his shirt. "She can feel him," I said, gasping for breath between the tears.

"What?" Luca asked, pushing back a little so he could see me.

"When he approaches, she knows he's evil as soon as she sees him. Her face changes immediately. She's terrified. She goes from a happy little girl to terrified prey in a moment. She can feel him … she has your gift."

He was silent. What could he say? What could either of us say? A child who had our eyes, who had his gift … a child who looked like the perfect combination of Luca and me was being hunted and we weren't there to protect her.

"We don't know who that child is or what your dream means. You're exhausted and so am I. We need to sleep so we can think more clearly."

"I try to sleep, but then he's there," I said.

"You need to try again," he said, kneeling beside my bed and helping me lie back. He pulled my quilt up and then one of the blankets my mom had made, on top of it. "I'll stay here for a while. You'll be okay."

I pressed the back of my head into the pillow. "Luca, what if my dream isn't wrong? What if she is who I think she is and she's being hunted?"

He shook his head. "Shh, you need to rest."

"But what if it's real?" I asked.

He was kneeling beside me, tucking the corners of the blanket around my chin. His expression hardened. "If she is who you think she is, we will protect her," he said, his voice strong and unafraid. "Our child will never be hunted."

I got the sense that though he was speaking to me, his words were meant for someone else.

Two

"Aaahh," I moaned, pulling my body away from my sister, whose freckled nose was practically touching mine. "What're you doing in my room?" I asked, staring at Avi, my way too energetic nine-year-old baby sister.

Avi's breath tickled my nose. "I was checking on you. When I saw Luca still sound asleep in his room, I figured you had another nightmare."

"You went to Luca's room?" My voice was hoarse from sleep.

"I wanted someone to play with and he's always awake way before you and Lisieux," Avi said as if it made perfect sense for her to go into Luca's room first thing in the morning.

"Isn't today Saturday?" I asked.

"Yes."

"He doesn't work on Saturday."

"That's the point," she said, blinking her emerald-green eyes at me.

"You should let him sleep in on Saturdays." I pushed myself up.

Her demeanor shifted. "Did you have that dream again?"

"Ugh," I groaned, and fell back against the pillows.

"Was it just as awful?"

Her voice sounded oddly mature when she wanted it to be. I nodded, my hair making a rustling sound against the pillows.

I felt bad that Avi knew about the dream in the first place. I hadn't meant to tell her, but she was the first one in my room the first night it happened. I was too panicked to think clearly, so I told her everything and she repeated it to everyone else when the rest of them arrived a few seconds later. Everyone except our dad, who could sleep through anything.

That was back when Luca also slept soundly … before he had to protect me every night from the boogeyman. Now he was in my room before I could even fully wake up. Some nights he was the one who woke me from the haunting dreams.

"It seems weird that you keep having the same awful dream," she said, her forehead pulled into little wrinkles as she tried to understand.

"People have bad dreams sometimes," I said, not wanting to discuss this with her, especially while still waking up.

She shook her head sorrowfully from side to side, saying in a solemn voice, "In a different family, it would be a simple bad dream. In our family—"

"Why do you talk like that?" I asked, sitting up.

"How should I talk?" she asked, tilting her head, her voice less ominous.

"Like the little girl you are."

"You're dreaming of a *little* girl being hunted. I don't want to be a *little* girl," she said flatly.

I stared at her. "It's a good thing to be a little girl," I said.

"Is it? It doesn't seem like it," she said, her clear green eyes staring back at me.

I felt my shoulders slump forward. "This is too much for so early in the morning."

I took the sweatshirt from the end of the bed and slipped it over the T-shirt I wore. Avi followed me as we made our way down the stairs.

The kitchen was flooded with sunlight and the smell of fresh blueberry bread. Thank goodness for Jason and Sam living here. Ever since the fire destroyed their home, Luca and his aunt and uncle had been living with us. Almost as soon as they arrived, Jason took over as the primary cook. It wasn't until the coldest part of winter—when we did our best not to leave the house—that he started showing off his baking skills.

Very soon after that, Jason's Baked Goods was born. A welcome and unexpected career change for him, but one he had secretly dreamed of for many years. All it took was encouragement and a bit of seed money from Gigi to get him to embrace his God-given gifts … gifts each of us is enormously grateful for on a daily basis. His creations have been so sought after that he already hired two other guys to help him.

"Where is Jason?" I asked, cutting a piece of bread and turning on the stove to heat the water in the kettle.

"Him and Sam went down to check on their house. Gigi went with them. She'll probably find something else the house absolutely must have, that will delay the move another few weeks. Like she did with the crown molding," Avi said with a grin, shoving crumbled blueberry bread into her mouth.

Our copper-colored, furry mutt, Jackson, stretched from where he was snoozing in his bed and wandered over to lick up the crumbs Avi was dropping all over the floor.

Avi was right about Gigi; she was a master at delaying the completion of Sam and Jason's house. When Mr. Jones was hired to rebuild the house that Thomas had burned down, the contractor said it would take four months max, even with winter weather delays. But we were now going on eight months.

Once Gigi learned how much Jason loved to bake, she had the kitchen redesigned to accommodate three ovens—something Sam and Jason were both opposed to, but Gigi assured them was a practical necessity. And since she was paying for it and it was on our property, she had the final say. After all, she was the one who built the original house because the shack Jason's squatter parents constructed wasn't fit for humans, especially humans with a young child trying to survive the Maine winter. Now that Jason's parents were long gone, and Jason, Sam, and Luca were essentially part of the family, Gigi was spoiling them as much as she spoiled the rest of us. Which is why she insisted the footprint of the house needed to be at least a thousand square feet bigger than the original, in order to accommodate a separate bathroom for the master bedroom, a third bedroom, and the much larger kitchen.

Two weeks before, when the house was almost complete, she said it absolutely needed crown molding in every room. There was no doubt she was down there now, doing her best to think up something else to delay them from moving out of our home. But to be fair, none of her changes came close to causing the delay that the skating rink build-out had caused. When Dad pulled Mr. Jones and his team off the house and asked them to focus on the skating rink, it caused months of delay. None of us, including Sam or Jason, were upset about it.

The kettle whistled, and I poured its contents over the chai tea bag in my mug. I took it and the slice of blueberry bread to the table. I held the hot mug as the tea steeped. The daytime temperatures were warm, but the nights were always cold in Maine.

Avi took some more bread and bounced her way over to the table, Jackson following at her heels. "Will you play with me now?"

I groaned. "I'm barely moving."

"Ugh, I'm so bored," she said, flopping onto the bench opposite me. Her unbrushed red hair almost reached the floor.

"There are moments, like this one, when I actually miss the calm, mopey Avi," I said.

"I do not!" she said.

"You have so much energy so early in the morning," I said.

"Siena, it's 9:00 a.m. I have been up for three hours, and it's practically lunchtime. This is not a lot of energy for lunchtime," Avi said, slapping the table with her hands.

I sipped my tea. I could drink espresso all day long and not be half as active as she was with no caffeine.

She leaned forward onto the table. "So, what do you think the dream means?"

She was staring at me with large, unblinking eyes. It was all I could do to not shiver at her expression.

"What's the deal with the not blinking?" I asked, trying to sound unrattled by her expression though it was freaking me out.

She gave me a tiny smirk. "I'm working on my 'intense stare.' "

"No need to practice, you're already a master." I sipped my tea.

She grinned. "Thank you, but don't try to distract me. What do you think the dream means?"

"You had the dream again?" Lisieux asked from the stairwell.

I moaned and slid lower on the seat. "It's just a silly dream." I wished I'd never told Avi.

Sitting next to Avi, Lisieux yawned, her brown wavy hair sticking up in different directions. She didn't resemble Avi and me, except for her green eyes and ghostly white skin, which we got from our mom.

"This is our family," she said, "and it's *you*. If Avi or I were having the dream, it might be silly and mean nothing, though probably not if we were having it every night for a week. But it's definitely not nothing if *you* are having it."

"What do you think it means?" Avi asked, now focused on Lisieux.

"It seems like there's a connection to evil that hasn't been broken," Lisieux said thoughtfully as she took the rest of the blueberry bread from my plate.

"I was eating that," I said.

"We broke Dad's curse," Avi said, with a sort of academic interest in the conversation with Lisieux.

Lisieux put the rest of the bread into her mouth. "Yes, the curse Dad made was broken, I think at least, but what about all the stuff before him?"

"The stuff before him?" Avi asked with great interest.

I cringed.

"It's not like our great-great-grandparents were good people," Lisieux said, pondering as she spoke. "Gigi's grandmother was the one who did the curse with Dad, after all. It doesn't seem like all of that would be washed away simply because the curse was."

"That was five generations ago," I said, no longer interested in the blueberry bread.

"Yeah, and our family isn't like that anymore. We're good now," Avi said.

"True, we have the sacraments and sacramentals to help us, but there are still spiritual laws, same as there are physical ones," Lisieux said while munching.

I said, "God created those laws to help us, not hurt us."

Lisieux licked her fingers, saying, "Of course he created them to help us. Everything was done out of love for us, but laws are still laws. If you go against them, you can be hurt. It's why farmers plant in sunlight, not in a forest. Crops need sunlight to grow. It's a law. Nothing personal against tomato plants planted in full shade, but they're going to fail."

Avi lifted her eyes to mine, her voice somber. "It's like if you jump off a cliff, you die."

I felt heat flush my face and my pale skin turned red as I tried and failed to force the memory of Thomas falling from the cliff out of my mind.

Lisieux said softly, "The point is, physical laws can hurt us too. And being unaware of them doesn't mean they don't affect you. A child can still be hurt by a hot stove."

"Or a frozen pond," Avi added intensely.

I shivered at the memory of almost drowning.

Lisieux continued, mildly oblivious to Avi and me. "Physical laws are like spiritual laws. Our family broke the law. If our family had been good for generations, it would offer some form of residual goodness, but it wasn't. It was bad. So we have residual badness."

Avi said, "Grandfather George wasn't bad."

"No, he was the good one, and from what Gigi has told us, his family was good," Lisieux responded. "In truth, it's his side, his and Mom's that allows us to have any chance at all."

"A chance at what?" I asked.

"Not being evil," Avi said, her green eyes unblinking.

I shivered. "Why are you so creepy? You didn't used to be this creepy."

A broad grin formed across her face. "I'm trying out creepy. What do you think?"

"I think if you don't want to seem evil, don't be so creepy," I said, leaning against the seat.

"Hmm, I'll consider that." She appeared to be taking my words seriously.

Luca's footsteps were heavy on the stairs. "Good morning," he said, running his hands through his curly hair, the same sort of curly hair as the girl from my dream.

I sipped my tea, concentrating on its warmth to avoid thinking of my dream.

"Good morning," Avi called out cheerfully.

"You're so weird," I said to Avi. How she could flip from totally creepy to totally normal in half a second was beyond me.

Luca studied us for a moment and then went to the fresh blueberry bread. He cut a piece about half a loaf thick and came and sat beside me.

"Do I want to know what you three were talking about?" he asked.

"Probably not," Avi said sincerely.

"I figured," he said, taking a bite of the bread.

It was amazing how much his body had changed since living with us and being able to eat as much as he liked. Working with Mr. Jones wasn't hurting him either. He worked hard every day with Mr. Jones's team, on whatever project they were doing, which lately had been Sam and Jason's house, as well as the skating rink build-out. The combination of food and manual labor meant that Luca had gone from gauntly thin, when I first met him, to gorgeously muscular.

Every time Luca and I went anywhere, I was reminded how attractive he was. All the girls smiled a little too much and stared a little too long. Luca never seemed to notice, but my sisters and I did. They were fiercely protective of him, and me, and us. In their minds he was already their brother and they would do anything to protect that. I loved them all the more for how they loved us.

Luca stuffed another giant bite of bread into his mouth and almost as quickly swallowed it. He said, "You three promised to take me skating today," as he took another bite.

"It isn't good to swallow food that quickly," Lisieux said. "You need to chew it."

He chewed for twice as long, swallowed, and then gave Lisieux a gorgeous smile that would melt anyone's heart.

She glared at him sternly and said, "That was not enough chewing either."

He used his fork to cut a smaller bite and said, "I promise to chew if you promise to go get ready."

"It's still early," Lisieux said.

"I'm serious. I've never been skating before, and you three promised to take me today."

"But the day just started," Lisieux said, wrapped in her fuzzy robe.

"It's going to get crowded and crowds aren't my thing. Besides, by the time you get ready, the day will be half over," he said, raising one eyebrow playfully.

Avi said, "I don't take nearly as long as those two."

"Aww, but you will," he teased. "Give it time, young one, give it time."

She giggled. "Come on." She pulled Lisieux and me up. "We don't want to keep our Prince Charming waiting."

Three

Half an hour later I sat in the driver's seat of my BMW, Luca sat beside me, and my sisters behind us.

"I love how green everything is starting to turn," Luca said, eyeing the tiny buds popping out everywhere.

Avi asked, "Does it remind you of Florida?"

Luca laughed. "It reminds me of Florida three months ago. The seasons here are way different."

"Do you miss it?" Lisieux asked.

He turned to face them. "Yeah, parts of it. I'm glad to be here with you all, but I miss it."

"You mean you're glad to be here with *Siena*." Avi had said my name in a sing-songy way.

"No, I mean I'm glad to be here with *all* of you. I wouldn't leave any of you, not for all the warm, sunny weather in the world."

I took his hand in mine. I loved him for so many reasons and his love of my sisters was at the top of the list. I drove past the streets that led to our church and the center of town. His love for our shared faith was also at the top of the list.

As we neared the farthest boundary of our town, I turned down a street that took us away from the ocean. The trees were thick leading up to the newly paved parking lot. Everything about the skating rink, except for the outside of the building, was new; even the idea of it was only a few months old.

It was a few weeks after Christmas, when we were sitting with Jody and her husband, Dave, after Mass. We were watching Avi pretend to roller-skate with their two young kids, and Jody said how it had always been her dream to open a roller-skating rink. Dad, being Dad, jumped on the idea. He already had the building and the perfect general contractor, Mr. Jones. The added bonus was that when Dad pulled him off Jason and Sam's house to work on the skating rink, it meant Luca and his aunt and uncle had to keep living with us a few extra months.

The extra added bonus was that when Jody and Dave mentioned they wanted to have a coffee shop and offer baked goods at the skating rink, Gigi knew exactly who they should partner with. Since they were completely renovating an old building, it was easy to add an industrial kitchen perfect for Jason's Baked Goods. A fantastically yummy partnership was born.

The previous weekend marked the grand opening and it was a huge success. Luca, Sam, and I stayed away due to the crowds … and the demons that often go along with crowds, but the rest of the family said the whole town was there and everyone loved it. Jody and Dave wanted the rink to be a gathering place for people of all ages, especially young families like theirs. So it's a bright, inviting space with a ton of natural light, lots of vibrant colors, an indoor play area for little kids, a mini ninja course for bigger kids, the café that sells the best bakery items in town, and of course a skating rink in the center.

"Isn't it so pretty!" Avi exclaimed, admiring the taupe building with brightly colored pink, purple, and blue stripes angling across it.

"You did an excellent job helping to pick out the colors," Luca said, putting his hand on Avi's shoulder.

She leaned against him. "Thanks," she said.

We pulled open the glass doors, and Jody waved to us. She was busy with barista duties, so we went straight to the skate counter.

"Good morning," Dave said in his typical upbeat way. "Here you go." He handed over skates to a mom with two little kids. "Have fun!"

"Oh, we will," the mom said, carrying the skates as she scooted her kids along.

"Do you think Elle and Noah want to skate?" Avi asked. Dave and Jody's kids were in the indoor play area.

"I'm sure they'd love to," Dave answered.

"Good. I'll go get them," Avi said, skipping off to the play area.

"Do you want your skates?" Dave asked us.

"Yes, please," I said, answering for Luca and Lisieux.

Dave reached behind the counter and handed us the roller skates Gigi had bought us. She'd said it didn't matter how pretty a place was, her grandkids weren't wearing other people's shoes. Luca officially counted as one of her grandkids. In truth, she'd probably choose him over me if there was ever a fight between us. Everyone would.

Luca gazed apprehensively at the skates.

Lisieux said, "I promise, rollerblades are easier than the old-style skates."

"I don't believe you," Luca said. "A square is going to be more stable than a straight line."

"You might think that, but no," Lisieux said, pulling him over to one of the seats.

"Then why does Siena have skates?" Luca countered as I followed them, giggling at his protests.

"Because they're cuter," I said, holding up my yellow lace-up skates with sparkly purple wheels.

Lisieux plopped him into a chair. "Trust me," she commanded as she unstrapped the Rollerblades and helped him put them on.

After she had strapped them up, she asked, "How does that feel?"

Luca moved his feet around. "Not totally awful."

"See, I told you. Let me get you one thing," Lisieux said, looking around and running to retrieve a neon-orange frame, a PVC walker on wheels.

"What's this?" Luca asked.

"It's how you learn. It's like a regular walker, but for skating. See? Some of the kids have them," Lisieux said, pointing to the little ones out on the rink slowly making their way around.

"Yes, but theirs are cute and little. This is like a barricade, and it's even painted to match," Luca said with a groan.

"Cute little kids get cute little walkers, big men get barricades," Lisieux said. "Stand up." She went behind him to help him stand.

Luca got up and his feet threatened to slide out from under him … but the PVC walker supported his weight.

"This is so embarrassing," he said, his arm muscles bulging as he struggled to get his feet beneath him.

"At least you're willing to try new things," I said with a giggle.

"Ignore her," Lisieux said. "She hasn't skated in years, and she's going to wish she had one of these too."

I finished lacing up my skates and rose from the seat. I skated around on the carpet and then stepped onto the rink. It was like I'd never stopped skating—like my mom was right beside me and we were doing the hokey-pokey as we sped around the rink. I only thought of my mom for a moment because in the next moment Luca was edging out onto the rink and I was swerving to miss him. I spun around in a controlled circle.

"What do you think?" I asked.

"I think next time we come I'll stick with Uncle Jace's breakfast sandwiches," he said, gripping the neon-orange barricade that surrounded his legs on three sides.

I laughed and said, "Take your time, go slow, one skate in front of the other."

"That three-year-old just passed me," he whined.

"That's Noah. He's been here every day for weeks, so he should be better than you. Besides, everything is easier when you're that close to the ground."

At that moment Noah tripped. Avi came up behind him and scooped him onto his feet.

"Did that make you feel better?" I asked Luca.

"Maybe a little," he said grudgingly.

"Nice job," Lisieux said as she glided past us. "See? Didn't I tell you Rollerblades are better than skates?"

At that moment Luca stumbled and resumed his death grip on the frame.

"Yeah, way better," he said sarcastically.

Despite Luca's apprehension, he learned fast—or fast for someone who wasn't a kid. After a few times around the rink he no longer needed his giant barricade, and after a few more rounds he even let go of the wall for a few seconds at a time.

"What do you think? A new Saturday staple?" I asked as the song "Walk Like an Egyptian" came over the speakers.

Luca grimaced. "I don't think I can handle this much fun every Saturday," he said, stumbling. His hands gripped the rail.

I stifled laughter. "Come on, I want a tea and you need a scone," I said, taking his hand in mine and gently leading him through the middle of the rink.

He grasped my hand with a death grip. His face was tense and his legs were locked so I was pulling him along.

Avi twirled around us. "He needs a break."

I smiled. "That's where I'm taking him."

"You want me to push?"

"No!" Luca sharply replied as she reached for his back.

I grinned at Avi. "I've got him."

"Okay," she said, giggling as she skated around us before leaving to find a friend.

We reached the opening in the rink. "There, we made it," I said.

He clung to me as he lifted his feet onto the carpet. He was breathing hard. "I like … the carpet."

"Yes, it is nice," I said as if I was talking to a child.

I led him to a bench nearby. He moaned as he carefully sat down.

I kissed his lips lightly. "You can take off your skates. I'm done torturing you … for this morning, at least."

"Thank goodness." He slumped back.

I could sense him watching me as I glided off to get our shoes. When I returned, he had his Rollerblades off and was hunched over, exhausted.

From behind him Lisieux hopped gracefully from the rink onto the carpet and glided toward us with her twin best friends behind her.

"You look rough," Lisieux said to Luca.

"Not falling is hard work," he said, leaning on his legs. His head angled upward and a few curls fell in front of his eyes.

Lisieux's friends giggled. Girls were always giggling at Luca. When you're gorgeous, apparently even the least amusing statements become hilarious.

"Oh, come on," Lisieux said as she shook her head in exasperation at her friends and went toward the bakery bar.

"That was funny," Luca said, arguing with my unspoken thoughts. "I agree, it's weird when they giggle and I'm not being funny. But that was funny."

I gave him a placating smile. "Yes, it was a tiny bit funny."

"More than a tiny bit," he said, taking the shoes I handed to him.

When we both had our shoes on, I said, "Come on," and helped him stand.

"That feels so weird."

"What?"

"The ground." He was moving slowly.

"Now, that's funny."

"I wasn't trying to be funny."

"That's what makes it funny." I kissed his cheek.

We slipped our skates behind the skating counter. Standing in the bakery line, we were a few people behind Lisieux and the twins. Her friends took turns glancing at Luca and whispering to one another. Lisieux jabbed them in irritation.

He whispered to me, "Why do they do that? Do I have something on my face?"

I took his hand and leaned against him. "They do it because they're fifteen-year-old girls and you're gorgeous."

"So you say," Luca said, not convinced.

"The fact that you don't know it makes you all the more beautiful," I said, wrapping my arms around him.

He leaned into me. "Shoot, they're out of Uncle Jace's breakfast sandwiches," he said, releasing me.

I peered around the woman in front of us. He was right; there wasn't much left. "I guess that's a good thing," I said.

He rubbed his stomach. "Not for me."

"They've had a steady crowd here all morning," I said.

"Have they? I didn't notice. I was concentrating too hard on not falling," Luca said.

I laughed.

"Who knew I was so hilarious," Luca said, stepping forward to the front of the line.

I asked, "Want to share a scone?"

Luca raised an eyebrow.

"You're right, that was silly of me to ask," I said.

"Can we please have two blueberry scones and a chai tea?"

"And a cup of water, please," Luca added.

"How did he do?" Jody called while she was steaming the milk for my tea.

"Great," I said, grinning.

Luca groaned.

"You did do great for your first time ever skating," I said.

"Maybe," Luca said.

"You did," I said gently, bumping my hip to his.

"If you say so," he said.

Jody handed me my tea. "Enjoy," she said before whirling around to work on the next order.

We sat at one of the tables in the center of the indoor eating area. Luca drank half his water and then started on his scone. I sipped the hot tea, enjoying the rich flavor and watched Avi twirling in the middle of the rink.

"This place got crowded," Luca said between bites. "Looks like half the town is here."

I nibbled a bit of my scone. "Are you feeling okay?"

Luca inhaled as if feeling the air. "Yeah, that's the great thing about little kids. They bring such lightness to the air. The adults probably have stuff, but the kids outweigh it."

"There are a ton of kids here," I said.

I leaned back in my chair, holding the cup of tea in both hands. Children were everywhere. Most with parents, some skating in groups or playing together in the indoor play area, parents at tables nearby watching them, chatting with each other.

I sat up straighter, trying to understand what I was seeing.

He watched me with concern, saying, "What is it?"

"That girl."

He swiveled in his seat. "What girl?"

I was standing now, staring at the girl with hair that matched Luca's. She was alone; her green eyes with amber flecks gazed past me. I spun to see what she was looking at. Was the man here, hunting her in this place, this place with so many children? I started to shake. She began moving quickly toward the side doors. I went toward her, but she didn't slow. She moved swiftly from the building—though the doors didn't open. I could see her on the other side of the glass, in the outdoor seating area. I dodged young skaters and made it to the door.

She was still there, inside the fenced seating area. She peered back as if waiting for me. … As if she wanted me to follow her.

Four

I went out the doors. She was now on the other side of the white picket fencing that separated the outside of the café from the parking lot. I unlatched the safety lock and went out the gate. I heard the building doors slam behind me. I turned and exhaled. It was Luca, not the man from my dreams—the man I was sure was nearby.

"What are you doing?" Luca called as he ran through the outdoor dining area. He caught up to me in the parking lot.

"Don't you see her?" I said, not slowing down.

The girl was not walking fast, but somehow I never got closer to her. When she reached the edge of the forest, she turned and stared at me. Her dress was dirty and torn. Her dark curly hair had leaves and twigs stuck in it. Her dress and hair were dripping wet.

I held my hands out … it wasn't raining. Her gaze stopped my approach. Her eyes were breathtaking and full of pain. She was so sorrowful I wanted to cry.

A moment later she turned away, and I watched her thick curly hair disappear into the trees.

Luca gripped my left arm. "Siena, stop."

I tried to pull away. "I have to find her before he does," I said, wrestling my arm from Luca's grasp.

"Who? There's no one here, not in front of you or behind you. There's not a girl or a man—there's no one other than you and me."

I stopped struggling against his hold. The day was bright. Squirrels were calling from the trees above us. He was right; there was no one else. Except the people sitting on the outdoor patio. They were watching us … I'd run out of the building and around their tables into the parking lot, and Luca had chased me and now he held on to my arm. Of course they'd be watching.

I gently wiggled free, saying, "I'm not crazy."

"I don't think that," he said.

"I saw her … the girl from my dreams." I moved to one of the large rocks that marked the edge of the parking area.

"Are you sure?"

"There's no mistaking that hair or those eyes. They're so much like,"—I gulped—"yours … ours."

His expression was worried.

"I have to find her," I said.

"Then I'll go with you." He started into the woods. "Which way?"

I came up beside him. "She went this direction."

With every step I was watching the woods and Luca was watching me, though he was trying to hide it.

In front of us, the woods seemed to go on forever.

After we'd walked a mile or so, Luca asked, "How far do you want to go?"

"There," I said, pointing to an outline of a structure up ahead.

Luca took my hand in his. It was his way of slowing me down and protecting me.

We stood in front of it. "What is it?" I said.

"I think it's the remains of a house or something," Luca said.

We stared down at a large rectangle covered in thick green moss. It was made of stone, but only a foot or so high. Inside the rectangle were the remains of walls and probably the roof.

"This moss is incredible," Luca said, gazing up at the trees.

"It seems to start in the middle and spread out from there," I said. "It looks magical—not in the occult way, but in the …" I struggled for the words.

"Beautifully enchanted way," Luca said.

"Yes." I stood there mesmerized by the carpet of vibrant green moss. "Did someone live here?"

"If they did, it was a very long time ago," Luca said.

"Do you think she was leading us here?"

"If I was a ghost I would live here. If I couldn't be in heaven, I mean," Luca said.

"But she isn't a ghost. She hasn't been born yet," I said, though I felt confused.

He took my hand. "Siena, you don't know that's who she is. You need to keep an open mind."

I laughed. "If my mind was any more open it would float away."

He chuckled and said, "Good point."

"I want to go a little farther." I felt the need to see what was deeper in the forest.

"Lead the way," he said.

We walked side by side through the spring forest, dappled light hitting our eyes from time to time.

Luca said, "This area is so pretty."

"Do you feel anything?" I asked.

He stopped and was silent for a moment. "No. But I wouldn't, without someone being nearby."

"You felt things at the inn," I said, inwardly cringing at the thought of the evil place that had haunted our land for generations.

"The inn was different," he said. "The cursed object with your dad's blood was giving evil a home. The evil was still there. There may have been evil here before, but it's not like I can see what used to be here."

I shuddered. "No, that's *my gift*," I said sarcastically.

"It is a gift," he said softly, "but not one I have. I only feel what's right in front of me, or, sometimes, a faint residual. Demons aren't interested in empty space."

I winced at the mention of demons. "It's hard to think of the woods as empty space," I said.

"You know what I mean. Demons want people, not trees," he said.

In the distance, I heard the call of gulls and the sound of cars.

"Are we near the beach?" I asked. A hint of salt air wafted around us.

"I get so turned around in the woods, I have no idea where we are," Luca said.

The sound of cars increased.

"I suppose we'll find out soon."

The land had a minor rise to it which kept us from seeing straight through the trees. After we crested the subtle hill the sky was open and seagulls circled in the distance.

We had to be close to the ocean. A few more steps and we could see far beyond the trees. The ground sloped down to the road that paralleled the ocean. On the other side was …

"The BayTree," Luca said with concern.

I was shaking. The mere thought of the restaurant that housed memories of those murdered children sent panic through me. Before I started dreaming of the girl, I had dreamt of the children … never seeing them clearly, only whispers of who they'd been. Every night they were there, not doing anything, and, thankfully, not being hurt—but they were always there. I might dream of other things, but in the periphery they were there, watching me. Not speaking, not moving. When they finally disappeared, the girl appeared.

"I had no idea we were near here," I said, feeling sick to my stomach.

"The woods must angle more directly than the road does," Luca said.

The restroom window was open. Near that, the attic window was dark. I stared at it. I didn't realize how centered the attic window was in the roof line and how much larger that window was than the restroom window. They were different styles too. The attic window was old-fashioned, with strips of wood creating the small panes. The restroom window must've been a newer addition. The attic window was the original, which made me wonder how large that space had once been and if it had been an actual room, not just the attic where kidnapped children were kept.

"You okay?" Luca asked.

"Yeah," I said, though we both knew I wasn't.

I didn't want to speak to him about the BayTree. I didn't want to ask if he thought there could be a connection. Of course there wasn't. It was simply a coincidence. Perhaps she'd wanted us to find the moss-covered structure or she'd meant for us to turn in a different direction. Or none of this was real and I was losing my mind.

"Come on, we should get back," Luca said, pulling my elbow. "I'm sure by now your sisters have noticed we're gone."

"Yeah, okay," I said, following him the way we'd come.

As we moved farther into the forest, I realized I was sweating, and not because it was hot out. I unclenched my fists and pulled my hair into a ponytail. My neck was damp. The sea breeze felt good. It reminded me that walking through the woods next to Luca was real and dreams were not.

"There you are!" Avi exclaimed. She and Lisieux were running toward us.

"How did you find us?" Luca asked.

Lisieux held up her phone. "I tracked Siena's phone."

I reflexively touched the phone in my back pocket. "I forgot I had it," I said, grateful for being trackable, at least by my sisters.

"What are you doing out here?" Avi asked, her face concerned.

Luca was silent. He didn't know what to say. Neither did I.

"What happened?" Lisieux asked. "I saw you two at the table and then Luca was suddenly following you out to the patio."

Avi piped up, "Then she told me, and we started tracking you."

Luca looked down at them. "You two shouldn't go into the woods alone, it's not safe. Next time we disappear, call us."

"Next time, have your phones off silent," Lisieux countered.

"Fair enough," Luca said. He pulled his phone out of his front pocket and switched the ringer on. On the screen were five missed calls from Lisieux and one from his aunt Sam. "Did you call Aunt Sam?"

"No," Lisieux answered.

"I bet Jody did," Avi said. "She saw us run out after you."

"What's going on?" Lisieux asked.

Luca glanced at me.

Above us an eagle chirped, circling high overhead.

There was no point in lying to them, so I said, "I saw the girl from my dreams."

Lisieux frowned and said, "You saw her while you were awake?"

I nodded.

"Creepy," Avi said. "Is she here now?"

"No. I didn't see her after she entered the woods."

"Then why are you all the way out here?" Lisieux asked, glancing subtly behind us at the BayTree.

"We kept walking in case we discovered something," Luca said. "We didn't find anything, only the remains of a super old shack and …"—his voice trailed off—"the BayTree."

"Creepy," Avi repeated.

I shuddered.

"You think the girl has something to do with these woods?" Lisieux asked, sounding as if she was trying not to sound skeptical.

Avi said, "Why else would she be here?"

"Because this is where Siena is," Lisieux said.

Something about the way she said it made me think *I* was the problem. Which I was. None of them were dreaming about hunted children, none of them were running out of skating rinks chasing a hallucination.

"It might be something about the woods," Luca said as the skating rink came back into view.

"Lisieux is right," I said, feeling angry at myself. "She was here because of me. The woods don't matter."

"Siena, you don't know that," Luca said.

I grimaced. "I do. She's here because of my mind, not any other reason."

They glanced at one another. I was going crazy and they knew it. They followed me to my car.

"Do you want me to drive?" Luca asked.

I wanted to cry. He really did think I was out of my mind.

"I'm okay to drive," I said, opening the door. I plopped into the seat and started the car.

The rest of them got in. The people at the skating rink's outside tables were staring at us as I pulled out of the parking lot.

Five

I drove in silence, careful to avoid glancing in my rearview mirror and seeing my sisters who were trying but failing to watch me without being noticed.

When we pulled up to the house, my sisters hopped out of the car. I felt relief with them gone, like I had been pretending I was normal and no longer had to pretend.

"I'm going for a walk," I said as I got out of the car, the gravel drive crunching beneath my sneakers.

The smell of fresh-baked cinnamon rolls wafted out the open garage door. "You should go in and get a cinnamon roll," I said to Luca.

"I'll go with you," he said, coming beside me and putting his hands on my shoulders.

"I'd like some time alone, and you'd like a cinnamon roll or whatever incredible creation your uncle has made," I said, forcing a weary grin.

"Are you sure you don't want me to come with you?" he asked.

"I need some time," I said. My mind was racing. I needed to quiet it and I needed to be alone.

He kissed me sweetly on the forehead. "I'll be inside waiting for you and only mildly enjoying whatever Uncle Jace has made," he said with a playful wink.

I hugged him and then released him. I made my way through my backyard, dodging foraging chickens as I went. When I entered the woods, I felt instant relief. I was alone for the first time all day. No one was watching me. I allowed the weight of the day, the girl, the dreams, the children in the attic, to fall on me and not pretend they weren't suffocating me.

For the briefest of moments, I wondered if this was what Luca's mom had felt like. Had it felt like that world was more real than this one? Did she feel like she had no choice? … *There is always a choice,* I heard from deep in my heart. I raised my shoulders and let them drop to shrug off some of the heaviness.

In the distance a dog was barking, the sound startling. Then it stopped. I turned around, feeling as if someone was watching me. No one was there. I turned to one side; it felt as if someone was going to emerge from the trees. I shivered. The dog barked again. It sounded like Jackson and it was coming from the beach. I didn't hesitate. I ran down the trail as quickly as I could. I wasn't sure if I was running more out of fear at whoever or whatever was around me or out of a need to know why Jackson was at the beach. If he was there, someone must be with him. I hadn't gone into the house, so I supposed it could be anyone, but I couldn't think of anyone it would be. Sam only went down there with Jason, and clearly, he was baking. My sisters had just been with us. Dad almost never went to the beach and Gigi barely even went on the trails.

When I reached the edge of the sand, the tree line ended and the sunlight was so bright it made it hard to see. I slowed to a walk and used my hands to shield my eyes. Jackson saw me and ran over to me, bouncing. He was playing—relief swept over me. Whatever he was barking at was not dangerous. He ran from me over to the ashen remains of the inn.

Gigi was there, and gave a faint wave from the rock she sat on.

It was a startling sight. She appeared so frail, leaning forward with her hands on her walking stick, her chin resting on it. As I approached I could tell her eyes were focused on the old stone fireplace, the only thing left of the burned-down inn.

Jackson bounced beside me as I neared her.

"What are you doing out here?" I asked.

She held up a finger. After a few seconds she made the sign of the cross and looked up at me. "At the moment, I was praying."

I sat on a large rock near her and pressed my legs against the cool stone. "You came all the way out here to pray?"

"I was missing my mother," she said, her blue eyes somehow old yet childlike.

"I'm sorry," I said, feeling guilty. I thought so often of my own mom, but it rarely occurred to me she'd do the same.

"Her birthday is coming up," she said. "I always think of her more around her birthday."

"I do the same thing," I said.

"We all do," she said with a smile. "That's why we have gooseberry pie every year on Rebecca's birthday."

"It's her favorite," I said.

"It is, and it's a nice way to remember her—not that you ever forget her. It occurred to me, as I was sitting here, that I may very well be the last living person who remembers my mother."

"Oh," I said, the thought startling. "But I remember her."

"Siena, you know her from my memories, but you have none of your own and neither does Paul. Even my George—God rest his soul—never met her. I don't believe anyone else living remembers her."

"That's a depressing thought," I said, and slumped onto the rock.

"Eventually each of us will be forgotten," she said easily.

"That's even more depressing," I said.

She chuckled. "It is, but it doesn't upset me. When I go, so do my memories. I suppose that's how it was intended."

A new thought occurred to me. "Are you dying?"

She didn't turn away. She said, "We're all dying, some of us faster than others, but no, I don't plan to leave anytime soon. Though this past year has taken a lot out of me."

"It's taken a lot out of all of us," I said, kicking some rusted metal that had once been something inside the inn.

She was silent, staring absently at the fireplace, or maybe she was staring past it, at the ocean.

In a resigned tone, she said, "Yes, I suppose so."

"Why did you come out here … to this place of …"

"Evil?" she said, raising an eyebrow. "This was her home, for better or for worse. It was where she was born, spent her childhood, and where she died. I have to believe that at some point along the way, she had some degree of happiness here."

"She must've, if she brought you back here," I said.

Gigi sighed.

"What is it?" I asked.

"That's always confused me. This place wasn't happy for her and it certainly wasn't happy for me, yet she brought me here. I've never understood that."

"Did she have much of a choice?" I asked.

"No," Gigi said. "She had some friends in New York, but none who would've welcomed me or kept me safe, for that matter. Still, I've always wondered. … There were orphanages, which would've been a better option than her parents."

"Maybe she thought they'd changed."

She exhaled. "People always hope that those who are troubled become better with age. In truth, they frequently become worse," she said wearily.

"At least they let you two stay here when she was so sick," I said.

She nodded. "They were never kind to her, but they did allow us to stay in the cooking tent. Thank God it was summer and we weren't freezing to death. And they gave us some food. We ate a lot of blueberries, but it was enough to get by. It could've been worse. I always remind myself of that. It could have been much worse."

Her clear blue eyes seemed to bounce from the past and back to the present.

She turned to face me. "What happened at the skating rink?"

"Oh," I said, "You heard about that?"

"It's a small town, Siena. You should always assume everyone is aware of everything. In this case, Jody was afraid you and Luca had a fight, since you ran out and then he and your sisters followed after you."

"What did you say to that idea?" I asked.

"I said perhaps they had gotten into a fight. After all, teenagers in love and all that," Gigi said, watching me.

"I turned eighteen months ago and Luca is almost nineteen," I said, taking issue with Gigi referring to us as teenagers.

"Like I said, teenagers in love," Gigi said, her watery blue eyes staring back at me. "What actually happened?"

I decided not to argue. "Why can't it be that simple?" I asked.

"Nothing in our family has ever been that simple." She scoffed in frustration but her eyes were loving.

It was as impossible to lie to her as ever. "I saw the girl from my dreams and followed her into the woods."

"Did you find her?" Gigi pulled up a little straighter.

"Of course not. She isn't real. She hasn't even been born yet," I said, mumbling the last part.

"Hasn't been born yet? How would you know that?" She stared at me.

I dug at a loose rock with the toe of my shoe. "I think she's my daughter."

Gigi exhaled loudly. "Seeing the future is rare and dangerous, even for those with gifts. I have heard of some dreaming of their future children. They are called announcing dreams, but they are rare and should be treated with caution. Though perhaps the Lord may have given you such a gift. Did this girl tell you she's your daughter?"

"No, but she's the perfect combination of me and …" I hesitated.

"Luca?"

I nodded.

She continued to study me. "But she didn't call you 'Mother' or anything similar. She is simply a girl who favors the two of you in one way or another?" Gigi said, minimizing my connection to the girl.

"She's never spoken," I said.

"Then you don't know who she is, so don't assume you do. You remember what Saint John said."

"Test the spirits."

"Demons lie," Gigi said.

"I know that," I said, feeling defensive.

"Yes, you do, yet here you are taking this dream, and now this apparition, as someone so connected to you as your future child. That's dangerous, Siena, to follow so blindly simply because she looks somewhat like you and your first boyfriend."

"Luca is more than my *first* boyfriend," I said to counter her stinging words.

Her features softened. "Luca is a remarkable boy, and there is nothing I'd love more than to see you two happily married and with a beautiful daughter. However, no one can predict the future, not even the dreams of my extraordinarily gifted granddaughter."

"If she isn't my daughter, then who is she?"

"Have you prayed about it? Have you asked the Lord for clarity?" she said, already knowing the answer.

"No."

"It's no surprise you have no answer," she said, standing.

I wanted to separate myself from her, but I remained, my gaze falling on the fireplace with the missing middle stone— the stone that had been soaked with my father's blood.

"What else are you thinking about?" she said.

"Nothing," I lied.

"Siena, I'm sorry I hurt your feelings, but you must pray about every single thing that is shown to you. It's dangerous not to."

I didn't respond.

She took one of my hands. "Help me walk back," she said.

It was startling how much she had aged since the inn last stood. I helped her pick her way across the rocks until she reached the sandy part of the beach, where the roses grew.

"What more are you thinking about? I promise to listen calmly," she said.

After a moment I said, "The woods we were in. When we followed her, or at least when we thought we were following her, we saw an old structure. It was probably the remains of a house."

"Many houses used to dot the woods around here. There's nothing surprising about that," she said calmly.

"I suppose not, but when we kept going, the woods ended at the BayTree."

Her expression became grave. "The BayTree?"

"We were on the low bluff across the street from it. We were eye level with the attic window," I said with some difficulty.

She stopped walking. "Hopefully, that was a coincidence."

"What if it wasn't?" I asked. The wind was blowing hard across the ocean, causing whitecaps.

She started forward again. "It was," she said, trying to convince herself.

I moved in front of her. "Is there something you aren't telling me?"

"I know nothing more than I've told you," she said, trying to pass me on the trail.

"But you have more to say." I again moved in front of her, blocking her way.

She placed both hands on her cane. "I've told you my grandparents were friendly with the people who built the BayTree."

"Yes," I said, feeling unsteady, "and your mother left when the … crimes … the missing children were discovered."

She rubbed the top of her walking stick, careful to avoid my gaze. "I have always felt there was more to that … more she didn't tell me."

"Why do you think that?" I asked.

"I'm sure I'm wrong," she said, leaning on her walking stick with both hands.

I felt the hairs on my skin prickle. "Your intuitions are usually right," I whispered above the wind.

"Yes," she said, turning and resting her eyes on the remains of the fireplace. "They are usually correct."

Jackson started barking furiously.

I turned. He was barking at a crab.

"It's just a crab," I said, feeling like I could pass out any second.

Gigi nodded and continued down the trail.

Six

That night I didn't dream of children—not mine nor any other. Instead, I dreamt of my mother. She lay beside me on my bed, like she used to when she was alive. She stroked my hair all night. When I awoke I prayed to fall asleep so I could be with her again, but Jackson was barking too much and Avi was shrieking too loudly. I didn't understand how she was so awake; she'd stayed up as late as I had.

My family and I had prayed the previous night, while Luca used his gift to watch for holy souls out in the yard. After that, Dad left for a meeting and Lisieux suggested a Star Wars marathon until he returned. I agreed, not because I wanted to watch Star Wars, but because I didn't want to be alone. I fell asleep on the couch halfway through the first episode. After the second one, my dad got home and went straight to his room. The rest of us headed up a few minutes later.

I pushed myself out of bed. It was already ten. No wonder Avi was so awake. I dressed for Mass as quickly as I could, twisting my hair into a low bun, and went downstairs.

Gigi said, "You look lovely."

I swished my flowy summer skirt from one side to the other, saying, "Thank you."

"I like your hair pulled back," Avi said. "It makes you look nicer."

"Avila, why do you say things like that? Your sister looks perfectly nice all the time," Dad said, already sounding worn out from a morning with Avi.

"I didn't say she didn't look nice most of the time, I said it made her look *nicerrr*," Avi said.

"I guess, thank you," I said as I took my keys from the counter.

"Good morning," Luca said as he and Lisieux came downstairs.

"I like your hair like that. You look nice," Luca said.

Avi said, "*Nicerrr*, you have to say the *errr* part or you'll get in trouble."

Dad hung his head and Gigi chuckled.

Luca said, "Are we missing a joke?"

"Always," Lisieux said, and placed a bookmark between the pages of the book in front of her.

Dad took his keys from the hook. "Come on, we're going to be late."

When we walked into church, Avi took Dad's hand and skipped beside him down the aisle. We slipped into the pew in front of Dave, Jody, Elle, and Noah. Jody gave Gigi a hug and whispered good morning. We may have given them a chance at their dream jobs, but it's because of them that people no longer hated us—at least not outwardly. That family was impossible not to love. Once people found out that Dad and Gigi were giving them a shot at their crazy roller-skating rink dream, our family reputation went way up.

The other big shift happened after Thomas's parents moved to Ohio to be closer to family, and away from the memories of our town. Without them in the parish, people no longer seemed to need to hate us.

The bell in the back of the church rang, the congregation stood, the choir began a hymn, and Father Luke, along with two altar boys, processed down the aisle. I was grateful I'd finally stopped imagining Thomas there as one of the altar servers.

After a few minutes of standing, it was time to sit and listen to the first reading from the book of Isaiah. The words "release to the prisoners" and "day of vindication by our God" echoed through the church. The responsorial psalm was based on the same theme of freedom. Psalm 146 seemed to repeat Isaiah's words: "The Lord sets prisoners free … the Lord raises up those who are bowed down." I was pondering these verses as the second reading from the First Letter of John began. I felt a chill and looked up from the missal I held. The blood drained from my face as the girl appeared, standing in front of the altar.

She moved easily across the space, stopping next to the tabernacle. She sat, in one fluid motion, huddled beneath the tabernacle which was in the center of the altar with the life-sized crucifix above it. She had her knees pulled to her chest, her clean white dress covering her knees. Her arms, in frilly long sleeves, were wrapped around her knees, and her light brown face, framed by loose curls, was resting on her knees. She wore tall black boots laced up to her shins.

The girl was perfectly still. Her eyes appeared open, but as if she was in need of a nap. I'd never seen her motionless before. In my dreams she was either playing happily or running—terrified. At the skating rink she was moving quickly. Here, she was resting peacefully, though her face wore the same sad expression. I recognized it; I'd seen it many times before on people who'd suffered. Even when they were not suffering, they were not at peace. Gigi was often like that … since Dad's addiction had resurfaced. Even now when he'd been sober for months, she hadn't returned to who she'd been before. I wondered if the girl was like that, if whatever happened to her had made it so she couldn't return to who she'd been. It was impossible. She didn't exist yet, or maybe not at all. So whatever suffering she might someday experience hadn't happened yet.

Luca leaned over and whispered, "Are you okay?"

"She's on the altar," I said, hearing the tremble in my voice.

He straightened his back. He was taller than me, yet he craned his neck for a better view of the altar, as if he was missing the figure I saw. Of course he wasn't. No one could see her except me. Seeing things other people don't … not a good sign.

Luca whispered, "Is the guy here?"

I sucked in air. I hadn't thought of that. I subtly twisted my neck from side to side. A moment later, those around us were standing. Luca casually helped me stand, and I took the opportunity to glance around. I didn't see the man. I turned back to the girl. She wasn't afraid.

"He's not here."

Luca placed a hand over mine.

The girl was now kneeling, facing Father Luke. He was reading from the Gospel of Matthew, chapter ten. The words floated around me, but I heard only parts here and there … about what is concealed being revealed. And there is no need to fear one who kills the body, only the one who can destroy both body and soul should be feared.

When Father was done, the girl moved back into a sitting position. Father Luke began his homily. She didn't appear to be listening any more than I was. She moved closer to the stand supporting the tabernacle, her head and shoulder leaning against it as if she couldn't get close enough to it. The way she sat, it was as if she was leaning against someone she loved and they had their arms around her.

Her expression of longing made me want to go to her, to put my arm around her, to tell her she wasn't alone, but even if it wasn't the middle of Mass and I could go to her, I doubted she would stay. Yesterday she had moved as I approached, and kept a good distance between us. Besides, she wasn't real. None of this was real.

Luca put his arm around me and whispered, "What's she doing?"

"Sitting down, leaning against the base of the tabernacle. She looks lonely."

He removed his arm from my back and again sat taller trying to see her.

Father Luke finished his homily and sat down as the altar boys readied the altar. The girl sat up a little taller. She wasn't afraid of the boys. She must see them, though, or she wouldn't have moved. In a moment she began to kneel, wrapping her left arm around the base supporting the tabernacle, again reminding me of how someone would lean against someone they loved. She remained this way throughout the Consecration, carefully watching everything Father Luke did. She seemed particularly focused when the bells were rung and Father Luke held up the consecrated Host and chalice.

The choir started singing "Here I Am, Lord," and Father Luke left the altar to give out Communion. She stood and walked dutifully behind him. On one side of Father Luke was one of the altar boys with a Communion plate. She stood on the other side. She carefully watched each person receive Communion, her focus always on the Host. Once that person had consumed the Host, her attention moved back to Father and the next person. She was not interested in the person, only in the Eucharist.

The row in front of us stood, and Luca subtly pulled me up. I felt weak, as if I was going to faint. I wasn't afraid and yet I could barely move. Luca casually steadied me, nudging me forward. Upon my approach, the girl's focus changed. She was no longer staring at the Eucharist; she stared at me. Her expression was blank, her eyes unblinking. She was not focused on anyone but me. My knees started to buckle. Luca grabbed my arms to keep me upright.

"Siena, I said 'The body of Christ,' " Father Luke repeated expectantly.

I shifted my gaze to see him holding up the thin, cream-colored wafer. "Amen," I said, and opened my mouth to receive the Eucharist.

Afterward, Luca moved me to the left. The girl was now directly in front of me. I was supposed to move, but I couldn't. I was frozen in her stare. Beside me, Luca knelt and received. He stood and gently pushed me forward. I had drawn attention to myself … I always did. I walked, with my head lowered, back to the pew. I knelt beside Avi. Luca slipped in behind me. He kept his body close to mine, knowing it would help.

"Are you okay?" Avi asked, sounding nervous.

I nodded and lifted my hands to cover my face, as if deep in prayer, though I couldn't do anything except watch the girl. She was no longer interested in me; she had returned to observing each person receive Communion. She didn't stare at any of the others: she watched them receive and then went on to the next person. It wasn't personal, like it had been with me. Gigi was wrong, how could she be anything but my daughter? She appeared in my dreams and in life, but only to me. She stood by Father Luke, transfixed on the Eucharist, except when I was there and then she was focused on me.

I studied her. Her clothes were of a style unfamiliar to me. Today she wore a bright white dress, trimmed with delicate lace. I thought back to the dreams and even to the skating rink. On those days she wore a pale blue dress that was covered in splotches of brown mud. The shoes she wore today were the same as in the dream and yesterday at the skating rink, but today they were shiny. The other times, they had been muddy. In her hair was a thin, pale blue ribbon. I hadn't noticed it when she was at the altar, but now I could see it. It was the same color as her dress on the other days, though on those days she had no ribbon in her hair, only twigs and dirt.

The Communion line ended, and Father Luke turned, almost bumping into the girl. She appeared unfazed by the near collision. He went to the altar and she followed reverently. As he began to clean the chalice and paten, the girl stood watching, her hands pressed together as if in prayer, her long dress falling above her ankles so only some of the laces of the black boots could be seen. She was beautiful and angelic, but not from this time. It made sense; she had not yet been born. She followed Father Luke and stood beside him as he reverently took what remained of the consecrated Hosts and placed them inside the tabernacle. She remained there, staring as if she could see inside it.

Father Luke gave the empty chalice and patens to the altar servers and returned to his seat, where he led the congregation in "Oh sacrament most holy, oh sacrament divine, all praise and all thanksgiving be every moment thine." After the third time, the girl disappeared.

"She's gone," I whispered to Luca.

He nodded slightly. "Try and breathe. You're even paler than usual."

He was right. I felt the room spinning. Thankfully, everyone sat at that moment. As inconspicuously as possible, Luca helped me sit.

"Your hand is like ice," he said, gently rubbing my arm to increase the circulation.

After a few minutes, Father Luke stood. I pulled myself up by the back of the pew in front of us. After what felt like years, Father Luke finally processed to the back of the church.

I started to push my way out of the pew.

Avi whispered, "Are you okay?"

Thank goodness she had the sense to ask it quietly. "I don't feel well," I said, and brushed past her to get into the center aisle.

Luca followed.

"I need to go home," I said to him as we made our way down the aisle.

Surely, my family was wondering why I was being so weird, but I couldn't do anything else. Luca kept me steady as we left the church. The warmth of his hands felt good on my chilly skin. I heard him tell people I wasn't feeling well. I tried to acknowledge them while they said they hoped I'd have a speedy recovery and to the suggestions that orange juice and donuts would help. Luca said it was my stomach and it was best to get home. That was slightly embarrassing, but better than telling them the spirit girl who had been haunting my dreams was sitting next to the tabernacle throughout Mass. That would not be easily forgotten, and my hope of fitting in would be forever gone.

Luca walked me calmly to my car and opened the passenger door. After helping me in, he hurried to the driver's side and started the engine.

"Are you okay?" Luca asked as he pulled out of the parking lot, carefully dodging the many young kids running to their cars.

"I think I'm losing my mind," I said while feeling like I was going to be sick.

"We've been over this. You're sane. So we need to accept that you aren't imagining any of this, that it's real. We need to figure out what it means," he said, pulling onto the main road that would take us home. He glanced at me. "There must be a reason she's appearing to you."

"I have no idea what it is," I said.

"Has she ever spoken?"

I shook my head.

"Not even in your dreams?"

"No."

I watched the trees blur by. "At least today she wasn't being hunted. That was nice. She wasn't exactly happy, but she wasn't running in terror. So that's something."

"What was she doing?" Luca asked.

"She was sitting next to the tabernacle. Leaning against it, kind of like a child would lean against a parent. She knelt when

Father read the gospel and during Consecration. When he was giving out Communion, she stood beside him."

"What was she doing there?" Luca asked.

"She was watching him hand out the Eucharist, except when I went up. Then she stared at me." I shivered.

"What was her expression like?" he asked.

I breathed into my hands and rubbed them together. I had to warm up. "Sort of blank. Watching."

"Not mad or angry?"

"No. Not happy, either. Neutral."

He nodded.

"Why does that matter?"

"I don't know if it does."

"Did you feel her?" I was scared to ask. I couldn't handle it if he said yes.

"No," he said. "I wouldn't, not with the Eucharist so close. That tips the scale in the good to an extreme, and I only feel when the scale is tipped to the dark side," he said, trying to be funny.

I didn't laugh.

After it was clear his joke fell flat, he asked, "What did she look like?"

"You know what she looks like … she looks like *us*."

His grip on the steering wheel tightened. He was silent for a while.

"What was she wearing?" he asked.

"Today it was a white dress. Usually it's a pale blue dress."

"She always wears a dress?" he said, his grip loosening a bit.

"Yes, but today it was a different dress. White, like I said, and it was clean. Usually it's muddy, like she … like she's been running from someone. She also had a pale blue ribbon in her hair today," I said, trying not to think about why her dress would be covered in mud.

"That's interesting," Luca said, leaning back in his seat.

"What is?"

"You don't wear a lot of dresses, other than to Mass," he said.

"Right, but why does that matter?"

"I have no idea if it does. Just thinking about stuff. Can you describe the dress? Is it like something Elle or Avi would wear?"

"No. Both dresses were long, reaching all the way to her boots."

"Would you think our … our daughter would wear something like that?" he asked, turning his head slightly toward me.

I thought about his question and hesitantly answered, "I like the style. It almost reminded me of something out of a Jane Austen novel. I'm not sure where to find clothes like that. Maybe that style will become popular in the next twenty years."

"Or maybe she's wearing the clothes that people wore when she *was* alive," he said pointedly.

"You think she's from the past?"

"I see souls who have lived and died. I've never seen one who hasn't been born yet, or I don't think I have." He tilted his head, thinking about this.

"That doesn't mean I couldn't see a future child," I said.

"Anything God allows is possible," Luca said as he pushed the button to open the gate.

I watched the tall grass waving in the wind. "If she has already lived and died … does that mean the man has been chasing her for a hundred years?" I asked, a sense of dread washing over me.

"If she's from a time when they wore clothes like that, then he's been dead for decades. For him to still be chasing her wouldn't make sense."

"But that's what I see in my dreams," I said as Luca parked the car.

"First of all," he said, turning to me, "we don't know what any of this means. If they were both real people and if he hunted her in life, then it's pretty unlikely he's where she is now—in the afterlife, I mean. It's possible he found God before he died and begged to be forgiven. I suppose we should pray for that, but if he was as awful as your dream implies, it seems safe to assume there is a great chasm between where she is and where he is."

I felt a sense of relief followed by confusion. "If she's from the past and she's not our child, and she was hunted by that guy, but she's not anymore, what does any of this mean?"

I prayed for clarity as Luca handed me the car keys. His fingers grazed my palm and I felt the heat of his hands. His amber eyes were trained on mine.

"It means she has been waiting a long time."

Seven

I grasped the keys and hopped out of the car, slamming the door and running to the driver's side.

"What are you doing?" Luca asked, staring at me as I rushed past him, into the driver's seat.

"Get in, I'm driving," I said.

Inside the house Jackson was barking; he'd heard us. Sam and Jason would know we were home. It didn't matter. I started the engine before Luca was in the car.

"Seriously, get in," I said through the rolled-down window.

He hopped in, and I spun the car around. He braced himself as I sped down the driveway.

"What's happening right now?" he asked, buckling his seat belt.

I brought the car to a sudden stop at the gate. As soon as it opened I inched through and sped down the highway.

"We need to go back," I said, finally sure of the next thing I was supposed to do.

"You could've said you want a donut," Luca said, trying to understand what I was doing.

"I don't mean back to church, I mean back to the BayTree."

He stared at me like I'd lost my mind.

"It's the same building. It's been remodeled a dozen times, but it's still the same building," I said.

"Yes, that's why you saw the children in the attic and why we've never gone back there," he said with a shiver.

"True, but if I touch the walls, maybe I'll find something," I said.

Apprehensively, Luca asked, "You want to find more memories from the BayTree?"

"I don't want to do any of this. But for some reason, I'm part of it and I have to find out why. I have to know who she is and why she's haunting me," I said, pushing down on the accelerator.

We passed the road that led to church and then the road that led to the center of town and the skating rink. I was driving way too fast. Thankfully, there was barely anyone on the scenic highway. I lifted my foot from the accelerator as we neared the bridge that bordered the bay. The tide was low, the tall docks sticking out into the middle of emptiness. Boats hoisted up near them dangled in midair. A few seconds later I was pulling into the gravel lot that was the BayTree.

"You think she's connected to this place?" Luca asked, hurrying out of the car to keep up with me.

"I don't think anything, only that I saw her in the woods and then we stood up there," I said, pointing to the top of the forest on the other side of the street.

"Why not go there and explore the woods. Maybe there were memories at the structure we found," Luca said.

"Because I'm like you, I sense evil. No, I don't sense it, I see it. And I already know there's a ton of evil here. So there are memories here. The woods might not even be connected to her," I said.

"This place might not be connected to her either," Luca said, jogging to catch up to me.

"I have to try," I said.

I reached for the handle of the door.

Luca put his hand on my arm, stopping me. "What are you even looking for?"

"I have no idea."

His amber eyes were searching mine. His grip on my arm loosened, his gaze fell and then met mine. "Fine, but don't leave my side. Promise?"

"Promise," I said, opening the door.

He took my hand in his and gripped it tightly. He wasn't kidding; he wasn't letting me away from him.

With my first step inside, the hairs on my arms stood up. I looked around, partially expecting to see the girl or the man chasing her. I saw neither.

The hostess asked, "Do you have a reservation?"

"Umm, no," I said.

"It's a forty-five-minute wait," she said.

I noticed the people sitting on benches near us, most on their phones, the others watching us.

"Oh, okay," I said.

"Do you want to wait?" the hostess asked.

Luca squeezed my hand and said, "We've heard your truffle fries are excellent. Can we get an order to go?"

"We don't do to-go orders during our Sunday brunch," the woman responded.

"Please, I'm seriously craving truffle fries," he said, leaning toward her. This action pulled his shirt tight against the muscles of his arms and chest.

Her face flushed and she appeared flustered. "Uh, okay, but you'll have to wait and it will be at least twenty minutes," she said, almost apologizing.

"I'm sure they're worth the wait," Luca said with a sweet smile. "Is it okay if we wander around? We've heard it's a historic building."

"Whatever you want," the hostess said far too eagerly.

"Thanks," he said, leading me toward the stairs.

As we went up the stairs, Luca said, "She was so accommodating."

"She was into you, Luca."

"Don't be ridiculous."

Despite being in the BayTree, I couldn't help grinning up at him. "You seriously didn't pick up on that?"

"Siena, I asked for fries and she took the order, that's it."

"If you say so," I said, trying not to laugh.

"She was not into with me," he said in a whisper as people passed us on the stairs.

"Whatever you say," I said, squeezing his hand and releasing it when we reached the second floor.

People were everywhere. The windows were open, allowing the sea breeze to swirl the smells of food.

"Did you see this?" Luca asked, going toward a wall with many framed pictures.

In front of him was a framed newspaper article. Beside him were more of the same. Each of them had a picture of the BayTree, but in each picture the building appeared slightly different. The one in front of us was the most recent. The article announced that the BayTree restaurant was opening. In the foreground of the picture stood several people I didn't recognize. I assumed they were the owners, and I assumed my dad knew each of them or at least knew of them. I moved down the line, from picture to picture.

"You were right. This place has been a lot of different things," I said, thinking back to when Luca had stayed up all night researching its history.

"I saw most of these online. At least the recent ones. I wonder where they got the really old ones."

"The frames look super old too. Maybe they found them during the remodel. Maybe the previous owners had kept them?" I guessed.

He leaned closer, examining the framed clippings. "Yes, that must be it. These are definitely original."

The last newspaper clipping showed the BayTree under construction. I stepped backward. In the foreground of the picture was a man looking proud and a woman lovingly holding a young boy. The boy clinging to her had big, clear eyes and his hair appeared to be made of golden curls, like the woman's. I stared at the man. His eyes were big and clear like the boys, not like the dark ones I'd seen before … yet there was no mistaking who he was.

"That's the man from my dreams," I said, feeling bile burn the back of my throat.

I turned away from the wall and tried to focus on the happy customers and the ocean beyond the building.

Luca put an arm around me. He read aloud the article that accompanied the photo. "Mr. Charles Padgett, our newly elected mayor, announces that his spacious new home will be completed within the next two months. Mr. Padgett reported it is his wife's deep love for the ocean that drew him to build a home so close to the sea. But as we are all aware, Mrs. Beverly Padgett, formerly Miss Beverly Richardson, is a member of one of the founding families of our beloved community. The land their home is being built on was a wedding present to the young couple from her grandfather, Mr. James Richardson. Mr. Richardson has jokingly reported that he gave them the land because he would do whatever it took to keep his granddaughter from moving out of town with such a scoundrel. Mrs. Padgett reported she is thrilled to announce that the Junior League spring function will be held at their new home. I've been told the table settings will be quite extraordinary."

Luca and I both stared at the glowing words of the article.

I said, "They were perfect. He was the mayor, she was small-town royalty. Even their son was beautiful."

"No one is perfect," Luca said in an ominous tone.

I hesitated, my hand nearing the framed picture.

Luca's hand gently grasped mine midair. "Are you sure you want to do that?" he asked.

I held on to his thumb, and the warmth of his hand made some of the chill fade. "I don't *want* to do any of this."

Eight

I released Luca's hand and moved my fingers swiftly to the frame.

Her brown eyes were shining in the afternoon light. She was laughing as the little boy came running toward her. She opened her arms and scooped him up. She held him with both arms, propping him on her hip. He was no older than two or three. His blond hair glistened in the sun. She lovingly pushed some of the curls from his face and wiped a smear of dirt from his cheek. He clung to her, nuzzling his face against her.

"You're tired," she said, combing her fingers through his curls. "As soon as the photographer leaves, I'll get you to Grandfather's and put you down for your nap."

"You spoil him too much," the man, Charles, said. My mind winced at his voice.

"How can I not spoil such a perfect little boy," she said, lovingly kissing the boy on the cheek. The boy buried his face in his mother's neck, carefully watching his father.

"Why do you always dress him in that outfit every time we're photographed?" Charles said in a sharp tone.

"It's such a handsome look for him. It makes the blue in his eyes so much brighter," she said, nuzzling the little

boy. "It makes his eyes look almost as blue as yours," she said, admiring her husband's eyes.

"The photograph will be in black-and-white. No one will see his blue eyes," he said, clearly thinking she was foolish.

"Oh, I suppose you're right about that," she said thoughtfully.

"Of course I am, and you dress him in that so often, people are going to wonder if we can't afford to buy him any other clothing." He sounded irritated.

"They won't think that, dear. We have plenty of money. Everyone knows that," she said.

"No one has plenty of money," he grumbled, "except your old cheapskate of a grandfather."

"Grandfather has been extremely generous with us. He gave us this land and the timber at cost. And he has allowed us to stay in his home these last three years as we have been building this one," she said softly.

"Yes, and he has given us a meager two rooms for our use."

"Why do you need a third? I never did understand that," she said, watching him and trying to understand.

"A man needs his space. Why does your grandfather need four rooms, plus all the living areas of the house?"

"It's his home. He can do as he pleases. He didn't have to let us live with him. We could've rented a place in town, but that would've cost money and you wanted all we could spare for your campaign," she said.

"A campaign you wanted me to win," he reminded her.

"Yes, dear, I always want you to win, if that is what you want, and it was, and so I did," she said.

He said, "Don't forget any money we saved went right back to him to pay for the timber."

"He sold it to us at cost," she said.

"He has plenty of timber. He could've just as easily given it to us."

"Given it? All the timber for the entire house? That would be asking far too much," she said, offended.

"Is that why you didn't ask when I told you to?" He spoke with quiet anger so the photographer couldn't hear.

"I did ask, and Grandfather said no," she stated.

"Cheapskate," Charles said under his breath.

"Don't let our son hear you speak that way about his great-grandfather," she said.

Charles responded, "My son will hear me speak whatever way I choose to speak, about whomever I choose to speak it."

"Everyone ready?" the photographer called from behind the box-shaped camera.

"Yes," Charles said, and placed a firm hand on his wife's shoulder.

I sucked in a breath as the restaurant returned with the smells and sounds of Sunday brunch.

"Are you okay?" Luca asked with concern.

I nodded.

"What did you see?" he asked, sounding worried.

I leaned against him, wishing I could plop to the floor in the middle of the room. The world suddenly felt very heavy. "It was them, getting ready to take the picture. He was complaining about what she dressed the boy in and that her grandfather was cheap, even though he gave them the land and lumber at cost. She stood up to him a little and told him not to speak about her grandfather that way, but he didn't care. He was being a jerk."

In a low voice, Luca said, "He kidnapped Black kids, hid them in his attic, killed at least one but presumably a lot of others, along with his wife and son, and you expected him to be nice?"

I leaned my head against the wall. This was so awful. "I suppose I never expected him to have a pretty wife and an adorable little boy. She was younger than him, not in a totally gross way, but in an easy to dominate sort of way. She stood her ground, though, and defended her grandfather. She must've really loved him."

"Who? Her grandfather or her serial killer husband?" Luca asked.

I hesitated. "Both, I think."

Luca studied the picture and asked, "Was there anything more?"

"The little boy was so cute and loved his mom so much," I said, feeling tears burn my eyes.

"I mean, nothing horrible happened?"

"No."

"That's weird," he said.

"Why is that weird?" I asked.

"In the past, you've seen evil, not simply memories," Luca said.

"My guess is, everything connected with him is evil," I said, wishing this was only a dream and I was going to wake up to a reality where I wasn't watching the memories of a killer.

A waiter approached us and asked, "Can I help you?"

"Just checking out these pictures while we wait for a table," Luca said.

"Why?" The waiter sounded confused and irritated.

Luca answered, "We like old pictures."

The waiter spoke with exaggerated articulation, as if we were stupid: "You should probably wait at the hostess stand so you will hear your name called."

"Good idea," Luca said, taking my hand and leading me toward the stairs.

"There were more pictures up there," I said as we went down the stairs, carefully avoiding the people coming up the stairs.

"If we cause a scene, it will be harder to come back," he said as we got to the bottom of the stairs.

"Yeah, okay," I said, both wishing we could stay and grateful we were leaving.

"Wait," the hostess called, holding up a to-go bag.

"That was sooner than expected," Luca said.

"The kitchen wasn't as backed up as I thought," she said, smiling up at him.

He released me and pulled his wallet from his back pocket. I quickly scanned the entryway. Another framed newspaper clipping announced the opening of the restaurant.

"Ready?" Luca said, moving me toward the door.

Behind us, the hostess announced, "Drexel, party of four."

We stepped aside to allow a husband, wife, and two college-age daughters to move from their spot by the door. Behind where they had been standing were some more photos. The one closest to me was of the little boy from the newspaper clipping upstairs. He was a few years older, but his curls were still there. He was sitting on the stairs. He held a miniature train in his hand. He was maybe five or six. It appeared to be in the room we were in, but more open, more grand. Walls had probably been added over time. My fingers started to move toward the frame when I noticed the image next to it. I stared.

There were two girls. One was taller, with white skin and long straight hair. The other … was the girl from my dreams.

Nine

The girls in the picture were looking directly at me. The taller girl was grinning broadly while the girl with curly hair, the one from my dreams, was holding her friend's hand and smiling, but in a reserved way.

My fingers trembled as I touched the frame.

They were on the beach, giggling, holding on to one another. Their bare feet splashed the water as they faced the sea.

I looked around … the ocean was on one side and the BayTree was on the other. I'd never seen it from this angle. It was imposing, to say the least, built up beyond the sand and rocks. The little boy from the other two pictures was there, digging in the sand. He was about the same age as he was in the photo on the stairs—five or six. His blond curls seemed to glow in the bright light of the beach. Though the girls were giggling and laughing, he was sullen. I realized he'd looked the same in the last memory. Now it was more pronounced.

His mother stood near him and ran her fingers through his hair. She'd also changed. She was still beautiful, but there was a heaviness, a resignation that seemed to be pushing her shoulders down.

For their part, the girls were entirely focused on each other. They held hands and jumped over the tiny waves and squealed with delight. The woman watched them with both admiration and pity.

"I'm ready," a man called from behind a large box-shaped camera.

The woman called out, "Girls, smile."

The girls stopped jumping. Their hands remained entwined. It was a calm day, so the taller girl's long brown hair hung straight. The girl from my dreams stood beside her.

"That's a good one," the man said, his blue eyes shining as he removed the large camera box from in front of his face.

The woman watched him take note of the girls, a glimmer of recognition in her eyes.

My body started to shake and my knees faltered. Luca grabbed me to keep me from falling.

The hostess rushed toward us, saying, "Is she okay? Should I call 911?"

"Her blood sugar's low. She'll be much better after she eats some of the fries," Luca said.

After the hostess turned away, he used his phone to capture the image of the two girls.

"Come on," he said, guiding me toward the door which someone was holding open.

The air outside felt fresh. I hadn't realized how hard it was to breathe in there. The slight breeze made my skin feel cold. I was sweating.

"The girl from my dreams was in that picture," I said as Luca opened the car door for me.

"I sort of figured, since you almost passed out. Here, get in. I'm afraid if you stand much longer you'll actually pass out." He shut the door.

I sat trembling in the front seat … the image of the man watching the girls play in the waves replaying in my mind.

Luca started the car and pulled his arm across me to fasten my seatbelt.

We drove in silence, passing the bay. The tide had begun to come in, changing the aspect of the bay.

"He was watching her," I said, feeling nauseated. "He was the one who took the picture."

Cautiously, Luca said, "The man from your dreams?"

I looked at him and nodded.

Luca leaned back. "I guess your hunch to look for clues at the BayTree was a good one."

I didn't respond. Why did I want to know more? I rubbed my hands up and down my arms.

"Are you cold?" Luca asked, turning the temperature up even though it was warm outside.

"Yeah, a little," I said, leaning forward and hunching my body into a ball.

Luca placed a hand on my back; the heat from his touch felt good.

After we'd driven for several minutes, he asked, "Who was the other girl?"

I shook my head. "No one said a name."

He asked, "What was happening in the memory?"

"The girls were playing in the waves. They were laughing, having fun, being silly little girls. From what I could tell, they were close, probably best friends. I would say sisters, but …"

"They didn't exactly look alike?" Luca guessed.

"If it was today, I'd say one or both were adopted and they really were sisters. But back then, …."

"Skin tone mattered more," Luca said for me.

"Yes, but they loved each other. That was clear."

"Is that all? They were playing and he took their picture?"

"Pretty much. The woman and the little boy from the newspaper article were there. The little boy was digging in the sand, and she was standing beside him. It had been a few years. He was five or six. The man said he was ready, and so his wife told the girls to smile. They did, and when he stood up, I saw who it was. And the memory ended."

I started to shake uncontrollably as images filled my mind. Terrified children huddled in the darkness of the BayTree attic mixing with the girl from my dreams running through the woods trying to escape the man who was hunting her. The man who just took her picture.

"She was a happy little girl. She was loved," I said through sobs. "All the children were loved, and he took them," I screamed, unable to stop the flood of emotions overtaking me.

I felt the car roll to a stop.

"Don't take on their pain. It won't help any of you," Luca said, placing a cautious hand on my back.

"She was so young," I said between sobs. "They were all so young!" I screamed and pounded the dashboard.

"I know," he said, wrapping his arms around me.

I fought not against him but against the world. He did not release me until my body had grown still.

"There's a reason for all of this," he said as I started to breathe more regularly.

"Is it to torture me?" I asked.

"No, that much I'm sure of. You need to try and keep things separate from you. You can't let the evil and the pain into your life. That isn't what God wants."

Angrily, I asked, "What does he want?"

"I don't know, but it's not to bring you pain," he said.

I shouted, "Then God is failing!"

"You asked to see the world as it really is," Luca said calmly, as if I got what I'd asked for.

I felt heat flush my cheeks. "I have begged God for so many things and he answers none of those prayers! And then this one he answers in the most awful of ways," I said, turning my anger on Luca.

He dipped his head and then raised it. "It doesn't make sense, but good will come of this. Good always comes of darkness."

"Aargh," I growled. "Luca, I don't need a saint, I need my boyfriend. The stuff that's happening to me is insane. Seeing that doting wife and adorable little boy, and there's Satan standing next to them. And then I see two happy little girls playing at the beach and who's taking their picture? Evil! I know what's going to happen to her! I may not have the details, but I know what happens to her and I don't want anything to do with it. She's not ours—thank God for that—she's not our child. So I have nothing to do with any of this and I want *nothing* to do with any of this!"

"Okay," he said, turning the car back on.

"Okay?" I asked as he started driving down the road.

"Yeah, okay. I get it. This is awful. You want nothing to do with any of it. I don't blame you. Let's pretend it didn't happen. Maybe wipe your eyes a little, so our families don't wonder what's wrong."

As he drove, he pulled the bag of fries open and started eating.

"You're eating?" I stared at him.

"I'm hungry, and we're not talking about any of this other stuff, so yeah, I'm eating."

I pulled open the mirror in the visor. I looked horrible. I found a napkin in the glove compartment and tried to wipe off at least some of the black mascara. By the time we reached our driveway, my face was red rather than streaked with lines of mascara.

"No one's here," I said, surprised.

"Your family stays a long time after Mass," Luca said. "Avi is probably still eating donuts."

We went into the house.

Luca picked up a note on the counter. "Aunt Sam and Uncle Jace are working in the woods between our houses," he said, placing the note from his aunt back on the counter.

"I think Aunt Sam is right. It won't seem so far away if we can see your house from ours," he said, throwing away the now empty bag from the BayTree.

"Are we going to talk about what happened at the BayTree?" I said, tapping my foot.

"I thought you wanted to pretend like nothing happened," he said.

"You know I can't do that."

"Yes, I do," he said with a smile. "Glad you do too."

"Don't do that."

"What?" he asked innocently.

"Be cute. This is not a cute conversation, this is an awful, horrible conversation," I said, shaking my head.

He came to me and put his arms around me. "Life is good. Don't forget that. God wants you to be happy and enjoy life. This stuff he's letting you see … it's not to make you depressed and freaked out."

"Really? 'Cause if it was, then the mission would be accomplished," I said.

"Siena, you have to figure out a way to witness the pain and to care deeply, but not let it inside. You have to keep things separate, or you really will go crazy."

"How am I supposed to do that?" I asked.

He thought for a moment. "Give yourself permission not to take it on. Tell yourself it's not yours. You're being shown this stuff to help, not fall apart."

"That's easier said than done."

"Yes, but you have to do it. Approach all of this like a mystery to be solved, not as someone who's witnessing a murder. Because you aren't. That happened a long time ago. That guy—now that we know who he is—is long dead. He isn't hurting anyone anymore."

"Then why is he still chasing her in my dreams?" I asked.

"Those are dreams. Dreams don't always mean exactly what they seem to mean," Luca said.

We could hear the garage door opening.

"Try and pretend to be okay, or at least more okay, so your sisters don't get upset," Luca said.

He was right. I inhaled and exhaled and uncrossed my arms.

A moment later the door opened and Avi rushed in, followed by Dad. Avi was jumping and twirling around the kitchen. Everyone looked exhausted as they watched her.

Lisieux said, "She had way too many donuts."

"Clearly," I said, watching my sister with the faintest amusement.

Dad came to me. "Are you okay? Avila said your stomach was hurting. You're so pale." He placed a hand on my forehead.

"She's always pale," Lisieux said.

"Paler than usual," Dad said, not taking his eyes off me.

"My stomach was hurting," I said. "I'm doing better now. Just tired. I think I'll take a nap."

He felt the side of my face with the back of his hand. "You don't seem to have a fever," he said, as if not having a fever meant I was completely fine.

"I told you I'm a bit tired."

"All right, if you're sure you're not sick, I'm heading to the office. I have some work to do," Dad said.

"It's Sunday!" Avi exclaimed, dropping to her knees dramatically. "The Bible says not to work on Sunday!"

"I don't have much to do, but it can't wait. I'm closing on some land purchases this week, and I want to review the contracts," Dad said, pouring himself a cup of coffee.

Lisieux said, "Isn't that your fourth cup of coffee today?"

Dad grinned. "Caffeine, good," he said playfully, giving Lisieux a quick kiss on the cheek.

"Can't you review them on your computer from here?" Avi asked, standing up and crossing her arms.

"It's easier for me to do it at the office." He kissed Avi. "I'll be back soon," he said, grabbing his keys.

"Feel better," he said to me, and was gone.

"That was abrupt," Lisieux said as we each stared at the closed door—even Jackson tilted his head at the door.

"Yes," Gigi mumbled. "Very abrupt."

After a moment, Gigi turned from the door to me and Luca. "Where did you two go?"

"I told you, I wasn't feeling well," I answered.

"Why not?" Gigi asked. Her eyes locked on mine as if trying to determine the truth.

I glanced at Luca, who nodded.

"I saw the little girl at Mass," I said, feeling no reason to lie.

"You saw her?" Avi said, coming beside me.

Lisieux asked, "What was she doing?"

"She was up on the altar. Watching the tabernacle or the Eucharist, whichever she could see better."

"Who is she? Has she told you anything?" Avi asked, as if it made total sense that a girl from my dreams would appear in our church.

"She's never spoken to me, but we found a picture of her," I said.

"A picture?" Gigi said.

I nodded.

"So," Gigi said cautiously, "she is not who you thought she was?"

"No, she's not," I said with relief.

"I'm glad," Gigi said, sitting at the table.

"Me too." I sat across from her.

Luca clicked on his phone. "This is the picture," he said, holding it so my sisters could see.

Lisieux asked, "Which one is she?"

"The one with the curly hair," I answered.

Avi held Luca's hand close to her face. "The other one looks like Lisieux, but with less crazy hair," Avi said, still admiring the picture.

Lisieux studied the photo. "Maybe a little," she said.

Avi took the phone that was still held by Luca and moved it close to Lisieux. "Not a little, a lot."

I got up and went to them. I stared at the photo, this time focusing not on the girl from my dreams, but her friend. "I didn't notice that before," I said, taking the phone from Luca's hand. "I guess from the right angle she does look like you." A wave of fear washed through me.

"May I see?" Gigi asked, not getting up from the table.

Avi snatched the phone from my hand as Luca and I exchanged a concerned glance. Why did the other girl look like my sister?

"See? Isn't she Lisieux's twin?" Avi said, sitting beside Gigi.

Lisieux said, "She's not my twin."

Gigi took the phone from Avi and focused on the image. "Oh my," she said, and then accidently dropped the phone on the table.

"See, I told you. She is, too, your twin," Avi said to Lisieux.

Gigi's hands were shaking as she tried to pick up the phone.

"What is it?" I asked, sitting across from her while Lisieux and Luca came with me.

Gigi's eyes grew wide as they met mine. "That's my mother."

Luca said, "Your mother?"

"Yes," Gigi said quietly.

"Really? That's Great-grandmother Dorothy?" Avi asked excitedly.

Gigi stared at the picture. "I never knew she laughed as a child. She was so lonely and isolated."

Avi said, "Every little girl laughs."

"Not if they have no one to teach them how," Gigi said.

"They were friends," I said. "Great-grandmother Dorothy and that little girl. They appeared to be the best of friends."

"I never knew she had a friend," Gigi said, confusion tinging her voice. "She never spoke of another child except the boy who lived at the BayTree, and he wasn't a friend. He was a good bit younger and she said she felt sorry for him."

"The boy was there too—not in the picture, but in the memory," I said. "From what I saw, Great-grandmother Dorothy and the girl from my dreams were the best of friends, like sisters."

"You saw the memory?" Lisieux asked with intensity that matched the situation.

I nodded.

She lowered her head as if realizing that wasn't a good thing.

"Where did you find this photograph?" Gigi asked with caution.

I didn't want to answer that question. They were all watching me.

"It was at the BayTree," Luca finally said.

There was a collective gasp, and then silence.

Lisieux spoke in barely a whisper: "When did you go there?"

Luca answered, "This morning, after Mass."

"Why would you go there?" Avi asked, no longer sounding like someone high on sugar.

"I-I had a feeling there might be something there to help explain why the girl was appearing to me," I said.

"Why was my mother's picture at the BayTree?" Gigi asked, staring at Luca's phone without touching it.

I looked at Luca and then at Gigi. I felt like crying. I waited for Luca to speak, but he didn't. "Because the man who built the BayTree was the one who took the picture," I said, wishing I could have told her anything else.

Ten

I closed my eyes, not wanting to think about the girls … but they were all I saw. I saw them laughing together, jumping over waves. I saw the expression on the man's face as he took their picture. It wasn't evil, but it wasn't good either. Something in between. I wondered if the girls recognized the expression. I could tell by their laughter they didn't. The scene in my mind switched to his wife. There was something … a hint of understanding and then it passed. She pushed it away, not wanting to see what he was becoming. How long would it be? How long before he started hunting? The curly-haired girl in the photograph was close in age to the girl in my dreams. It would not be long ….

***

"Aunt Sam and Uncle Jace are doing good work over there," Luca said, bringing me some chai tea.

I was in the gazebo. After Gigi had gone upstairs, I had come outside. I needed some fresh air. The only sound was the buzz of Jason's chainsaw. They were not taking down any established trees, simply clearing away some brush and low branches to open things up.

I took the tea as Luca sat beside me.

"Yes, they are," I acknowledged, and sipped the tea.

We were silent together, listening to the distant sounds of Sam and Jason and the occasional chirping of birds and clucking of chickens. A storm was brewing far out over the ocean, which was causing the breeze to pick up. Jackson was lying near us in a patch of sunshine, too tired to care about the chickens or the storm. It was his naptime—most of the day was his naptime.

I sipped my tea. "I need to talk to Gigi."

"Siena, she doesn't want to talk about it. That's super clear. Besides, every bit of this happened way before she was born. She didn't even know her mom was friends with that girl."

"She's the only living person who could possibly know anything. She's the only one who remembers her mom. She told me so herself. I have to talk to her."

"She's an old woman, leave her alone," Luca said, leaning forward onto his forearms.

"If she ever heard you call her old, you would be in such trouble," I said, teasing.

"She has aged a lot recently," Luca said, sounding concerned.

"I noticed that too," I said, no longer in a teasing mood, "but I hoped I was wrong."

"Maybe we both are."

"Unlikely," I said as the chainsaw was turned off and the sounds of birds and insects were more audible.

After several minutes, Luca said, "I guess Aunt Sam and Uncle Jace are done clearing for now."

I shifted so I could see toward their house. "I can see through the woods a little easier," I said. "At least in some parts."

"Me too," he said, over the far-off rumble of thunder.

Jackson raised his head and whined.

"Do you feel that?" Luca asked as he sat taller.

"What?" I said, trying not to feel fear, though I did.

"It's cold," he said. He stood and spun around, looking for something.

"The wind was blowing," I answered, wishing I could believe that explanation.

"It wasn't the wind," he said as the breeze picked up and warm air swirled around us.

"It feels warm now," I said, feeling relieved.

He sat down. "Yeah, you're right."

I leaned against him, grateful for his strength. I was watching two squirrels chase one another up a nearby pine tree when I saw something. I sat forward and put down the mug of tea.

"What is it?" he said, as if he already knew what was happening.

"I see her."

"What's she doing?"

"Watching us," I said, my throat going dry.

She was standing next to the tree the squirrels had been playing on. As if they sensed her too, they had fled. I wished I could do that. I wished I could run away and never see her again, but something told me the only way to make her go away was to find out why she was there.

"She's in a blue dress, but it's clean," I said, feeling some sense of relief. "Maybe that means she's not being hunted."

"Where is she?" Luca asked.

"By that pine tree next to the trail," I answered.

She moved. She had been partially hidden by the pine tree and now she stood away from it, in the middle of the trail. Jackson stood and left the gazebo.

"Jackson," I whispered to him.

He stopped and stared at me.

"Come here," I said as the girl began to move down the trail.

He ignored me and went toward the trail.

I whispered, "Jackson, no."

"He's going to her?" Luca asked.

"Yes," I said, panicking.

Luca took my hand. "It's okay. I don't sense any evil and apparently neither does Jackson."

"What if you're wrong?" I said.

"Don't you remember how he reacted to Thomas?"

My mind went back to Thomas … when he was trying to persuade me to go on a picnic with him—a picnic without food. Jackson was more aggressive than I'd ever seen him. He was barking and growling. He wasn't doing any of that now.

"She isn't evil," Luca said. "I'd feel it if she was, and if I didn't, Jackson would."

I asked, "What does that mean?"

"Is she going down the trail?" Luca asked.

I nodded.

"Then it means we should follow her," Luca said.

I lowered my head. "I was afraid you were going to say that."

He held his hand out for me. I took it and stood up.

Jackson was waiting for us at the start of the trail, as he had done hundreds of times before. The girl was moving slowly along the path, her hands outstretched as if she was touching tall grass—though nothing was there. We made our way down the hill. The chickens scattered around us, but they were calm, not squawking. All the animals were calm. The squirrels and birds were merely watching, and Jackson was plodding along between her and us. Maybe Luca was right and she wasn't evil.

"He's next to her now," I whispered to Luca as the girl's hand reached down and seemed to touch Jackson's head. He wagged his tail and remained by her side as she led us down the side path, the one that went toward Luca's house. When we neared the cutoff for the pond, the girl stopped.

"She's looking toward the pond. She's smiling, I think," I said, watching every move the girl made.

Jackson whined as if he wanted to go that way. She petted him and together they moved toward the pond. They didn't go to the giant rock that hung over the pond. Instead, they went around it. Her feet left no prints in the soft mud; only Jackson's paws left impressions.

He followed her dutifully around the pond and into the woods.

"I've never been out this far," I said, suddenly aware that none of this was familiar.

"Me either," Luca said.

There was no trail. He was walking behind me as we wove through the ferns and fallen trees. The girl did not bother finding her way around things; she simply went through them. Our pace was slower now that we had to pick our way around trees and rocks, both of which seemed to be getting bigger the deeper into the forest we went.

I glanced up at the sky to get a feel for where we were. The ocean was on our left, the main road that marked the edge of our property on our right, but both were far enough away that neither could be seen or heard.

Luca said, "This place feels eerie and magical."

"We're on a trail," I said, realizing it was easier to walk.

"It's a game trail," Luca said. "She must have brought us to it to make it easier for us to walk. That was thoughtful of her," he said, as if she was a regular little girl leading us through the woods.

The girl started to skip, winding her way around boulders. It was as if it was a habit, like skipping was what she did in this place and she couldn't not do it, even now.

"I had no idea we had boulders like this. It's like a giant was throwing them around and they smashed into the earth, and now they're covered with moss," I said as thunder broke somewhere closer to shore.

Luca said, "The moss reminds me of the moss that covered the remains of the building near the skating rink."

The girl turned and focused on him.

"She's looking at you," I whispered, having come to a stop.

"Did I say something that means something to you?" he asked her.

"Can you see her?" I asked.

"No, but you can," he said.

"She's stopped watching you. Now she's going to that boulder. … She touched it," I said. "She's walking again, now she stopped and she's staring at the boulder."

Luca said, "Touch it where she did. Maybe there's a memory."

"I don't want to touch it," I said, crossing my arms and holding my shoulders. The air was suddenly cool as the rain started falling over the ocean. "I don't want to see evil."

The girl looked at me with a troubled expression, and went to the boulder again and placed her hand on it. She stepped away from it again and seemed to wait.

Luca said, "Maybe you won't see anything bad. You saw the girls playing in the picture frame, so maybe this will work the same way."

"I saw the girls playing and *he* was there," I said, cringing.

"He didn't hurt them. Give it a try. You said yourself you had to have answers. Maybe she's trying to give them to you," he said.

I looked at the girl, whose expression was blank. I started forward. I placed trembling fingers on the boulder, trying to find where she had touched.

"I don't see anything," I said with relief, quickly removing my hand.

"You aren't touching the stone. That moss hasn't been there for decades, only the stone," Luca said.

He was right. I put my hand back on the moss and carefully wiggled my fingertips down to touch the smooth stone.

The scene around me changed.

Eleven

The boulders were covered with snow. I heard young girls giggling somewhere nearby. I stepped around the boulder. It was like I was moving in a dream. The girl was there, stifling laughter as she busied herself making snowballs. From behind me, I heard more giggles. I spun, it was Great-grandmother Dorothy. She had two snowballs behind her back.

"Okay, I give up," Dorothy said with a mischievously playful grin.

"Ah-ha!" the girl said, leaping from the boulder and launching snowballs.

Dorothy was ready. She dodged the snowballs and threw one that got the girl right in the face, which made the girl laugh hysterically. She laughed so hard she missed her target, and Dorothy got her the second time. The girl recovered and launched some more snowballs. This time she hit Dorothy in the neck. Dorothy made a silly face, pretended she'd been hurt, and fell into the snow. The two wound up in a heap of giggles in a snowbank shaped by wind drifts near the boulder.

The scene changed. It was spring. I blinked, thinking maybe I was back in the present moment, but then I heard a girl calling: "Nira."

I turned to see Dorothy coming through the forest, calling to her friend. The moss was almost a neon color, it was so vibrant. Everything was alive: little ferns were unfurling and chipmunks scurried across my feet.

"I'm here," the girl, Nira, said, skipping toward her friend. "Ma sent me with treats."

She pulled two pieces of fried dough from the pockets of an apron she wore over a brown skirt. Her black curls were pulled back into a tight wrap. She was clean and neat, a clear contrast to Great-grandmother, whose dirty skin was covered in clothes that were worn thin. Her long brown hair was unwashed and uncombed. Nira's cheeks were plump, the way a young girl's face should appear. Dorothy's were gaunt—she was near starvation.

"Are these mulberry?" Dorothy asked excitedly as she took what Nira offered and began to eat hungrily.

"Yes," Nira answered, watching Dorothy with concern. "When was the last time you ate?"

"Yesterday, for breakfast," Dorothy said, not bothering to stop chewing.

"Here," Nira said, handing her the other fritter.

"No," Dorothy said, "that isn't right."

"We have plenty right now. Spring is a good time for us," Nira said, pushing it back to Dorothy.

Great-grandmother Dorothy took it and began eating it, this time slower, actually enjoying it. "Thank you,"

Dorothy said. "I don't deserve the kindness you and your ma show me."

"'Course you do," Nira said. "You would do the same for us if you could."

Something about Dorothy's expression shifted ever so slightly.

"Do you have any guests?" Nira asked as Dorothy finished the second fritter.

"No," Dorothy said, "but we will in a few days. Things will be better then. We always have food when guests are around, and I'm allowed to eat whatever scraps I want," she said with excitement.

A flicker of revulsion flashed over Nira's face. "That will be good," she said. "It's hard to see you so thin."

"It happens every winter," Dorothy said, trying to make light of it. "Once the weather warms up, we'll have an inn full of folks and plenty to eat."

"And a great deal more work for you to do," Nira said.

"I don't mind it so much. Ma and Pa are nicer when guests are around, so it's better for me," Dorothy said, sucking her fingers.

"I suppose that's true, but then we can't come to our enchanted forest," Nira said, twirling her long brown skirt, which floated a little.

"You can," Dorothy said. "You can keep everything in order. The guests never come this far out. I don't even *think my pa has been this deep in the woods. Definitely not my ma."*

Nira giggled. "No, your ma hates the trees. She'd never come out here."

"That's true," Dorothy said, hopping onto a fallen log and using it as a balance beam. "I'll come out when I can, maybe on a Wednesday, if Ma ever sends me into town alone."

"Every time I'm in the cave, I'll light a fire so you can see the smoke coming out the upper window and come, if you can," Nira said. She started to move away from the boulders.

"Good idea," Dorothy said.

She followed Nira … and the memory faded.

Luca was beside me. I pushed my hand hard against the rock, but nothing else came. "It's gone," I said sadly.

"What did you see?" he asked.

"Her name is Nira," I said to him as the girl raised her head slightly at the sound of her name.

"Nira? I like it," Luca said.

"It fits her," I agreed. "I was right. They were the best of friends. This was their secret place. They called it their enchanted forest."

"If it looked like it does now, that was a fitting name," Luca said.

"It was the same," I said. "Funny how so much changes, but the forest doesn't. The trees grow, but that's all."

"There's something nice about that," Luca said, looking around at the moss-covered trees and boulders.

"The memory started in winter. They had a snowball fight that ended with them laughing in a pile of snow. Then it was spring. Dorothy was so thin, she was half starved to death. Nira brought her some food. They talked a little about the inn and Dorothy's parents. It sounds like she had to work hard and wasn't well fed. Nira brought food for both of them, but gave all of it to Dorothy because she was so hungry."

Thunder broke, this time over the shore. Nira moved deeper into the woods.

"She's moving again," I whispered, noting the sky was becoming angrier every second. The tops of the trees were leaning in the wind, but the wind remained high so we couldn't feel it.

"The storm is over the land now," Luca said, sounding worried.

Jackson barked. The girl was moving quicker, and he was chasing after her.

"Come on," I said, starting to jog to keep up.

"Where are we going?"

"I have a guess," I said as the rock cliff that marked the end of our property and the beginning of the state park came into view.

Luca said, "We can't climb the cliff."

Large drops of rain were falling on us.

"We're going into it," I said, "not up it."

"What does that mean?" Luca shouted from behind me.

The storm made it hard to hear.

"There," I shouted as I saw Jackson's tail slip into the face of the rock.

"It's a cave," Luca said when we reached the low opening.

I was about to go into it when Luca held my arm. "Wait! Let me go first," he said, pulling out his phone and shining his light inside. He had to crawl to get through the opening. A moment later, he shone his light through. "Come in," he said.

Now the rain had begun sliding down the cliff wall. I crawled through the opening, my knees and hands getting covered with mud.

Jackson was in the center of the space, gazing up at me. He sat next to what appeared to be a fire pit. To the right of us was a small table with two chairs. To the left, a bench with a back and a blanket made of braided cloth of every color. In front of the bench lay a rug made of the same braided cloth. Everything was covered with a thick layer of dust; still, it looked like a little house.

I got out my phone light and shone it around. "What is this place?" I said.

"I have no idea," Luca said, equally amazed. "There's an opening up there." He tilted his light upward.

He was right; the rock face jutted out and there was a crack in it.

"That must be the upper window Nira spoke about in the cave. She told Dorothy she would light a fire anytime she was in the cave and Dorothy could watch for the smoke that would go out the upper window as a signal that she was there."

Luca shone his light up to the window, a rough diamond-shaped slit in the wall. "That's incredible. It lets smoke out and light in, but because of the angle of the rock face, the rain stays out."

"This whole place is incredible," I said, kneeling and touching the soft rug.

"How did they get this furniture in here? Some of it would fit through the opening, but not the table, or the bench," Luca said as he shone his light onto the roughly hewn wooden table, with equally rustic chairs on each side.

"They must've put it together in here," I said, appraising the opening of the cave.

In amazement, Luca asked, "They did all this themselves?"

"Nira's mom seemed pretty involved, so maybe she helped."

"That's a seriously nice mom," he said.

I ran my fingers along the table. "It's so pretty," I said.

In the center of the table was a slightly chipped ceramic vase with what appeared to be sticks jutting out of it. I reached my fingers toward the sticks.

"Siena, no," Luca said, whirling to reach for my hand.

He was too late. The sticks crumbled at my touch. It didn't matter. The memory remained. Pain seared through my body.

Jackson barked furiously as shrieking overtook my mind. I fell to my knees, the pain unbearable. I couldn't breathe. I was drowning. Luca grabbed me, knocking the remains of the purple lupins out of my hand. We fell together onto the ground. The shrieking had stopped and so had the pain, but the memory … the memory would never leave.

Twelve

I lay on the ground, panting and crying. Luca was holding my head on his legs. A fire burned in front of us. I could hear murmuring … Luca praying. His words were becoming clearer as the room came into focus. It wasn't a room … it was a cave. I felt cold. The fire's heat reached me, offering comfort. Luca was holding me and Jackson was near my feet, his nose pointed toward the entrance of the cave. I could hear the rain falling. I pushed myself up to a sitting position.

"Are you okay?" Luca asked, his hand holding my arm to keep me steady.

"What happened?" I asked.

"You passed out."

I looked down at the fire. There were glowing embers; it had been burning a long time. "How long ago was that?"

"A few hours," Luca said.

I rubbed my head. "Where did the wood come from? It's raining outside."

Luca pointed to a stack of thick branches piled in the corner. "It's well-seasoned wood, but not rotten, which was a surprise."

I sat hunched over. The fire made strange shadows on the walls, strange shadows that reminded me …. "I touched the lupins. That's what the sticks in the vase used to be."

"Yes," Luca said, sounding guilty. "I realized too late that there was evil in them."

"You could feel it?"

"It was so subtle, I couldn't feel it until I focused on it, when you reached for them," he said.

"I saw Nira's death," I said, staring at the fire and trying not to remember.

"I'm so sorry."

"How can that much evil exist?" I said. Tears started to burn my eyes.

"Don't let it in," Luca whispered, holding me against his chest.

His skin smelled damp; his shirt was wet from the rain.

"That pain isn't yours," he said. "Don't let it become yours."

"How do I stop it?" I said, crying.

"Look at me," he said, turning my face toward his. "Open your eyes. Think of the good. Think of me. Think of Jackson."

At the mention of his name, Jackson came over, his face almost touching mine. He licked my nose. I threw my arms around him. His fur was dry; he had come into the cave before it started to rain. I buried my face into his thick coat—think of Jackson. It was good advice. I thought of him as a puppy, chewing up anything he could find, and chasing chickens, and bounding in the snow. I squeezed him tighter. He was still, allowing me to immerse myself in memories of him.

I thought, too, of Luca, of the way he laughed, the way he worshiped.

Then I thought of God. How … how could a loving Father ever allow such evil to exist? I knew the answer I was taught: Evil exists because God wants us to freely choose him. If he took away evil, he'd be removing our choice to create evil, and he loves us too much to remove our free will. That was the answer in books, not in my heart. In my heart I heard: *She is loved, she was never alone, she is free.*

"If she's free, why is she here?" I asked angrily, not believing the words I'd heard within me.

It's not about her.

This thought made me stop. I released Jackson and slumped forward.

Luca asked, "Did you get an answer?"

"It's not about her."

"It's not about her?" Luca said, studying the words as he spoke them. "Do you think it's about him?"

I wanted to vomit. "If it is, he can rot in hell. I'm not helping him."

"That's not a Christian response," Luca said softly.

"You didn't see what he did," I said, eyes glaring.

He stopped. "You're right, I'm sorry. And you're probably right. He's probably in hell, though I hope not," Luca said, tilting his head upward.

"I appreciate that it's practically impossible for you to sin since the slightest thought of sin makes you sick, but there are times, like right now, when your goodness is obnoxious."

"God wants each of us, even the worst of us," Luca said simply.

I stood up and brushed myself off. "If he wanted me to help the devil, he shouldn't have shown me what he did," I said, glaring at Luca.

"Good point," Luca said, standing beside me.

I said, "Come on, we need to get back."

"It's still raining."

"We won't melt." I didn't want to be in that cave for even a second longer.

"Yeah, okay," he said, stomping out the fire.

Once it was out, he turned on his phone light. "Here, I'll go first." He knelt next to the opening.

"No," I said, terrified at the thought of being in the cave without him. I thrust my body into the freezing mud that was pooled at the entrance. Muddy water filled my shirt and shorts … the memory of the girl being drowned in the ocean encased me like the freezing water. I pushed hard, scrambling out of the cave, out of the freezing water, away from the memories. I let the tears fall, mixing with the rain. No one could see my tears.

Jackson came next, shaking the mud from his body as he exited the cave. And then Luca. He was not panicked like me, just dirty.

"Come on," he said, taking my hand and pulling me up from where I was crouched next to the rocks.

I walked beside him. His phone light guided us through the darkened forest. It wasn't late, only dusk, but the storm had blotted out the sun.

"Do you ..."—he hesitated—"do you know why the flowers were there?"

"It was him," I said, my voice robotic, trying only to remember and not to feel. "He brought them to the cave. He placed them on the table ... a sort of calling card."

"For who?"

"I don't know."

"Did you see ... all of it? What he did to her, I mean?" he asked.

"Yes," I said resolutely.

It was time for me to stop pretending. Stop pretending I was still a child, that I was innocent. I had witnessed the sort of evil that was found in hell.

Luca said, "I'm sorry."

"I understand why people go crazy," I said.

"There is good. You know there is good," he said.

"It's hard to remember that sometimes," I said.

He clutched my hand. "You have to choose to focus on the beauty, not the evil."

He was gazing down at me, willing me to see him. He didn't want to lose me. And I didn't want to be lost. All around us were the giant boulders covered in moss. The clouds had faded, the rain barely a sprinkle. It was twilight and the smell of the fresh spring earth surrounded us.

"I choose beauty," I said, looking into his golden eyes.

He leaned forward, kissing me with such intensity, an intensity that I matched. I kissed him with more passion, more life than I ever had before. I refused to give in to the darkness. Love, in its truest sense, could never exist in darkness. My love for Luca could not exist if my soul was consumed by darkness. I kissed him as if my life depended on it and he kissed me the same. He wanted me to fight the evil I witnessed, to stay with him, to understand what it meant to be alive.

Lights shone on our faces, and we pulled slightly away from one another. He held me next to him, his arm protectively around me. I held a hand up to shield my eyes.

Dad yelled, "You two are gone for hours in the middle of a storm, and we find you making out."

"We weren't making out," Luca said, holding up a hand to shield his eyes from the bright flashlight beams.

"I thought you were better than that," Dad said, approaching us. "I thought you were both better than that."

"Dad, stop," I said, embarrassed by how angry he was.

"You've put me through hell these last hours! I've been losing my mind with worry. Your phone signals stopped, and then the storm, and now I find you making out. What did you do, turn off your phones so you could be alone?" he shouted.

"Paul, calm down," Sam said, her voice sounding scared.

"That's easy for you to say," Dad yelled back at her. "She isn't your daughter—he isn't even your son."

His words cut Sam the same as a knife would have, and she stumbled back. Jason kept her steady and remained silent.

I shouted to Dad, "How could you say that!"

Luca held my hand to try and calm me. "You seriously think we came out here to be alone together in a rainstorm? We could do whatever we wanted, whenever we wanted, in your house."

"How dare you," Dad said, coming nearer to us.

Luca stepped in front of me. "You've been drinking," he said with disappointment but not surprise. "I smell it on your breath."

Dad's face contorted with rage—the rage of an addict who'd been caught. He shoved Luca into me. I fell back against one of the boulders and slid onto the muddy ground.

"Paul, stop!" Sam screamed, and ran to me, helping me up.

"Get up! You think you're a man?" Dad screamed at Luca. "You think you can do what you want with my daughter? Then get up and fight like one."

Jason stepped between them. "That's enough, Paul," he said. "You aren't thinking straight. You've been doing more than drinking. The kids make good decisions, always have. It's you I'm not so sure about."

Jason turned to help Luca stand. Before anyone saw it coming, Dad punched Jason in the face. Sam and I screamed. Sam ran to Jason, but it was too late. He had barreled into Dad, knocking him onto the ground. Dad was taller. Jason was stronger—the result of a life of hard work.

"Stay down," Jason growled, shoving Dad into the mud as he himself staggered to his feet.

Dad was breathing heavily and groaning as he rolled to his side in the mud. He vomited.

I started crying, which made me even angrier. "I … thought … you … were better," I said through the tears.

The pain hidden in the lupins decades ago may not be mine, but this pain was. This was my father. His addiction was overwhelming him … and all of us.

Breathing hard, Dad leaned against one of the boulders. He wiped his mouth with the sleeve of his shirt. "I haven't been drinking, Siena. You have to believe me." He reached for me.

I pulled my hand away from his reach. "Don't you dare touch me!" I said, enunciating every word with the fury I felt. "And if you ever lie to me again, it will be the last thing you ever say to me."

Thirteen

"What happened to you four?" Gigi asked when she saw us enter the house, caked in mud.

"Dad," I said. "He's using again."

I would not lie. I would not pretend the truth wasn't the truth.

Gigi slumped back as if she'd been shot, and in some ways she had. Her only son was an addict, an addict who treated his friends horribly and tried to beat up his daughter's boyfriend, a boy he loved and had welcomed into his home. But that was the addict. Nothing made sense; nothing was believable.

Fighting back tears, Lisieux asked, "Where is he?"

"The gazebo," Jason said, nursing a swollen face. "Jackson's with him. He's as muddy as the rest of us."

I was grateful Jason didn't mention that Dad was also covered in his own vomit or that Sam had cried the whole way back to our house.

Gigi tried to sound strong, as always. "You four should shower. I'll have Paul give Jackson a bath outside."

When no one moved, she said, "Go."

We each started toward the stairs.

She turned to the girls. "You go, too. I want to speak with your father alone."

My sisters hesitated, and then did as they were told. Upstairs, Luca, Sam, and Jason trudged toward their rooms, but my sisters stopped at my door. They stared up at me, each looking despondent.

"I have to shower," I said, feeling the mud drying on my skin.

"What's wrong with Dad?" Avi said, sounding as if she was about to cry.

Lisieux held her.

I picked at some mud drying on my hand. "I don't know," I said, wishing I could explain or at least understand our dad. I couldn't.

"I'll shower, and then we'll talk," I said, feeling the mud hardening as I stood still.

"Okay," Lisieux said, leading Avi away to her room.

When their light flicked on, I turned and entered my darkened room. I went to the window where the light from the kitchen was lighting up the yard enough to see my dad on his knees in the gazebo.

My heart softened. I'd been feeling hatred toward him. He was messing everything up *again*, but seeing him like that … I saw him for what he was, a man who was profoundly broken and intensely lost. I shivered. The air felt cold against my damp skin and drenched clothes. I sensed someone near me. I turned, expecting to see one of my sisters, but no one was there. In my head, I heard my mother's voice. I gasped at the sound—a sound I'd longed to hear for years.

"Help her."

"What?" I asked, swiveling my head.

"Help her," my mother's voice repeated.

"Where are you?" I whispered, trying desperately to see what wasn't there.

If I could see the girl and her memories, why couldn't I see my mother? She wasn't there, that's why. My mind was playing tricks. I told myself I was upset for my father and wished my mother was around to help. My mind was filling in that gap. The explanation was simple enough.

Down below, Dad was coming toward the house, with Jackson beside him. Both of them went slowly toward the back door. I imagined Gigi was waiting there. I could picture the disappointment and anger her expression held.

I went to my bathroom and stepped into the shower with my clothes on. As the warm water sent the mud streaming down the drain, I stripped off my clothes and laid them at the end of the shower. The brown water turned soapy. I scrubbed my hair and body, grateful to be clean.

"Help her." The words reverberated in my mind.

Was that really my mother's voice? I shook my head and the stream of water hit my ears. How could it be her? Who else could it have been?

I stood motionless, allowing the hot water to rush over me. If it was her, why didn't she say to help *him*? That would've made sense. She loved my father more than anyone else, and he needed so much help. If it was really my mother, she would've asked me to help him.

If my mind created an auditory hallucination of her, it would have said to help him, not her. I turned off the water and took my towel from the rack.

"Ugh, why is my life so bizarre?"

I wrapped the yellow towel around my red hair. The mirror was fogged from the steam of the hot water. I went into my closet and slipped on my pajamas. I hadn't eaten dinner, but I didn't care. The day had been long enough. I wanted to be alone. I wanted to sleep.

I kept my door closed and turned off the bathroom light. I went to my bed and wrapped the blanket my mother had made around me. I felt bad not going to my sisters, but what could I say to them? What could anyone say to any of us?

"Help her."

The words began again on a loop in my mind. I flipped over on the bed and covered my head with a pillow, trying to drown out the thoughts. After a few minutes I gave up and sat up in frustration.

"Okay, fine," I said under my breath. "You want me to help her, and Nira keeps appearing to me, so you want me to help Nira? Nira is dead. I saw her die." I choked on the last words. "There's nothing I can do for her."

I curled into a ball and pulled my mom's blanket around me.

"I miss you," I whispered to the voice.

Fourteen

For several hours I bounced between sleep and wakefulness: thoughts of the cave, the horrific memories, my dad—all of it mixing together. I heard voices throughout the house, more than usual. I didn't have the strength to listen. I reached for the rosary on my nightstand and wrapped it around my wrist, grasping the crucifix like the lifeline it was.

"Help me," I whispered into the night.

My body relaxed. Finally, the night and my mind were quiet …. I slept.

I stood in front of a gigantic castle—not one like our house, but a true castle with spires reaching high into the sky. It was a night with heavy clouds and no moon. There was no source of light, yet somehow I could still see. Everything was black-and-white or shades of gray. No color. Nothing was alive here. I was surrounded by stone. There was not the first blade of grass or fallen leaf.

I didn't want to go into the castle, but at the entrance was Nira. I went toward her. She turned and faced me. Her face was no longer neutral, as it so often was when she looked at me. Instead, she looked determined. She held out a hand for me. I took it. It did not feel like a ghost's hand; it felt, instead, like the hand of one of my sisters. Upon contact, we were suddenly inside. Not inside the front door, but inside somewhere up high.

All around us, people were walking quickly, as if they needed to be somewhere and do something right away ... but they weren't going anywhere. They were simply walking from one place in the room to another, each appearing so rushed. But no one was doing anything other than appearing busy. I began to pray out loud. It wasn't a conscious decision—more like a reflex. The world was so dark, it seemed to call for prayer. A man in a suit stopped in front of me. He listened for a second and then started to pray along with me. A moment later he disappeared.

"Where did he go?" I asked, looking down at Nira.

"He talked to God," she said. "You don't stay here if you talk to God."

"I'm here and I talked to God," I said.

"In some ways you are here, but in more important ways you're not," she said, leading me forward.

As we walked, I prayed without thinking. It was as if all the prayers I had prayed throughout my life started to pour from my lips. The ones I knew the best came the easiest. Around us everywhere were busy people, busy people who were hurriedly going nowhere. When one approached us, they either started praying and disappeared or kept walking.

"They aren't ready to hear you," Nira said as I was wondering why some kept walking instead of praying. "It takes so long for some to be ready," she said with a sigh.

This whole time, Nira was holding my hand, or maybe I was holding hers. I was afraid to let go of her. I was afraid that without her, I'd be lost. She was leading me through the darkness, though I somehow had no trouble seeing. In the corner there was a giant of a man. He didn't look like any other man I'd ever seen. He was as tall as two, maybe three men, and every muscle on his body was perfectly defined. He was beautiful in every sense of the word.

"He's a guardian," Nira said.

The beautiful giant was smiling at her with such genuine love that I felt a longing to move closer to him.

When we approached, he stepped aside. Behind him there was a form huddled in the corner.

Nira released my hand and knelt beside the form. I could somehow tell it was a human being, though it looked nothing like it. It was more like an indistinct animal, a sort of blob.

Nira tilted her head lower to try and get the form to focus on her, but the creature would not. I began praying. The form gradually became less of a blob and more of a person. It slowly lifted its head. It was a girl not much older than Nira. I continued to pray. As the prayers went on, the girl's features became more distinct. She lifted her eyelids. She did not appear to notice Nira, who was directly in front of her, nor the guardian who seemed to be anxiously watching her every move. Rather, she was slowly lifting her gaze to me. I began to tremble. Her eyes were dark and shattered from years of sorrow. How long had she been here? Who was she? I continued to pray and then she was no longer hidden.

I stumbled backward as Dorothy stared back at me.

My arms hit my mattress hard as my torso thrusted upward. I frantically felt for my bedside lamp. I tried to turn the light on, but I was shaking so hard I couldn't get my hands to work. The room was freezing and my fingers were numb. I clicked the light on as Luca rushed into the bedroom. He came to me looking as panicked as I felt. I clutched him. He held me close.

"I'm here," he whispered, "you're safe." He was moving his head from side to side. "Is anyone else here? It's freezing," he said, sounding worried.

"It was a dream," I answered, though it was much more than that.

"Did he catch her?" he asked, his voice growing quiet.

I shook my head against his chest, feeling the softness of his sweatshirt against my face. "It wasn't that dream."

"What was it about?" he asked, bracing himself for another awful vision.

"It was better and worse," I said. My throat felt like cotton. I swallowed to try and clear it. "No one was being hunted, but Nira was there."

"Did anything happen to her?" he asked, holding me a little tighter.

"She was okay. She was my guide, I think. We were in a castle of darkness. There were people everywhere, all of them were rushing around, but no one was going anywhere. It was a horrible place. There was no light anywhere, yet somehow I could see. Everything was in black-and-white. There was no color. Nothing living anywhere."

"You said there were people," he said.

"They weren't alive. They were souls. I'm not sure how I know that, but that's what they were."

"Was it hell?" Luca asked, his voice faltering.

"I don't think so. I was praying. It was like a reflex more than an active thought, and as I prayed, some of the people, or souls, prayed with me and then they disappeared. Not all of them did. Some kept rushing around going nowhere, but some stopped and listened and then prayed with me and then disappeared. Nira told me they left because you couldn't be there and talk to God. So it couldn't have been hell, or none of them would've prayed."

"Nira spoke to you?" he asked.

I thought for a moment. "Yes, she had such a tender voice. Maybe she can speak to me in dreams, but not when she appears when I'm awake."

"Maybe," Luca said. "Did she pray along with you and disappear?"

"No, she wasn't there. I mean she was beside me the whole time. Actually, she was holding my hand most of the time. She seems like a sweet little girl. But she wasn't really in that place. She was like me, just visiting."

"Why would she visit somewhere like that?" he asked.

"I guess for the same reason I dreamed of it. There was someone there who needed us, or at least I think that's why I was there."

He pushed back a little so he could see my face. His expression was questioning.

"Nira led me to the back wall. A man was there, a giant man …"

"The hunter?" Luca asked, his tone panicked. "The guy from the BayTree?"

"No." I shook my head. "I don't think either one of us would visit him. Nira called him a guardian."

"Like a guardian angel?"

"I think so. He was beautiful and so good. I could see him perfectly even though the place was dark, but it was like the darkness couldn't cover him."

"Was he Nira's guardian angel or yours?" Luca asked, sounding intrigued.

I paused. "He was guarding someone else. She was stuck in the wall. At first I couldn't see anything other than a sort of formless blob, like a small boulder or something. I kept praying, and she became clearer and clearer. Nira was so happy when she came out a little and could be seen. Nira tried to get her to notice her, but she wouldn't. It was like she couldn't see Nira or the guardian … only me."

"She saw you? Who was it?" he asked, sounding scared.

I whispered, "Dorothy."

Fifteen

Luca sat on the edge of the bed, his gaze falling on the darkened hallway beyond my open door.

"Maybe it was just a dream," I said.

Luca gave a chuckle. "We both know it wasn't 'just a dream,' " he said.

I sighed. "It was an awful place."

"But it wasn't hell?" Luca said.

"It wasn't hell, but it was still far from God, and that separation was suffocating. But it wasn't God who was away from them. They were away from God."

"Isn't that always how it is? Us going away from God, not the other way around," Luca said.

"Yeah, I guess so. I don't think I've ever been that far from God. At least I've never felt like that before. I get why Dorothy was crumpled into the wall. If I had to stay there any longer, I probably would've done the same thing."

"I'm sorry," Luca said.

"I guess my mother was right," I said.

Luca pushed backward so he could see my eyes. "Was your mother in your dream?" he asked.

I ran my fingers through my knotted hair, tugging at it. "No. She spoke to me while I was awake. She said 'Help her.' I thought I was imagining things or that she meant to say help him, meaning my dad, but I kept hearing 'Help her.' So then I was thinking, maybe it was about Nira. But now I wonder if maybe it's about helping Dorothy."

"That's a lot to take in," Luca said.

I laughed. "It always is."

We sat together listening to the stillness of the night.

Luca asked, "How can you help her?"

"I have no idea," I said, sitting up a little away from him and leaning against my bent knees.

"You can pray," he said.

"We can always pray, and Dorothy did come out of the wall a little as I prayed, but she was so different from the others there. When I prayed in front of them, they either prayed with me and then disappeared or they ignored me. She didn't do either. It almost seemed like …"

"Yes?"

"Like she was so lost she wasn't able to let the prayers in."

"She saw you?" Luca asked.

"She stared at me. It freaked me out."

"You said she didn't see Nira," he said.

"She didn't seem to. She had no reaction when Nira was there, kneeling right in front of her. Nira and the guardian definitely noticed each other, but with Dorothy it seemed like Nira wasn't even there."

"Maybe she wasn't there. To Dorothy, I mean. I think the world of spirits is much more …." Luca hesitated, searching for the word. "Dimensional, like layered or something. Maybe Nira is in a different layer for some reason and so Dorothy can't see her."

I thought about his idea. "Maybe. It wasn't that Dorothy was actively ignoring Nira. She seemed to legitimately not see her."

Luca got up and walked to the fireplace.

"What are you doing?" I asked.

"Thinking," he said as he ran his fingers along the hand-hewn beam of the mantle. "You said Dorothy was a *girl* in your dream, not an adult?"

"Yes, the same as I saw her in the memories and the photograph."

"But she didn't die as a girl. She left here at fourteen, moved to New York, had Gigi, came back here, and then passed away. So she definitely wouldn't have looked like a young teenager when she died, right?"

"Right. She would've been in her early thirties or late twenties, I think, and Gigi said her life was hard and had taken its toll, so she definitely wouldn't have looked like she was thirteen when she died."

"Were the other people in the castle children?" Luca asked, coming back and sitting in my desk chair.

"No," I said, thinking through the forms I'd seen. "All the others were adults."

He nodded thoughtfully.

"What does that mean?" I asked.

"I'm not sure," Luca said, "but I wonder if whatever is keeping her there happened when she was a child."

"Nira died when she was a child," I said softly.

"Yes, but many people lose people close to them as a child, but I doubt their souls are represented that way. Most of the people I see passing are adults, mostly older adults. And you said the other souls in the castle were adults. It makes sense that you would be seeing Nira as a teenager. That's how her living body last looked. But Dorothy … she should appear older."

I asked, "What do you think it means?"

He leaned forward in the chair, his gaze intense. "It means you have to talk to Gigi."

Sixteen

From somewhere down the hall, Jackson whimpered.

Luca said, "He's having a bad dream."

"Must be something in the air," I said, pulling the blanket my mom had made for me around my shoulders.

"Must be." He leaned back in the chair, gazing toward the darkened hallway.

I said, "Didn't you tell me to leave Gigi alone?"

"Yes, but that was before I heard her talking to Aunt Sam last night," Luca said.

I stared at him.

"It was after everyone had yelled at your dad."

"Did you yell at him?" I asked in surprise.

"He's your dad. I couldn't yell at him even if I wanted to, which I didn't. Plus, I didn't need to. Gigi said more than I ever could've thought up and your sisters' tears really drove home the points she made."

"Gigi was actually yelling at him?" I said, mouth slightly agape.

"Big time. I felt bad for him. She was going way back, bringing up stuff from when he was a kid. Saying how just because she didn't say anything about what he was doing then, doesn't mean she didn't notice, and how she shouldn't have defended him to his dad, and how hurt Mr. George would be, and your mom, to see him acting like this."

"What did he do?" I asked, feeling my stomach churn.

"What could he do? He cried."

"He cried?"

Luca nodded. "Not loud, but tears were falling as she was making her points. He just sat there, silent. It was difficult to see him like that, and her. In a way it was sort of like both of them were at their worst. I could tell she blames herself for a lot of it. She didn't say that, but she talked about how she never should've tried to protect him from his dad, that Mr. George had wanted to take a much stricter approach and she had argued against that. You could tell it haunts her. At the end, she said she was glad Mr. George and Rebecca were dead, because for either one of them to see Paul like this would've killed them. At that point, he was no longer crying in silence."

"He loves them," I said.

"He loves each of you," Luca said, leaning forward and touching my toes with his fingertips.

"That's hard to believe right now." I turned my head toward the cold fireplace.

Luca said, "He's not thinking clearly."

My anger surfacing, I stated, "That's his fault and his choice."

"You sound like Gigi."

"That's because she's right. She should've been harder on him as a kid, questioning every lie he told. Letting him get away with stuff … that made things worse."

"It's easy to look backward and realize what should've been done," Luca said.

"If your kid is lying to you—if anyone is lying to you, repeatedly—do you simply go along with it or do you stop them?" I said, wishing Gigi had done a better job when my dad was young and wishing none of this was my life.

"To face the lies is hard. My mom was lying to me. I knew it and I let it go," Luca said, looking down.

"You were the kid, not the parent. What were you supposed to do?"

He shrugged. "I wonder if I had done something different, if things would be different."

"You can't change the past," I said, willing him to look at me.

He lifted his eyes to mine. "You can't either. Your dad is a grown man. You can't blame his mom for his choices, Siena. He's in his fifties."

"You're right," I said, "but I wish I could. It's easier to blame Gigi from forty years ago than to blame my dad now."

"That's kind of the same thing Gigi did," he said softly.

I gave him a puzzled expression.

"Don't you get it? At the time, she was blaming her grandmother, or his friends, or hormones, or who knows what? Anybody but him. You're doing the same thing. You're blaming your grandma, who made mistakes like everybody else—but not huge ones—instead of blaming your dad. It was the same with me and my mom. I spent a long time blaming

133

others … my loser dad, Aunt Sam, me, the demons. Finally, one day I accepted that it was her. All that stuff in her life made a difference, but in the end she was the only one who could choose to stop allowing the demons in. At the end of the day, your dad is the only one who can stop using whatever he's using."

I said softly, "It's really hard to accept that there's evil in someone you love."

"It is."

"Did he say how long he'd been using this time?" I asked.

Luca exhaled. "He said tonight, right before going to look for us. He said he was so worried about us that he took something to help with his anxiety."

I felt like crying. "Do you think he believes his own lies?"

"I hope not," Luca said. "I wasn't down there the whole time. Maybe he was honest later, when it was just the adults. At some point Aunt Sam realized how bad it was for your sisters to be there and she asked me to take them upstairs. Lisieux went right into her room and closed her door, but it took a while to get Avi settled. She was crying, so I kept telling her one silly story after another. By the time I left her room, I saw your dad's light on. His door was closed, so I figured they were done. I was hungry."

"That's a surprise," I said, grateful for Luca's never-ending appetite.

"I can't help it. No one ate dinner. I was starving, so I went down to the kitchen, but I stopped on the stairs because Aunt Sam and Gigi were talking."

"You eavesdropped?" I was shocked. Luca never did anything even remotely wrong.

"I did not," he said emphatically. "I simply walked a little slower so I wouldn't interrupt their thoughts too abruptly. I was on the stairs for a few seconds before I went into the kitchen, but I heard Gigi mention her mother."

"Why would she bring her up?"

"All I heard was Gigi comparing your dad to her mom," Luca said.

I stared at Luca for a moment. "Had you told them about the cave?"

He shook his head. "With all the stuff with your dad, no one seemed to remember that we'd been momentarily missing. I figured it was better to leave it that way."

"Yes," I said. "I don't want my sisters to go searching for it."

I shivered at the thought of Avi or Lisieux anywhere near that horrible place. "Did Gigi say her mom used drugs?" I asked, convinced the answer was no. I couldn't imagine that being a common thing for women to do almost a hundred years ago.

"I don't think it was that sort of comparison," Luca said. "They stopped talking when I went into the kitchen. The whole thing wasn't much, but it was enough to make me realize that maybe you're right. Maybe Gigi does know more about what happened."

I sat back, staring at the heavy drapes covering the three bedroom windows. When the drapes were pulled back, you could see through the windows. Now everything was blocked. It was how I felt about this situation. There was a clear answer, but something was blocking it.

Seventeen

At some point during the night the rain started again, stopping off and on to allow the lightning to illuminate the sky. As I lay listening to the droplets pelting the windows, I found myself grateful for the house sheltering me. I thought again about the cave and wondered how the girls had used it. It was so much like a home—a special hidden place they shared. They'd been so happy in their enchanted forest. Was he watching them even then? Would I have seen him in the memories if they had no memory of him being there? I doubted it. I pulled the blanket up around my shoulders and tried to sleep, but couldn't. All I thought about was Dorothy, melted into the wall.

The thunder shook the house, and I rolled over to face the windows. I stood and went to them, pulling open the drapes. The rain rolled down the panes. The lightning danced between the clouds. Most of the storm remained above the sea, but some of it stretched inland, over our house. I wondered if it stretched past our property or if it was contained within our boundaries. It was funny how storms were like that. At our house, so close to the coast, storms would be violent, even hurricane-like, and yet in town there would barely be a sprinkle. Sometimes ferocious storms hit in town and at our house, but not a drop hit the sea. We were the place of convergence, where the air above the sea and the land met—in that place where the storms were strongest.

I lay back in bed with my head where my feet typically were, and wrapped up in my blanket. My room was no longer freezing, my mind no longer racing. I watched the storm and soon fell asleep.

"Why are you sleeping like that?" Avi asked when I opened my eyes.

"Why are you watching me sleep?" I pushed myself into a sitting position.

"I asked you first," she said.

"I was watching the storm," I said.

"Hmm, I didn't hear a storm." She stepped to the window and peered out.

"That's because you could sleep through anything," I said, swinging my legs off the bed.

"I went to bed late, so I was really tired," she said sullenly.

"That makes me sleep extra heavy too. It's no wonder you didn't hear the storm," I said, putting an arm around her and pulling her red tangled heap of hair back.

I sniffed her hair. "When was the last time you washed your hair?"

"I can't remember," she said morosely. "No one reminded me."

I wanted to tell her she was now nine and no one should need to remind her, but she was right. If our mother had been alive, she would have reminded her. Before our dad slipped back to his addiction, he had reminded her.

"I'm sorry, Avi, I'll remind you tonight," I said, holding her to me. She deserved better than all of us, certainly better than our dad.

"How long have you been awake?" I asked her. Her head leaned against me and I had an arm around her.

"A few hours," she said.

The gloominess in her voice made my heart break. "Have you seen Dad?" I asked, feeling nervous to mention him.

She shook her head. "He and Lisieux are still asleep."

I glanced at my clock; it was after nine. "It's Monday, right?"

"Yes."

"Shouldn't he be at work?"

"He should be a lot of things," she said.

I swallowed the lump in my throat. "Where's Gigi?"

"In the kitchen, drinking tea and staring out the window."

"Is she okay?"

"I don't think so," Avi said, her words heavy, her head hanging down.

"Let me get dressed." I squeezed her before hurrying into my bathroom where I quickly brushed my teeth. I went into my closet and pulled on a pair of shorts, a T-shirt, and a sweatshirt. It would be hot outside, but the nighttime temperatures had cooled the house down.

"Ready?" I said, holding my hand out for Avi as I stood near my door.

The old Avi of yesterday would've pounced and grabbed my hand with such force I would have had to fight to stay upright, but the new Avi simply slumped slowly toward me and gently took my hand in hers.

The new Avi was a lot like the Avi after Thomas had died and a lot like me after our mom died. That Avi made me want to cry.

Downstairs, Gigi was exactly as Avi had described: sitting at the table, a warm mug of tea between her frail hands, her focus on the slightly open window.

"Good morning," I said.

She turned toward us. "Good morning," she answered, though by her voice it didn't sound as if the morning was good.

"Where is everyone?" I asked, and squinted at the sun pouring through the windows.

"Sam and her family are at work, as one would expect. Lisieux is sleeping, as one would expect, and I believe your father is too," she said, trying to hide how angry she was with him.

Avi released my hand and slid in next to Gigi.

"Good morning again, Avila," Gigi said, and kissed her messy hair.

I poured a mug of hot water from the kettle and brought it to the table. From a jar, I took a pinch of dried roselle petals and placed them into the water to let them steep.

I said to Avi, "It rained last night."

"Siena, we already talked about that. There was a storm, I slept through it." Her head was resting against Gigi.

"That means," I said with a grin, "there will be lots of earthworms out."

Avi was silent. I could tell she was thinking.

"Oh, all right." She pushed herself up from the table, her limbs flopping like a rag doll. "Come on, Jackson, let's go play with the chickens," she said, sounding gloomy.

Jackson scrambled to his feet and went to the back door, waiting for her. At the door, she slipped her feet out of her slippers and into her boots. Almost as soon as the door closed behind her, she started to run and jump in the mud puddles.

"Thank goodness she's easily distracted," Gigi said, leaning back. She sipped her tea.

I swirled the roselle calyces around in my cup and sipped from it. "It's hard for her to resist earthworms and mud."

Gigi grinned. "Who can blame her?"

We laughed. I was grateful for the laughter and grateful my sister was still young enough to jump in mud puddles and feed worms to chickens.

I took another drink of tea. "It's too bad Dad is asleep. He'd enjoy watching her have so much fun."

"It's too bad your dad is how he is most of the time," Gigi said, no longer trying to hide how she felt.

I supposed that had been for Avi's sake, not mine. "He's been good most of the time, and I'm sure he wants to be good all the time," I said defensively.

"Most people *want* to be good. Very few want to be bad, and even those who *do* want to be bad can probably blame it on someone else, especially their mothers," she said, her tone biting.

"I meant that Dad isn't horrible," I said.

"He isn't, and you're right that his intentions are good. But he's not a boy anymore. He has his own daughters. He needs to raise them!"

"It's not easy without Mom." Even as I said it, I wondered why I was defending him. Why had it been so easy for me to vilify Gigi for defending him as a boy, and yet, here I was, doing the same thing. Only now, he was a grown man.

"Of course not," Gigi said, slumping forward. "It isn't easy for me without her or for you three, but somehow we have made it through without drowning our minds in a world of synthetic reality. If Rebecca were alive—" She seemed to crumple in on herself. "To be honest, I'm almost grateful she isn't. I can't imagine how much his actions would have hurt her. She wasn't like us. She was not surrounded by darkness and she had no capacity to tolerate it. She was too good for us, too good for this world."

I was silent, thinking of my mother, hearing her voice from the night before. She may not have been able to handle darkness when she lived, but she was not afraid of it now. Now she was fighting for us. I could sense it. I could sense her, and she gave me strength.

"Maybe you're right, maybe Mom wouldn't have been able to handle this side of Dad, but I don't think so. I think she was stronger than you give her credit for."

Gigi exhaled a long sigh. "Perhaps you're right, Siena. Perhaps it's me who wishes I had no knowledge of any of this. But your mother was like your grandfather. They had a goodness about them that the rest of us don't."

"Even Avi and Lisieux?"

Gigi held up her mug and said, "Even Avila and Lisieux."

"How can you say that? They're just kids."

"It has nothing to do with them or how old they are. It's part of our family," she said.

"You think evil runs in our family?" I focused entirely on my grandmother.

"It probably does, but that's not what I meant. The darkness I feel isn't evil—at least I don't think it is. It's more like a shadow. It has always been around me. Somehow I hoped destroying the inn would finally remove it. The land feels different, healthier, but I still sense it around us. A shadow that has always been there." Gigi shifted her focus from the tea mug, back to me. "It was around me from my earliest memories. And then when your father was born, it went around him too. Not the first few years, but it settled in around him and got quite dark as his relationship with my grandmother grew. It left him when he married your mom. Rebecca was so good, it was like she had a protective shield around her that also protected her husband and kids. Once she died, the shadow returned to your father."

"Is it around me and my sisters?"

"Sometimes. It seems to come and go from you three, but it's always around your father."

I said, "Dad invites the darkness in with drugs."

"Yes, he does. But it was there before, when he was a child. It came from me, I think. It must have. It wasn't around George, but it was always around me and my—"

"Your mother," I said, completing her thought.

She nodded sadly. "It was always on her. After she died, I felt it stronger around me and eventually your father, and now you three."

"Luca has never told me he senses evil around you or Dad."

"Samantha doesn't sense it either. Like I said, I don't think it's evil. More of a covering, a sort of cloud in front of the sun. It doesn't create darkness, it blocks the light."

"How do you know any of this?" I asked, realizing how strange this conversation was.

She looked down at her mug and then back at me. "I can see it."

"You can see it?" I almost choked on my tea.

"Yes. It's the most visible around your father, though it's on me too. It's a sort of thin dark film completely covering us.

I can ignore it if I want, or see it. Most of the time, I try to ignore it."

"Why haven't you told me this before?" I stared at her. After all I'd been through with my gifts, why had she never mentioned this?

She stared down at her tea. There was no steam rising from it and the room was cold. The tea would be cold, but still, she held it as if it were hot.

"I suppose," Gigi said, "I hoped it had gone away with the inn. And things did get better. The evil left. That was nice, and it made the shadow lighter, like its thickness got thinner. So I guess I hoped it would continue to fade. But it hasn't. It's remained the same since the inn burned. And before then … how on earth would I have brought something like this up?"

I thought about what she said. It made sense, all of it. If Luca wasn't in my life, I would never have told anyone about the memories I see. I would've kept them a secret and thought I was losing my mind.

"I don't blame you for not telling us," I said. "Can you see anything else or feel anything else?"

"I expect spiritual gifts are as varied as physical ones. I do not possess the gifts that you and Luca have, or Samantha, for that matter. I can detect nothing other than the shadow that covers us."

I hesitated before saying, "What about your mom?"

"My mom?" she asked, puzzled.

"You said it was around her and then around you. Could she see it?"

Gigi stared out the window, not avoiding me, but thinking.

"When she was dying, she was terrified. Nothing like when George died, or other friends through the years. Their deaths were peaceful. They weren't afraid of what was to come. Sad, perhaps, to leave those they loved, but not terrified. My mother was different. She was absolutely terrified. Her mind had become childlike and she was so scared. It was very difficult. I myself was a child, and there was nothing I could do other than tell her it would be okay. We weren't Christian, but I still had a sense of God and I think she did too. And so I had hope that she'd be okay. But all she spoke of was the darkness. Maybe that was because her eyesight was failing or because she didn't open her eyes. She was out of her mind, so I suppose nothing she said at that point should be taken too seriously."

"It was serious to her," I said, horrified at the thought of a young Gigi being left alone to care for her dying mother. Especially when neither one had any understanding of God's love for them.

My own mother had died before she reached the hospital— before any of us could get to her—but I can't imagine there was ever any fear. She didn't want to leave us. I had no doubt about that. Still, she wasn't afraid to die. I was equally sure of that. If we weren't so young, she probably would've welcomed it. Everything she did was to serve God and she looked forward to the day she would see him.

"Yes, it was extremely serious to my mother. She was so scared and she held on for so much longer than she should have. I wish I'd prayed for her. Maybe it would've helped," she said, slouching forward. The cream-colored shawl she wore fell forward to the edge of the table.

I said, "You can pray for her now."

"I always do," Gigi said.

"Do you still pray for Grandfather and Mom?" I asked.

She was thoughtful. "Rarely. They don't call to me like she does."

"What do you mean, Gigi?"

"I never thought about it until now, but I feel my mother in a way I don't feel the others. It's not in a good way. It's more of a need. Your mom and George feel close to me. With George, especially, it's a feeling of love and closeness. With my mother, it's different. There is love, but there is … separation too. It feels as if she needs prayers in a way the other two do not."

We heard Avi shriek joyfully as she splashed in the mud.

I tried to slow my racing heart, but it was pointless. "Do you know anything about Nira?" It felt as if I was jumping off the high dive. There was no going back … not now.

"Nira?" Gigi appeared puzzled.

"She's the girl I keep seeing. She was Great-grandmother Dorothy's friend," I added, my heart beating so loud, I wondered if Gigi could hear it.

"The girl from the photograph? Did she tell you her name?" Gigi said with concern.

"No, she's never spoken to me—at least not while I was awake. But Great-grandmother Dorothy called her Nira," I said, watching Gigi closely and wondering if she knew this ghost girl.

"You saw them together again? Did you find another photograph?" Gigi asked with concern.

"Not a photograph, but another memory. Every memory of one contains the other," I said, my hands trembling. "They were best friends, more like sisters."

"That remains difficult for me to believe. My mother never spoke of her or anyone other than her parents and the people who lived at the BayTree, and none of those were positive memories."

I closed my eyes. "Nira died," I sputtered. "The man from the BayTree killed her. It might have been too hard to tell you about a girl she loved who was killed."

"How do you know this?" Gigi asked, frowning.

"I saw it," I said, trying not to remember the gurgled screams.

Gigi reached over to my hand resting on the table. "I'm sorry," she said, staring at me even though I was looking away. "I'm so sorry you saw that. No one should ever have memories like that."

Her kindness brought tears. "It's okay." I sniffled. "I can handle it."

"Yes, with the Lord beside you, you can handle it. Stay close to him," she said, rubbing my hand as if she felt I needed the reminder.

Maybe I did. It was so easy to see the darkness—much too easy. Now that I had my gifts, it was harder to see the good.

Avi shrieked with delight again.

I turned to the window. *All is made good,* the quiet voice in my mind reminded me.

"I see the evil, and it's hard. I see the good, too. God has never abandoned me and he never will. He never abandons any of us," I said, remembering how he'd been with Nira as she died. She hadn't been alone, not really.

"I'm glad you understand that, Siena. It's not easy, with the life we have."

The heaviness was evident in her words. Her soft hands loosened around mine.

I placed my other hand on hers. "We have a beautiful life," I said.

Jackson was barking as he and Avi splashed in the mud.

Gigi's shoulders straightened and she said, "Will you tell me about the memories? The good ones, I mean."

It was nice thinking of the two girls joyfully enjoying each other's company. I refused to think of anything beyond that. "The first memory was in the snow," I told Gigi. "They were surrounded by giant boulders. They were having a snowball fight, like Avi and I do sometimes. They were giggling and laughing, two sisters being silly together. And the second was in the springtime. The same giant boulders were covered with such vibrant moss, they appeared almost neon green. I bet if yesterday had been sunnier, they would've been the same bright green as in the memory."

Gigi leaned closer. "Giant boulders."

"Yes, ginormous, bigger than this table," I said.

"That's a real place?" She looked startled.

"Yes, far past the pond, almost to the edge of the state park," I answered, intrigued by her interest.

"It's on our land?" Gigi said, mouth almost falling open.

I nodded. "They called it their enchanted forest, and that's the perfect name for it. I've never seen anything as magical."

Gigi asked, "They were there together—my mother and this little girl?"

I nodded. "Have you seen it before?"

"In dreams. Many times, in dreams. I had no idea it was a real place."

"I can take you there," I said. "If you're up for the walk."

Gigi's eyes brimmed with tears. "I would love to see it."

"Do you want to come?" I asked Lisieux, who had stumbled down the stairs in her mismatched slippers. Her long brown hair was sticking up everywhere.

Her voice groggy from sleep, she asked, "Where are you going?"

"To an enchanted forest," Gigi answered, sounding like Avi.

Eighteen

We waited fifteen minutes for Lisieux to get dressed, put on real shoes, and pull her hair back into a messy ponytail.

"Are you finally ready?" Avi said impatiently as she leaped off the edge of the gazebo bench and landed with a splash in a mud puddle.

Lisieux told her, "You're getting filthy."

"It doesn't matter. Gigi said I could, didn't you?" Avi said.

"What I said was if you get any dirtier, you'd have to hose off before I let you into the house."

"See?" Avi said to Lisieux as if this had proved her point.

Lisieux shook her head.

"Come on," Avi said, taking Gigi's hand and helping her start down the hill, toward the trail. Jackson was right beside them.

Lisieux and I walked behind. When the trail split to go toward the pond, I made sure we went to the right. We continued on the winding trail, my hand automatically sliding across the bark of the trees that had been rubbed smooth over the years.

Avi said, "I hear Luca and the guys working."

Electric saws started and stopped in the distance. I imagined the smell of sawdust.

"Yes," Gigi said, "they're finishing up the trim this week. It won't be long. Only a few more days until they're done."

We each grew quiet. The thought of Luca, Sam, and Jason moving out was not a thought any of us liked.

"Sam told me I can have a sleepover anytime I want," Avi said, cheering herself up. "She said we'll make white-chocolate-covered popcorn and watch movies."

"That will be a lovely time," Gigi said.

"Yes, Sam and Jason let me get away with everything," Avi said with a fake maniacal laugh.

Gigi said sternly, "I'll have a talk with them beforehand."

"We need to go around the pond," I said as my feet started to sink into the mud. It had rained more than I realized in the middle of the night.

"Walk gentle," Avi said, and released Gigi's hand to jump into the mud.

"I thought you just said to walk gentle," Lisieux said. She moved off the trail to avoid the mud.

"I meant you three. Me and Jackson like the mud," she said, grinning as she hopped down the trail, throwing up splatters of mud as she went. Jackson was bounding around beside her, his fur no longer the color of copper.

"This way," I said. I proceeded around the pond using the same path Nira had taken me on the night before. The buzzing of the saws in the distance made me wish Luca was with us.

"This is the trail she took us down," I said when we reached a game trail which stretched deep into the forest.

Lisieux said, "Why would a ghost girl use a game trail?"

Avi said, "She was probably being nice to Siena and Luca."

It felt strange and yet totally normal to hear my sisters talking about a girl that only I could see. Did that make her a ghost? Was that better than a figment of my imagination?

"This feels familiar," Gigi said as the air started to cool.

"Why is it so cold?" Avi said, shivering.

Lisieux whispered, "Is she here?"

"Yes," I answered.

Nira had suddenly appeared in front of us.

Avi whisper-yelled, "Where is she?"

I said, "She's leading us."

Jackson passed each of us to walk beside Nira.

Again, Avi whispered, "Is she next to Jackson?"

"Yes."

Avi ran and caught up to our dog. "Hello, Nira. I can't see you. Can you see me?"

In an impatient tone, Gigi said, "Avila, don't talk to ghosts."

"It's rude not to tell her hello," Avi said. "What did she say? Can she see me?" Avi turned to me.

"She never talks to me when she appears like this," I said. "I've only ever heard her speak in the memories and in a dream."

Nira was leading us to where the enchanted forest began, at the moss-covered boulders.

In my heart, I was afraid she would take us to the cave. I would not follow her to a place that held that much evil, not with my sisters with me.

"It's just like my dreams," Gigi said, amazed at the beauty of this place that had been ours all along, while hidden well enough that we'd never found it.

"It's like nothing I've ever seen," Lisieux said, twisting around, taking in the enchantment.

"It's magical," Avi said, twirling around and around, reminding me of Nira.

"My mother knew of this place?" Gigi asked me.

Nira appeared to shift her focus to Gigi.

"Yes," I answered, aware that Nira was paying attention to the exchange.

Gigi asked, "Why did she never bring me here or at least tell me about it?"

"She did tell you, in your dreams," Avi said, still twirling, and leaping like a ballerina from the base of one boulder to another.

"What happened in your dreams?" Lisieux asked. She gently touched the vibrant moss on the boulder next to her.

"I saw the beauty of this place in my dreams, and wandered around, and ...." Gigi stopped talking in order to study the boulders.

"What, what?" Avi said urgently.

"I found something."

"What?" Lisieux asked.

All of us were now watching Gigi.

"I don't …." She touched a flat part of one of the boulders. "A box, I think."

Avi clapped. "Oooh, a mystery!"

Gigi went around the boulder. Nira was watching her. Nira suddenly appeared beside Gigi on the other side of the boulder. Jackson barked and ran to stand next to Nira.

Gigi inspected the boulder. "This looks familiar."

"How can you tell?" Lisieux asked. "It looks like every other side of a boulder."

"That indentation," Gigi said. "I remember that somehow."

Jackson barked, not stopping. Avi grabbed my hand when we heard someone in the trees.

"It's me," Luca called as he came out of the forest, and Jackson ran to him.

"You scared us," Avi yelled. "Well, not me, but Siena."

"I didn't mean to," he called back.

"Why are you here?" she asked when he was closer.

"I wanted to check on you." Luca placed his hands on her shoulders.

"That's so nice," Avi said. "How did you know where we were?"

"He tracked Siena's phone," Lisieux said with an expression that made it seem like Avi's question was a foolish one.

When we got home, I'd need to put my phone in my pocket before she saw it on the counter.

"Yeah, I tracked her," Luca said, winking at me so the others couldn't see. "I didn't realize you three were with her. I wouldn't have come searching for her if I'd realized she wasn't alone."

"Thank you for worrying about me," I said, kissing Luca.

Avi said, "Why do you always have to kiss? It's so disgusting."

"Avila, don't be rude," Gigi said before she returned her focus to the boulder.

"What are we doing?" he asked, following our eyes to the boulder with the flat spot on the top.

Lisieux said, "Gigi used to dream of this place and she says this spot is familiar."

"And she said she thinks she found a box in her dream," Avi added, as if Lisieux had left out the most important part.

"That indentation looks familiar," Gigi said, pointing with her walking stick at the indented spot low on the boulder.

Luca knelt on the damp earth. He gingerly touched the indented spot. His hand went right through it.

Avi gasped. "Your fingers disappeared!"

"It's an opening," Luca said, pulling away the moss.

Behind where the moss had been was a minor indentation in the boulder, like a miniature cave. He put his hand inside.

"Careful," I said, "who knows what might be in there."

He smiled up at me and then contorted in pain, jerking his hand out.

Avi screamed.

"I'm kidding," Luca said, putting his hand back in the hole. He felt around and pulled out a rusty green box barely larger than his hand.

Nira stepped forward, inches from Luca, who was studying the box.

Lisieux said, "That's a lot of rust."

Avi squealed and said, "Careful not to cut yourself."

Luca gently tried to open it. "It's rusted shut," he said. "I don't want to force it open without gloves on."

Avi said, "I wonder if it's cursed."

Lisieux said, "He wouldn't be able to touch it if it was."

"Lisieux's right," Luca said. "It isn't cursed, but there is some darkness. Not a lot, or I'd be sick. I do feel something that isn't good." He was turning the box over in his hands.

I asked him quietly, "Like you did with the lupins?"

"No, those were evil," he whispered back to me. "Whatever is in there isn't good, but it isn't like that. It feels like a memory of evil."

"Weren't the lupins the same?" I asked.

He shook his head. "Evil was still attached to them, until they disintegrated at your touch. There's no evil attached to this, only the memory of evil. Or at least that's my best guess."

"May I have it?" Gigi asked, holding a hand out to take the box.

I marveled at the difference in their hands when he placed the box in hers. Hers were pale, and so soft and frail that it seemed anything could pierce them. His were the opposite: a tanned-brown color with thick calluses. He'd always had large hands, and now, after working with Mr. Jones and his team, his hands had grown as muscular as the rest of him.

Gigi used the edge of her shawl to hold the box.

"The rust will ruin it," Avi said, and gasped to see the dainty cream fabric turning an orange-brown where it touched the box.

Gigi didn't seem to care about her shawl or anything else. Her attention was riveted on the rusty box. I glanced around. Jackson stood beside Avi. Nira was gone.

"Here, let me help you up," Avi said, trying to pull Luca to a standing position.

He hopped up, towering over her.

"Nira's gone," I said.

Gigi had already started walking back toward the pond, her focus on the box in her hands.

"I need to get back to work," Luca said as the rest of us started after Gigi.

I said, "Thank you for tracking me."

"Anytime," he said, and kissed me goodbye before turning toward the sound of saws.

"I always miss him when he's gone," Avi said wistfully.

"Me too." I took her hand in mine.

Lisieux said, "He'll be home for lunch, and based on those clouds, he might be staying at the house."

"I hope so," Avi said as we neared our yard.

Gigi climbed the hill with her walking stick in one hand and the box in the other. She went into the house without a word. Avi watched her and then started hopping around in the mud with Jackson.

I said, "Don't forget to hose him off—and yourself—before you come in."

"I'll wait for the rain," she said, sniffing its scent on the wind.

"Don't stay out if there's lightning," I said as Lisieux went into the house.

"I'm not stupid," Avi said, still jumping in the mud.

"Avi, I need you to promise me if you hear thunder, you'll hose the two of you off and come in, preferably through the garage so you can grab a towel and dry off first."

"Okay, fine, I promise," she said.

I didn't fully believe her, but I went inside anyway. Lisieux sat on a chair at the kitchen table, holding the book she'd left there.

I asked her, "Where's Gigi?"

"Upstairs," she said without shifting her eyes from the page.

I went toward the garage, inconspicuously grabbing my phone from the counter and putting it in my pocket. I opened the garage door. "Dad's car is still here," I said, partially disappointed, partially relieved.

I wanted him to be functioning and on his way to work. But at least if he stayed home, he wasn't buying more drugs.

"Maybe he's in his office," Lisieux called out, already so engrossed in her book she didn't bother looking up.

She hadn't read like this in a while. These last few months since my dad had gotten sober—or seemed like he was sober—they'd been playing chess. It was her primary focus, that and baking. She played chess with each of us and online as much as she was allowed. But like our dad, she was now returning to her drug of choice.

I went toward his office. The door was open. The only light came from the large bay window behind his desk. The room was empty.

Back in the kitchen, I said, "He must be upstairs."

She mumbled some form of response.

I went to her. "Hey."

She looked up at me.

"Don't hide. I feel overwhelmed too, but we need to be here for Avi. I'll try and be better for you too," I said.

Tears started to form in her eyes.

I hadn't expected that.

"It's awful when he's like this."

"Yes, it is, but the rest of us are still here, and Dad is going to get better. I can feel it," I said, wishing I was telling the truth.

Lisieux said, "You've never been good at lying."

"There's a reason this is happening. Why Nira is appearing and Dad is struggling," I said.

"What's the reason?" she asked.

"I haven't figured that out yet, but I'm working on it," I said.

She nodded. "Thanks for trying," she said, and slowly returned her attention to the page in front of her.

I kissed her on the top of her head and said, "Don't give up," and hurried to the stairs.

I needed to check on Dad, but even more than that, I needed to find out what was in that boulder.

Nineteen

Upstairs, Dad's door was ajar. I pushed it open. He was sound asleep—or perhaps passed out would be a better word—on his bed. He hadn't opened the door; it must've been Gigi. She must have had the same thought I did, which was to make sure he was still alive. It was an awful thought, but it was almost noon. I moved closer. He lay on his stomach, his body gradually rising and falling with his breath.

I exhaled. "At least you aren't dead," I mumbled, and left the room.

I went directly to Gigi's room and knocked on the closed door.

"Who is it?" she said, sounding hurried.

"Siena," I answered. A moment later I saw her shadow move under the door. The lock clicked and the door opened.

"You locked your door?" I said in complete surprise. I had never known Gigi to lock her door.

"I was afraid Avila would come up searching for what we found. I didn't want her to see the notes."

"Notes?" I asked.

"That's what was in the box," Gigi said, gesturing toward the loveseat at the far end of her room. I followed her to the loveseat. The windows behind it were open, allowing warm, rain-scented air into the room. There, on a faded gray towel, was the opened box with flakes of rust surrounding it.

I said, "How did you get it open?"

"I'm not quite as feeble as I appear," Gigi said with a weary expression. "In truth, it was not hard to open, as long as you weren't touching the rust with your bare hands. I tapped it around the opening, pulled, and it opened."

The wind blew in, bringing with it the smell of spring, of new birth, of hope. I felt the heaviness in the room. Spring was the hope I had to hold on to.

"My mother loved the smell of rain," she said. "I wanted to think of her in a good way while I read these."

"What did she write?" I asked, steeling myself for some sort of horrible response.

"She didn't write anything—at least not as far as I can tell. This is not her handwriting. Like you, she always made sure her penmanship was precise. There was never a line out of place. This is written quickly in an old-fashioned ornate cursive."

"I've never known you to think so much about handwriting," I said.

"I have never cared so much to try and understand the meaning behind it," she said with resignation.

I lowered my eyes. "If your mom didn't write the notes, then why do you think she's part of this?" I asked, though I also believed she was.

"She's the one I saw in the dreams, hiding the box where we found it. The writer is clearly addressing a young woman, though if I'm right and it is my mother, she was no older than Lisieux," she said with an edge of disgust.

Cautiously, I asked, "Who is the writer?"

"A married man with a son," she said, looking up at me.

Both of us knew what that probably meant.

"The man from the BayTree?" I asked as I felt the world spinning.

"That's my guess," she said, leaning back in a defeated manner.

I plopped down onto the other side of the loveseat, and my long red hair fluttered up with the wind.

In barely more than a whisper, I asked, "What did they say?"

"They spoke of his …." She paused for a moment. "Intense desire to be with her."

I felt my stomach heave.

In a whisper, I said, "He killed kids … he killed Nira."

"I am aware," she said softly, pulling her shawl tighter around her. "It's difficult to understand what was meant."

I looked down at the slips of paper. The paper itself was in good condition. The sprawling cursive writing was clear enough, but thankfully the ornateness of it kept me from being able to easily read it upside down. "Why is it difficult?" I said, my stomach churning.

"There are no notes from her, just from him, or I assume from him. The handwriting is the same on every note. It's like reading one side of a conversation. I have no idea what the other side is saying. Though I suppose in some ways I can tell," she said, sniffing.

Gigi loved her mother. And she always spoke of her in a way that was clear she not only loved her but respected her. Her life had been hard and she hadn't always made the best choices, yet she did the best she could. But this … being in a relationship with a murderer … a serial killer who killed your best friend …. I felt dizzy.

"Part of me wants to tear them to shreds," Gigi said, "to never let them be read by another living soul."

"Maybe that would be a good idea," I said, afraid of what they must contain.

"But why were we led to them? Why were *you*?" she asked, eyes boring into mine.

Thunder burst. The storm was fully upon us. I quickly closed the windows as water began to splatter the sills. In the distance, I saw Luca running home. I sighed in gratitude when he entered the yard. Avi greeted him. At least now she'd get washed off. Luca would be disappointed he didn't get in a full day's work, and after last night I was sure Sam and Jason were more than ready to move out of Dad's house. Still, I was glad Luca would be with me. I needed him here.

He quickly scooted Avi in toward the garage. She might not understand the danger lightning posed, but he did.

I returned to the loveseat. "Luca is bringing Avi in," I said.

She nodded. "He's a good boy. My mother never knew what that was like."

"What do you mean?" I asked.

"She never had a man like that in her life. Her father was awful, and then there was this man." She indicated the notes. "And then my father. After that, there may have been others, but she kept them away from me. She protected me, no matter what. She loved me and protected me, though she herself had never been shown either," Gigi said, dabbing at the tears.

I touched her hand. "Nira loved her. She had a real friend in her."

Gigi nodded. "I'm grateful for her," she said. "Without her … I suppose there's a significant chance my life would be very different."

I'd never thought of that. Nira changed our family. She loved Great-grandmother Dorothy, and because of that, Dorothy was able to love Gigi. I existed because Gigi was able to love not only my grandfather, but my father.

There was a knock on the door.

Gigi sighed and hastily straightened the notes, putting them back in the box. She secured the lid in place and wrapped the box in the towel. "Come in," she said.

Luca opened the door. "Sorry, I didn't mean to bother you, but Lisieux said she thought you were up here."

"We were just finishing," Gigi said, and I could tell she was too overwhelmed to continue this conversation.

I stood to leave.

"Will you take them?" she said, reaching out to me with the towel-wrapped box.

I glanced at Luca. He didn't respond.

"Luca said they held the memory of evil. So if I touch them, I'll see those memories," I said, wanting nothing to do with them.

"Please," she said. "Maybe I'm wrong. Maybe things are not how I thought they were. That is my prayer."

I sat back beside her. She held the box on her lap.

"What if I take them and what if … things are exactly as they appear to be?" I said with concern.

"Then I will know that. And I will also know he was at least fifteen or twenty years her senior, and as Thomas was quick to point out, young girls are easy to manipulate."

I cringed.

"I'm sorry," she said, lowering her head. "It was wrong of me to mention his name, but he was not wrong, not in that case. And my mother was a lonely girl. She would have been easy prey … she was easy prey."

Luca was watching the exchange. "I think you should take the box," he said. "Nira wanted you to find them. There must be a reason."

"You don't know what's inside," I said.

"I don't," he said, his hands in his pockets, his clothes clingy from the rain.

I said, "They're notes from the man at the BayTree, to Dorothy."

He stumbled and then straightened his posture. "Nira wanted you to find them. There must be a reason," he said.

Gigi held the box up for me. I hesitated and took it, careful to make sure the towel was fully covering it.

"Please, do not let your sisters see them," she said in a defeated tone.

I stood up and said, "I won't."

We started from the room, and Gigi said, "Remember, she had nothing that you have."

Luca placed his hand on my shoulder.

"The love Luca shows you in one simple gesture is more than any man ever showed her," Gigi said, sniffing. "It is not fair."

Luca answered, "It's not."

"I won't judge her. I promise," I said, hoping I could keep my promise.

We were walking out of the room when Gigi called out, "I will be praying for you."

Twenty

When we entered my bedroom, Luca said, "That sounded like an intense conversation."

"Yes," I said, placing the towel-covered box down onto the hearth of my fireplace. "I've never seen her like that."

"It's been a hard day and a half," he said. "She found out her son is using again, and whatever those notes are, seemed to challenge the memory she has of her mom. That's not a good feeling."

"I don't want to read them," I said, trying not to tremble at the thought. I sat on one end of the hearth.

He knelt beside me. "You don't have to and you definitely don't have to yet."

I leaned against him. "You should go change, you're soaked," I said as I ran my fingers through his sopping wet curls.

"Yeah, I'm pretty miserable." He laughed, pulling his shirt away from his skin.

"Go. I'll be okay."

"I'll be right back," he said, and left the room.

I pulled my legs up, feet on the hearth. I stared at the gray towel, with my head tilted to one side and leaning against my knees. I tried to work up the courage to unwrap the box. I couldn't do it.

I was sitting and staring a few minutes later, when Luca returned in dry clothes. His hair was still damp.

I said, "I'm sorry your workday got rained out."

He shrugged. "It's okay. I sort of had a feeling you needed me. Guess I was right."

I gave a sad laugh and said, "I always need you. I have the damsel in distress thing down."

He sat on the other side of the box. "That's not your fault."

"No, but it's exhausting," I said in a mopey voice.

He leaned forward to kiss me at the same moment as Avi popped her head into my room. Luca used his body position to subtly move the towel behind him.

"What's that?" Avi asked. Her hair was a wet tangled heap, but at least she had changed into dry clothes.

She really didn't miss much.

"A dirty towel," I said. "Luca was going to take it to the laundry room."

"I can take it if you want," Avi said, being her usual helpful self.

"That's okay," he said. "My hair is still dripping a bit. I'll keep it for now."

"All right. I'll go down with you. I was up here checking on Dad."

Luca asked, "How is he?"

"Awake," Avi said, excited.

"That's something," Luca said, trying to sound hopeful.

"Yeah. I told him he slept most of the day away. He asked me to bring him some orange juice and toast. He said his head hurts. Lisieux is with him now," Avi said.

"She's with Dad?" I asked.

"Yep. We've decided he can't take drugs if we're always with him, so we're not leaving him alone even for a second," Avi said.

"All day?" I asked.

"Forever, if we have to. We aren't letting him out of our sight. You two can help if you want."

I hesitated. Watching Dad every second of every day. Was that actually going to help him get better?

"Yeah," Luca said, "we'll help."

Avi grinned and said, "Thanks. Are you coming downstairs?"

"In a minute," Luca said.

"Okay," she said, and skipped from the room, her tangled red hair darkened from the rain.

I whispered, "We can't watch him every second for the rest of his life."

"We aren't doing it for him, we're doing it for your sisters. This is something they think they can do to help, so we need to help too."

"It's not going to solve anything," I said.

"I know what it feels like to watch a parent fall apart and have no power to stop it. Letting them think this will help, at least for a few days … we can give them that. And besides, it will make it more difficult for him to use."

"Yeah, okay, maybe it will," I said, not believing it. Luca was right, though. If it was important to my sisters, we might as well help.

Luca said, "So since your whole family is upstairs, I'm thinking we should read the letters downstairs."

I didn't move. "You told me I didn't need to read the letters," I said.

"That's true, but that doesn't mean I can't read them to you."

I got to my feet. "Luca, I don't want anything to do with those letters. My great-grandmother was in love with the man who killed her best friend. I just … that's where I draw the line."

Luca stood beside me. "I get that, Siena, but Nira took *you* to the box. Your mom told *you* to help Dorothy. Your grandma asked *you* to read the notes. It sort of seems like *you're* supposed to do this."

"To be fair, we can't be sure my mom asked me to help Dorothy. All she said was *help her*. There are lots of hers in the world. Besides, maybe it wasn't my mom at all. Maybe it was a demon pretending to be my mom or maybe I imagined the whole thing. Maybe none of this is real," I said, hoping I was right.

"The notes are real," Luca said.

I lowered my head and ran my hands through my hair. "Yeah, I guess they are," I whined.

Avi walked by, carrying a glass of orange juice and a plate of toast. "Are you feeling okay?" she asked me from the hallway.

Before I could answer, Luca said, "I told her we should go clean your dad's study. You know how messy it is, and she's being lazy."

"Oh, you should do that. He would appreciate it," Avi said, and continued down the hall.

"Yes, we should," Luca said, loud enough for her to hear. "Come on, you can do this."

In an angry voice, I whispered, "You're not the one who saw him murder Nira."

"This isn't about the memories, it's about the words," he replied.

"That's what you say right now," I said.

"Okay, fine. Come help me clean his study. I wasn't lying. It's a wreck. It's that or go babysit him," Luca said.

"Fine." I picked up the sweatshirt from my bed.

"What's that for?" Luca asked.

"I have a feeling we're going to have a visitor," I said, grumbling as I slipped on the sweatshirt.

Twenty-One

As we went through the kitchen, Jackson rose from his bed and followed us.

"It's like he knows what we're about to do," I said.

"Dogs pick up on more than we give them credit for," Luca said, placing the towel-covered box onto the coffee table in my dad's office. Luca started lighting a fire.

I sat at my dad's desk. Luca hadn't been lying. It was covered with random papers. I had no idea where to begin straightening it. I found the wooden cross that my mom had given my dad all those years ago. I placed it on top of a stack of papers. Then I started opening the drawers.

Luca said, "What are you doing?"

"Searching for his stash," I said.

"Do you think he'd be stupid enough to hide stuff in here again? Besides, I thought we were going to read the notes."

"He's a creature of habit," I said as I pulled out a bag of pills from the back of the bottom drawer. "And *you* are going to read the notes and I will listen."

I stood and took the pills to the fire. I opened the bag and dumped the pills onto the flames. The flames changed to blue and green before going back to yellow.

"Why are you burning them?" Luca asked.

"Because I'm pretty sure this time he'd dig through the trash for them," I said while hoping Luca was going to disagree with me.

He remained silent.

"Want me to help you look for more?" Luca asked.

"Nope," I said. If the search was finished, I would have one less reason to avoid the notes.

Luca said, "You're sort of taking the easy way out."

"I'm searching my dad's office for the drugs he's doing. This is not the easy way," I said, trying to make him feel bad.

"Yeah, okay," he replied. He unwrapped the box.

I cringed at the sight of the rusty metal and started searching the bookcases.

"The first note says *'Hello,'*" Luca said, placing it on the table.

"That's all?" I asked.

"Yep."

"How did she even know who it was from?"

Luca asked, "Do you want to touch it and find out?"

"No, thank you," I said, continuing to rummage behind the books.

"The next note says, *'I hope your day was pleasant.'*"

I mumbled, "Her day would've been more pleasant if she hadn't gotten a note from a serial killer."

He ignored my remark and picked up the next piece of paper. "The next is, *'You made me smile today.'*"

"He's making me gag," I said.

"I'm not sure your commentary is helping," Luca said.

I found a bag of powder and took it to the fire.

"Careful not to touch it," Luca said.

"Trust me, I don't want to touch whatever this is," I said. I carefully turned the bag in on itself and allowed the powder to fall into the fire. The flames momentarily turned blue.

Luca read the next note. " *'I'm glad you figured out I'm your admirer. Though there was some fun in keeping things mysterious. I hope you like the gift.'* "

"Admirer, stalker. Tomatoes, tomahtoes," I said, carefully sealing the bag and stuffing it into my pocket.

He shot me a grin. "It's a shame you weren't around to help Dorothy see the truth."

He pulled out the next note. " *'Thank you for showing me this place. You're right. It's beautiful, though not as beautiful as you. Forgive me, that was too forward.'* "

I asked, "What did she show him?"

Luca held the note out for me. I hesitated and walked to the other end of the room, putting more distance between us.

"It's not fair," Luca said. "He's manipulating her."

I stood at the bookcase, no longer feeling snarky. Now I felt the gravity of what was happening around me.

He picked up the next note, and I quickly returned my attention to the bookshelf in front of me.

Luca sighed, and then read: " *'Watching you with my son yesterday brought me both joy and sorrow. If only my wife was as much a woman as you are. You will be an excellent mother.'"*

"His wife loved their little boy," I said, feeling a knife pierce my heart as the lies became clearer.

Luca frowned when he picked up the next note. " *'How I wish I was with you. You will tell me I shouldn't say such things, but I can't help myself. I am under your spell.'"*

"Gigi's right. My sisters can never read these," I said from my spot at the bookcase.

Luca picked up the next note, scanned it, and put it back down.

"What is it?" I asked.

He stared at the note. "It's starting to get more real. *'You're right, it was wrong of me to kiss you. Yes, I'm married, but you're so enchanting! It isn't fair what you do to me. I lose all sense when you're around.'"*

"He kissed her?" I said, feeling like I was dangerously close to passing out. My face felt tingly as the blood drained from it.

Luca said, "Notice how he keeps blaming her? It's supposed to be in a sort of playful way, I guess, but it's really disturbing. What would a fourteen-year-old girl think of that or of being kissed by a man who was fifteen years older than her?"

"Twenty years," I said, my face slightly numb.

"What?" Luca said.

"He looked at least twenty years older than her, and not attractive. It's so gross. Why would she fall for him?"

"Dorothy was a kid no older than Lisieux. There's no way she could understand how messed up he was. And remember what Gigi said? She never had anything like you have or even like I had. We've been loved our entire lives. She wasn't. And he was a big deal. The newly elected mayor—or at least when he was building the house, he was. She must've felt flattered. A girl whose parents didn't care about her starts getting all of this attention from a man who was sought after by lots of people …. Wouldn't that make her feel special, getting attention from someone everyone wanted attention from?"

"But he's playing her," I said, sitting beside Luca.

"How could she have known that?" he said empathetically.

I was silent.

"We know what he did. All she knows is this guy that everyone thinks is so great thinks she's great."

I gasped and covered my mouth.

"What?"

"Do you think he was … do you think he had already … do you think there were victims already?" I asked.

Luca's expression changed. Apparently, he hadn't thought of that.

"Maybe."

We sat silently, watching the fire, the box with the remainder of the notes sitting ominously on the table in front of us.

"We need to get through these," Luca said. He read the next note. " *I wish I could take you away from here. You deserve better, but no one would understand. You're the only one who has ever truly understood me.'"*

Luca picked up the next slip of paper and read: " *'Where are you? It's been days! I'm beside myself with worry. I must see you!'"*

"I wonder if she's trying to put some distance between them," I said with the lift of an eyebrow.

He read: " *'I understand now. She has poisoned you against me. I'm a gentle man. You know that better than anyone. But I am a man and a man fights for those he loves.'* I think it's backfiring," Luca said.

I lowered my eyes.

Luca picked up the last note and read: " *'I give you my word. No one will get in our way. We will be together— soon!'"*

Twenty-Two

He sat beside me on the couch, the two of us watching the fire.

"How did my life get this messed up?" I said, leaning forward and pushing my hair away from my face.

Luca placed a hand on my back. "It's not that messed up."

I turned to him and said, "My great-grandmother was in love with a serial killer who killed her best friend, probably because he was mad at her for trying to protect my great-grandmother. And my dad is upstairs being guarded by my two little sisters so he doesn't use drugs. And my boyfriend—who I adore—feels evil and sees dead people, which I guess I do too since I see Nira, and I can't even touch those notes unless I want the memories associated with them … which I do not."

He sat back against the couch. "Yeah, that is pretty messed up," he admitted, staring at the fire.

I groaned.

"At least it isn't boring," he said.

I fell back against a cushion. "I mean, really, how did I get here?"

"For the record, we don't know if she was in love with him or had any feelings for him at all," Luca said.

"She saved the notes," I said. "You don't save notes that some creepy guy sends you unless you have feelings for him. Argh, this is so gross and so bad!" I stomped my feet and got up. I couldn't sit still any longer. "How? Why? Why would she have ever had anything to do with him?"

"It wasn't her fault," Luca said. "She wasn't the one going after him."

"First of all, we don't actually know that," I said, "but I agree it isn't likely. But don't you see? She didn't stop it and he killed her friend. That is so far beyond messed up, I can't even … I don't even understand how to think about it." I leaned my head against the mantle, near a picture of my family which included my mom.

Luca said, "You could touch the notes and then you'd understand more."

"Never. I never want to touch them. I don't want to see what he was doing. It was bad enough I saw the kids in the attic, and then Nira's … death. I can't take anymore, because once those memories are in my head, they never leave!" I was on the verge of screaming.

He came near me at the fireside. After a while he said, "That's okay. My reading the notes is probably enough."

"For what?" I asked.

"To help Dorothy," Luca said.

"Help Dorothy?" I stared at him.

"Yes. Isn't that what we were trying to do?"

"If she wanted help, she probably shouldn't have been involved with a psychopath who killed kids," I said, feeling disgusted by the idea of helping anyone associated with him.

"Do you honestly believe it's that simple? Do you think a child who had no one to love her would be able to resist someone who was a master manipulator? Did you resist Thomas?"

I felt like I'd been punched in the stomach. "I did not have feelings for Thomas," I said.

Luca crossed his arms and replied, "Then you fooled me."

"I-I didn't—" I said, starting to argue.

He held a hand up in front of my lips. "It doesn't bother me," Luca said, "or at least not much. He was popular and you were lonely. It wasn't hard for him to get you to begin to fall for him. Thankfully, you quickly figured out who he was, and we fought to protect you. But Dorothy had no one to fight for her, except maybe Nira."

I stared at him.

"I'm sorry. I didn't say any of that to upset you, but it's not fair for you to turn your back on Dorothy. She had no one in life. She needs someone in death and that someone, for whatever reason, is you."

I mumbled, "Thomas was not a murderer."

"Agreed, and he was our age. So you didn't fall for some creepy old guy, but that's not the point. The point is you were falling for a popular boy who was definitely not good for you and you did this even though you have a great family. We don't know how Dorothy felt about that guy, but we do know she had an awful family. It's not fair for you, of all people, to judge her."

Tears began spilling down my cheeks. He was right—he was right about everything. I was no better than Dorothy. The reason I didn't fall for a killer was because Thomas wasn't one and now he was dead and that was my fault too. I stood and ran out the door, grabbing my car keys as Jackson barked and I sprinted to the garage.

"Wait! I'm sorry," Luca called after me.

I didn't slow.

I drove without thinking. My vision was blurred by tears. The rain was so heavy I could barely see. I thought he loved me. How could he bring up Thomas and compare me to Dorothy?

He told the truth, a voice in the back of my mind whispered, causing me to cry harder. I had fallen for Thomas— only for a moment—but a moment was long enough to allow him in. A moment is what started all of this. He hunted me just as the BayTree man, Charles, had hunted those children.

Nira's last moments entered my mind. They were horrible moments, moments no one should ever imagine, let alone experience, and they were now in my memory. I was sobbing as they tortured me … sobbing as he tortured her. I made the turn without thinking. I parked diagonally and ran up the church steps two at a time.

I flung open the door. The building was empty. The red candle flickered in the darkness. The goodness was there.

I could breathe.

I went swiftly to the front of the building. The goodness was calling me, the same as it had called to Luca. I understood so clearly why he'd come in here that day of the festival. It seemed like a lifetime ago, but it was only last fall. How had so much changed that quickly? How was I now in this place, feeling the same draw to goodness he'd been feeling?

I didn't stop as I stepped up to the altar. I didn't bow as I should have. Instead, I fell to my knees, my arms grasping the base of the tabernacle. The consecrated Hosts were inside above me. I envisioned myself curled up at the feet of Jesus, only he was huge and I was tiny, and I fit perfectly next to his ankle. I clung to him. Memories flashed—memories that were not mine. I cried out, gasping for breath between sobs. I clung to him in my mind and in real life. My hands were grasping the stone pillar supporting the consecrated Hosts. The memories became fuzzier, my breathing slowed, and so did the tears.

My body relaxed a little. The pain was starting to fade. My mind started to clear. It was real, it was all real. The good, the bad, the memories, the dreams of the castle of darkness— all of it was real. It didn't matter that others couldn't see it, that others believed what happened before had no bearing on the present. The past mattered. What happened to Dorothy and Nira mattered, not just for their own sakes, but for mine too. I didn't understand that part, yet I felt it. I was connected to them … my family was connected to them … my father was connected to them.

There was silence, beautiful silence. My mind was slowing, listening to the sound of my breathing and the rain pelting the roof. From the corner of my eye, I saw movement. I shivered as the cold pressed onto my damp skin.

Nira came closer … into the sanctuary. I clung tighter to the base of the tabernacle. She came toward me. As she stepped up to the altar, she bowed and then went to sit on the other side of the tabernacle, like she'd done the day before during Mass. *Was that only yesterday?*

My mind raced. What was she doing? Why was she next to me? I released my hold as she leaned her head against the opposite side of the pillar. I shuddered. She was so close to me. She didn't appear solid, but not opaque either. It was like she was there and not there at the same time. I wondered what would happen if I reached for her. Would I feel anything? The air was frigid, as if I was surrounded by ice. It was how I felt every time she was around. I wondered if that happened because her world entered mine. I doubted spirits cared how cold it was or that they could feel any temperature.

Despite being right next to me and my sneaking glances at her every few seconds, she was paying no attention to me. She must have been able to see me; otherwise, why would she be here? I decided she wasn't interested in me. She was interested in our consecrated Lord, the same as I was. She wasn't that different from me, not when it came to what mattered. She was a girl, a girl who lived and died a long time ago, yet still a girl. She loved God; she must, or she wouldn't be here. And she was trying to help me. I wasn't sure how I knew that last part. Still, I did. All the times I'd seen her, it wasn't about me helping her, it was about her helping me … helping my family … helping Dorothy.

In that moment the memory of the previous night's dream flashed in my mind. In the dream, Nira smiled at the guardian and tried to engage my great-grandmother. In my dream of that awful castle, Nira was not afraid; she was not stuck there, she was just visiting, along with me. She was acting as my guide. She did not need me to help her then or now.

Starting to understand, I said, "You were there to help Dorothy … all of this has been you trying to help Dorothy."

Nira vanished.

Light streamed in when the doors opened. The sound of Luca's heavy steel-toed boots echoed through the empty building. His loose-fitting jeans and gray T-shirt were as black as his curly hair in the darkened church.

"I'm sorry," he said, rushing toward me. "I shouldn't have said those things. What happened with Thomas wasn't your fault."

He bowed as he went up to the altar and knelt in front of me.

"You weren't wrong," I told Luca. "I don't want to believe it, but I did fall for him … only for a minute, but I should've known better."

"How could you? You're an honest person. Honest people believe people until they have a reason not to."

I shook my head. "I was lonely, I didn't have any friends, and I wanted some. He showed up and that's all it took. It's embarrassing how easily manipulated I was."

"It could happen to anyone, Siena. That was my point. Not that you or Dorothy were somehow bad, just that it's easy for anyone to be manipulated. Especially when the person doing the manipulating is doing it on purpose."

"I understand," I said, not wanting to be angry at him anymore. I never wanted to be angry at him.

"Thank you," he said, and touched his forehead to mine.

"This is all so confusing," I said.

"Yeah, but it's what life really is. The world beyond this one is real, and God has allowed you and me to see and feel it in a way others never will. That's a gift. How could we ever turn from the Creator when we can see his love so clearly?"

I laughed. "That's true. There's no way we could ever deny God's existence or his goodness," I said, leaning against Luca's damp shirt.

"It makes life a bit more complicated," Luca said.

"You think?" I said sarcastically.

"And way better," he added.

"The jury is still out on the better part," I said. "Nira was here, before you came in."

"I wondered why it was so cold in here. I'm sorry I missed her," he said as if she was a dear friend.

I sighed. "You're funny, the way you talk about her."

"She's helping us. Whether you realize it or not, she is."

"I get it now. It's all connected: her, Dorothy, me, my dad, all of it's connected. I understand that now."

"In truth, we're all connected," Luca said. "That's one of those strange spiritual laws."

"Don't get philosophical. I need to stay focused on my family … my family and Nira," I said as I stood and bowed respectfully before stepping away from the altar.

"That's a good place to be focused," Luca said.

He copied my movements and we started down the aisle.

He said, "So where are you going now?"

"Home. I need to talk to my dad," I answered as I pushed the church door open to sunlight breaking through the clouds.

Twenty-Three

It was late afternoon, but with the parting clouds the day felt more like morning. I drove slowly. I was no longer in a hurry. I wasn't sure what I was going to do next, only that I needed to talk to my dad and I didn't want to.

Sunlight streamed into the greening forests around me. The sun brought hope in the most basic of forms. Nature understood this; all of nature reached toward the sun. As I drove down our driveway, the sun seemed to bounce off the grass that had been dormant and covered in snow for so many months. Now it was alive and growing tall enough to move in the breeze. Gigi had been the one to cut it my entire life. Jason had always offered or we could have hired someone, but she did it. She said mowing grass provided instant gratification, something that rarely existed anywhere else in life. But she had aged so much this winter, the thought of her on the riding lawn mower going up and down the driveway didn't fit the woman who now used a cane—though she made us call it a walking stick. I pushed that thought away. Who mowed the grass didn't matter.

Inside the kitchen Jason and Lisieux were baking. I decided the smell of apple twists also gave me hope. Perhaps not as much as a bright, sunny day, but enough to get me through a cloudy one.

"Where have you two been?" Lisieux asked as Luca shut the door behind us.

"Church," I said, and hung my keys on the rack.

"Told ya," Jason said.

He was the least religious person in the house, but at the same time he had an uncanny understanding of our need to be with Jesus.

Lisieux said, "I figured you were right."

I went around to where the apple twists were cooling and slid one onto a napkin. Luca hung up Gigi's car keys and then took a twist, not bothering to use a napkin. He'd have it eaten before it could leave crumbs. We each took a bite.

I said, "These smell amazing."

"Mmm, they taste even better than they smell," he said with a mouthful of pastry.

"Do you like the cinnamon to vanilla ratio?" Lisieux asked, her cooking notebook beside her.

Luca chewed. "Hmm … yes. Yes, I do," he said, trying to take Lisieux's question seriously.

"He doesn't exactly have the most discerning palate," Jason commented in his Down East Maine accent.

I said, "It needs more vanilla, or maybe almond."

"Ooh, almond would be good!" Lisieux made some notes.

"How's Paul?" Luca asked as he finished his first twist and took a second.

Jason glanced toward Lisieux and then away. He loved each of us, but he loved her the most. She was his kitchen protégé and with that came a sort of friendship the rest of us didn't have with him.

Lisieux's expression became sullen. "He's about the same," she said. "Avi is up there with him. She brought some Legos into his room and is playing with them in there so she can keep an eye on him."

"Did you search for stuff when you were in there?" I said, wishing I didn't need to ask that question.

Lisieux nodded toward the trash can. "I took what I found. There wasn't much. Just a prescription container that was half full with different types of pills in it."

"Did you look in his closet?" I asked.

"No. Should I have?" Lisieux asked, her normally bright green eyes appearing dull.

Jason was reassembling the red stand mixer Gigi had given him for Christmas. "Always check the closet, under the mattress, and behind the toilet," he said.

"Avi checked under the bed," Lisieux said.

"That's under the bed," Jason said. "You need to check under the mattress."

Lisieux slumped against the counter. "Oh, I didn't think of that."

"It's all right. Next time ya get him out of his room, I'll search it. Don't ya think about it again," Jason said, giving her an encouraging wink. "How much almond extract should I add?"

"Let's try a teaspoon," she said.

"Is that all? I think we need two," he said, sufficiently distracting her.

I thanked God for Jason, for his being there for her when our dad wasn't. I started up the stairs. Luca sprang after me.

"Do you want me to come with you?" Luca asked as we reached the second floor.

"Yes, but no. I need to have this conversation alone."

"I understand. I'll ask Avi to come with me. She could probably use a break, and the chickens are out in the yard. You know how she loves to play with them after it rains."

I felt like gagging. "Oh, I know, but she did that all morning."

"True, but not with me," Luca said with a grin.

He was right. Avi would happily go out again with Luca.

We stopped at my dad's open door. He was lying in bed, awake, and looked horrible. Avi was sitting cross-legged on the floor, entirely focused on her Legos.

I knocked on the doorframe.

"Hey, Avi," Luca said, "it stopped raining. Want to come play with the chickens with me?"

Dad's face turned a shade of green. He must've been thinking about the worms, the same as I was.

"I do, but what about Dad?" Avi asked, shifting her eyes to him, trying to signal that he couldn't be left alone.

I said, "I'll stay with him."

"Promise?"

I nodded. "I won't leave him."

"Not even if he needs to go to the bathroom?" Avi asked.

My face contorted. "Nope, I guess not."

Avi hopped up, scattering the Legos across the floor. Dad sat up a little taller, causing the scar on his left arm to become visible.

"I'll be back soon," Avi said. She went to kiss him on the cheek as she always did, but then stopped and turned from him, her expression confused and hurt.

She didn't want to kiss him and that hurt her. I didn't blame her. He looked almost nothing like our father. He hadn't shaved or showered. His skin was waxy and his eyes distant. Whatever he'd been taking, it had been for a lot longer than a day.

"Come on," Luca said, holding out his hand.

She took it. He squeezed her hand as if to say it was going to be okay.

"There are chickens to feed," he said, swinging their arms.

She started to skip as they reached the hallway.

Once they were on the stairs, I went and sat in the oversized chair across from the bed. I used to play behind the chair when I was a little girl, waiting for my mom to get ready. Tears threatened to come as I thought of how she'd feel if she saw her family falling apart.

"Have you come to yell at me, too?" Dad said with a biting tone.

My sadness was replaced by anger.

"It's your life, it's your choice," I said, feeling the power of the firstborn. "But it's our lives too. Don't expect me to sit back and watch you destroy *my* family."

"What're you going to do about it?" Dad asked with an edge of threat.

"Whatever it takes," I said, leaning forward on my knees.

He glared at me. I didn't flinch.

How had he changed so much in such a short time? He was in the middle of withdrawals—at least, I hoped he was. I hoped he hadn't taken something recently without our realizing it. The drugs leaving his system made him angry; it wasn't him, but still it was uncomfortable.

I said, "You told me once you were very much like Thomas. I hadn't believed you then. I have believed it since then, and it's totally obvious now. You remind me of him when he was possessed by the demons of the inn."

Dad flinched, unconsciously rubbing the scar on his left arm—the scar which had helped create the evil that had saturated the inn and killed Thomas.

"Don't compare me to him," Dad said, but his posture was softening.

"Then don't act like him," I said.

"You didn't used to be like this," he said.

"Like what?"

"Disrespectful … talking back to me."

I let out a frustrated laugh. "You think the issue is that *I* have changed. I have changed, we all have, because we have had to. Our father, who had been sober our entire lives, no longer exists. So, anything you are seeing in me, Lisieux, or Avi that you don't like … you can take full credit for that!"

He sat back, turning his head toward the window. After some time, he said, "It isn't easy."

"Nothing ever is, except the bad stuff. That's pretty easy. The good stuff takes a lot of work," I said.

We were quiet for a long time. He was staring out the window, and I was staring at him with my arms crossed—waiting for him to step out of line so I could pounce. If he wasn't going to act like my dad, then I wasn't going to act like his daughter.

He said, "I had a dream about your mom last night."

His words caught me off guard. I unfolded my arms. "You did?"

He turned to face me. "The dream wasn't actually about her, I don't think. But she was there."

"What did she do?" I asked.

"She smiled at me," he said, his face grimacing in pain as he fought back tears.

If we couldn't reach him, maybe Mom could. My anger toward him lessened. "She loves you … we all do."

He pinched the bridge of his nose a moment, and then said, "It was a strange dream. Maybe it was a warning. I hope not. I pray things haven't gotten that bad for me … for my soul." His eyes were fixed on me. "Or maybe they have," he said, sounding defeated.

"What did you dream?"

"I was in a giant castle. Everything was dark and dreary. I was wandering around, totally lost. Much like real life," he said with a self-deprecating chuckle.

"Mom was in the castle?" My face betrayed my concern.

"Sort of yes and sort of no. She was there, but she didn't seem to belong there. Most of the people, I guess they were people, were dark and hunched over, but Rebecca stood tall, taller than me, actually, and seemed to glow. Like … she was an angel," he said with love. "She was an angel on earth, so I suppose there's no reason she wouldn't be an angel in my dreams."

I tapped on my lips. "She must've been visiting. Was there a girl in your dream? A girl with lots of curly dark hair like Luca's?"

"No," Dad said, confused. "Why would you ask that?"

"I had a similar dream," I said.

"Of your mom?" Dad's eyes opened wide.

"Of the castle. In my dream, Mom wasn't there, but others were."

"You dreamt of that place?" Dad asked.

I nodded.

"Is it a real place?" Dad asked, sitting forward, his eyebrows scrunched in concern.

"I'm not sure. The girl from my dreams, with the curly hair … I've been seeing her."

He gawked at me. "You've been *seeing* her?"

"Yes. … She's been appearing to me. I guess that's what you would call it."

Dad ran his left hand through his stringy hair. He still wore his wedding ring. He said, "I suppose I need to let go of the idea that there is anything normal about our family."

I burst out laughing. "Nope, not the first thing normal around here. Besides, normal is boring."

"I think I could be okay with a little more boring," he said with a wince.

"Boring is not the hand we were dealt," I said.

Dad leaned back on the pillow. "I suppose not." After a few moments he spoke again. "The girl you described wasn't there, but there was another girl. At least I think it was a girl. She was almost completely distorted, but from what I could tell, her hair was straight. It seemed to hang around her face or what should have been her face," he said with a shiver.

I took my phone from my pocket and scrolled through to find the picture of Dorothy and Nira that Luca had sent me. I went to Dad, holding the phone out for him. "Is the one with the straight hair the one you saw?"

He took the phone from me and studied the picture. "I can't tell. The girl in my dreams was barely a form. Who is she, and," —he zoomed in—"why does she look like Lisieux?"

I took the phone back. Nira's expression caught my attention. Before, I thought her smile was a little off, like how so many people posed in old photographs, but now I realized there was fear behind her smile. I clicked off the phone and stuffed it in my pocket. I said to my dad, "The girl with the curly hair is the one who's been appearing to me. The one with the long, straight hair … is your grandmother."

Twenty-Four

Dad looked confused. "I met my grandmother. That's not her. Even as a girl, that couldn't have been her."

"Not your great-grandmother, your grandmother. This is Dorothy, Gigi's mom," I said.

"Dorothy? How do you have a picture of her on your phone?"

"It was hanging on a wall at the BayTree."

"You went to the BayTree? Why would you do that?" Dad asked with true concern.

I stood and went toward the window. "Nira, the other girl in the picture who has been appearing to me, sort of led me there. I needed to find out who she was, so Luca and I went after Mass yesterday. This picture was by the front door."

I opened the window to allow fresh air into the room. Down below, Avi was again jumping in the mud, her joyous squeals bouncing against our stone castle and making their way up to Dad's room. Luca looked upward and smiled. I wondered if he could see me or if he could sense that I could see him. I touched the window screen with the tips of my fingers. I longed to be with him and for our lives to be simple.

"How did their picture get in the BayTree?" Dad asked.

I turned to face him. "I don't know for sure. The frame was as old as the photo, so I guess they found it during a remodel or something."

"Why would their picture have ever been there in the first place?" Dad asked with growing concern.

I fidgeted. "The man who built the BayTree took the picture."

Dad was silent as the information sunk in. In a low whisper, he asked, "The man who killed those children?"

I nodded.

"How can you know that?"

I swallowed and met his gaze. "Remember how, sometimes, when I touch things, I can see the memory?"

He nodded slowly.

"I touched the frame of the picture and I saw the memory."

"Did he … he hurt them?" Dad asked fearfully.

I sat down in the chair across from him. "In that picture they were playing at the beach. His son and wife were there. He took the picture of them, that's all. But later … yes, he hurt them."

Dad got up, careful not to step on any of Avi's Legos as he came and sat on the bed, facing me.

"Your mom was right," he said. He was shivering and sweating.

I remained in the chair.

He said, "She told me you were gifted, that you could sense things others couldn't. She said your life would be beautiful, but hard. I told her I'd do everything I could to protect you so that your life was only beautiful."

"What did she say to that?" I asked.

He closed his eyes for a couple seconds and opened them. "She touched the side of my face and gave me the saddest look. She said it was far beyond my control. I hoped she was wrong. I knew she wasn't, she never was. She had her own gifts. Different from yours. She could read people and situations."

"Like Avi?" I said.

Dad said, "Uhm … somewhat, though their personalities are nothing alike."

"No one in the world is like Avi," I said in a tired voice.

"It's probably for the best," Dad said. He crossed his arms over his chest and bored his bloodshot blue eyes into mine.

Tentatively, I said, "Mom came to me last night. I think she asked me to help Dorothy."

"I thought you said you hadn't dreamt of Mom?" he asked, his eyes troubled.

"She wasn't in my dream. It was while I was watching you and Jackson in the yard. You were going into the house."

"You saw her while you were awake?" he asked, mouth open.

"No, I felt her. She was right beside me. I could feel her as strongly as I can feel you, and I heard her voice."

"What did she say?" Dad asked.

" 'Help her.' I'd have expected her to say 'Help him,' for me to help—." I stopped, realizing what I was about to say.

"Me."

"You were down in the gazebo, and you clearly need help," I said boldly.

"Yes, I'm clearly in need of help," he said, and I had the feeling that in his head he added "more than you know."

We stared at each other for a moment, reading the other's thoughts.

I said, "But she didn't say to help you. She asked me to help *her*."

"She wants you to help the girl who has been appearing to you?" Dad asked.

"That's what I was thinking, but then I had that dream, and found … some more memories and now I think she was talking about Great-grandmother Dorothy."

"She's been gone a long time," Dad said. "I'm sure she's at peace."

"She's been gone a long time, but that doesn't necessarily mean she's at peace," I said.

"Did he hurt her too?" Dad asked, looking away as he asked the question.

Neither one of us wanted to be having this conversation about the ways the local serial killer hurt our family.

I said, "They were in a relationship. I guess that's what you'd call it."

"Gigi told me her mom left here when she was fourteen," Dad said, his face growing even more concerned.

"Yes," I said.

"He was a grown man and she was fourteen. That is not a relationship," he said with disgust.

"She seemed to think it was. He wrote her notes and she kept them."

Dad looked as if he was going to be sick. "A grown man and a teenage girl can never have that sort of *relationship*, no matter what she may have thought. Whatever happened between them was evil."

"I don't know the details, but yes, whatever it was, was evil."

He studied me. He could tell I wasn't sure of Dorothy's role in this. He was like Gigi and Luca, who believed she was innocent.

"Siena, whatever happened, she was a child. It wasn't her fault."

I said, "Kids make awful choices and those choices have consequences. You, of all people, should get that."

He flinched. "You're right," he said with a nod, "I deeply understand that my choices as a kid had, and are still having awful consequences. But I am also an adult and I'm telling you that to think that if I … I pursued a teenage girl and anything that happened afterward would be her fault is ridiculous. I am the adult. I am the one who understands *exactly* what I am doing, not her."

I stated flatly, "She could have stopped it before it ever started and she didn't."

He rubbed his face. "You said there were notes?" He sounded frustrated with me.

I nodded.

"Have you read them?" he asked, clearly irritated.

"Yes, and he was very into her," I said.

His face contorted again like he was going to be sick. "What about her?"

"All we have are notes from him to her."

"Then you don't know how she felt," he said.

"You don't save love letters if the guy who sent them grosses you out," I argued.

"What about the memories? Do they have memories connected with them?"

"I haven't touched them," I said, surprised he'd ask me that.

"You should," Dad said.

"You want me to watch the memories of a murderer?"

"Maybe they won't be his. Maybe they will be hers," he said.

"He wrote them, so they'll be his," I said, trying to keep my voice steady.

"You're supposed to view them," Dad said.

I looked at him skeptically.

"Why else would you find them and then your mom tells you to help *her* and then you dream of that awful castle?"

"You're starting to sound like Gigi," I said with growing frustration.

"That's a good thing," he said.

I turned away in anger.

He leaned forward. "Siena, that castle … it was … it was not like other dreams. It felt real in a terrifying way, and it felt … like there was some part of me there."

"A part of *you*?" I said, turning back to him.

"I can't explain it, but the same way I could tell your mom wasn't part of that world, was the same way I could tell I was," he said, his voice trembling.

"How could you feel you're part of that world? It's for the dead!"

He stared at me and said, "A part of me has felt dead for a long time. I thought it was simply that I'd grown up, I was no longer a child, or that I was an addict … or am an addict. But something makes me think it's not those things. Something makes me think it has to do with the inn and the curse."

"We destroyed it," I said, leaning forward.

"Yes, and that helped, a lot, but when I was in that dream, when I saw that girl stuck in the wall, it felt the same as how I feel. Stuck in a place I don't want to be, but I have no way to escape because some part of me can't leave it."

"That's called addiction," I said.

"It came before the addiction. It came over me after the inn, and when I started using, it was like even more of myself got sucked into it. Then I got sober and met your mom, and most of me got unstuck. Then she died, and I felt it come back … but I had you three to keep me sane. After we destroyed the inn, I felt better, but it still felt like my foot was stuck in that place and I couldn't get it out. The drugs have brought more of me into the wall. If I … when I get sober again, I'll still feel like I'm stuck in that wall."

I compared his words and Gigi's, and said, "Gigi said she sees a shadow around you. That it was around her mom and then around her, but when you made that curse it seemed to leave her and settle on you. She said when Mom was alive, her goodness kept the shadow off you, but once she died, it came back and …"

"And?"

"She said it's on me and my sisters."

There was a knock on the doorframe. Jason and Lisieux were there. She held a tray with a grilled cheese sandwich and a bowl of tomato soup. Jason held her travel chess set.

"Are we interrupting?" Jason said, noticing our tense expressions.

"No. Siena has some things she needs to do," Dad said with a glance at me before shifting his focus to Lisieux and Jason.

I stood up from the chair. Jason was watching me and Lisieux was eyeing Dad.

"We thought you might be hungry," Lisieux said, sounding nervous.

Jason nodded subtly to me as I passed him. Then he spoke to Dad. "We also thought you might want to take a shower, which is why I'm here. Avi made us promise not to leave you alone, even when you showered."

"She's wise beyond her years," Dad said, trying to sound like it was not humiliating that his daughters didn't even trust him to take a shower. "Jason, maybe you can also help me … help me"—he struggled with the words—"dispose of some things."

"I can do that," Jason said. "Eat first, while it's hot. I promised Lisieux a game." He held up the chess board.

Dad nodded.

Lisieux didn't budge.

"It's okay," Jason whispered, "I'm not leaving you."

In the hallway, I let my shoulders fall forward. Our dad was so messed up, my sister didn't even want to be alone with him.

In a hopeful tone, Dad asked, "Lisieux, could I play you after I eat?"

I stood in the hall waiting for her answer.

"I guess if I play without my queen," she said, "it will be a little more even."

"That would be kind of you," he said.

I sighed with relief and made my way down the stairs.

Twenty-Five

I did not allow myself to hesitate. I went straight to my dad's office and shut the door. The drapes were open, but I couldn't see Luca or Avi out in the yard—though I could hear her shrieking with delight. How Dad ever thought we were normal was beyond me. No normal nine-year-old girl has that much fun feeding earthworms to chickens.

The room turned colder, and I felt Nira's presence. "Why would anyone want to be normal?" I said aloud.

She was sitting on the couch.

I said to Nira, "I would … but that's okay. 'Life with Christ is a wonderful adventure.' Pope John Paul II wasn't wrong about that." I stood tall as I went toward the fireplace.

Nira watched me silently, not so much in a creepy way, but more in a "one person intensely watching another person without speaking" sort of way … so, a creepy way. However, it wasn't creepy; it was comforting having her with me. I didn't want others around, while not wanting to be alone. With her here, I was basically alone, but not exactly. I added logs to the coals of the fire Luca had started earlier in the day. I used some scratch paper to revive the flames. The seasoned wood caught easily. I watched the dancing flames grow as I tried to get enough courage to retrieve the box.

Nira followed me with her eyes as I went toward the box hidden on my dad's bookcase. I carefully moved the books. I hesitated … I had to touch it at some point. Maybe there was no evil associated with it and there would be no memories. Or maybe I would go into his mind, his memories, and not Dorothy's.

I stepped backward and said to Nira, "I can't do it. I can't handle his memories."

To my surprise, she got up from her place on the couch and walked toward me. She stood beside me, looking from me to the box.

"You really want me to see these memories?" I said to her.

She didn't respond, yet in her silence I felt braver.

I rested my head against the bookcase. "God protect me," I mumbled, and then grabbed the rusty box.

I was inside the inn. I cringed at the awareness, though I'd never imagined the place could be so inviting. There was a welcoming fire in the fireplace and fresh wild roses in vases throughout the room that made the whole place smell sweet—nothing like the putrid smell of rotten eggs and dead fish. Happy guests were making their way up the stairs; another couple was going out the front door. There was nothing evil about the inn. It was cheerful. Nothing like what it had become. Dorothy was there, her long brown hair neatly brushed and pulled back into a braid which made her appear even younger than she was. Her clothes were worn, yet clean. She held the green metal box in her hands. She was looking around as if she didn't

214

I was back in my dad's office. I carried the box to the
coffee table and quickly set it down. Bits of rust flaked off onto
the polished oak.

"I didn't see him. Only her," I said to Nira, who was sitting
on the couch opposite me.

I pulled a blanket around me. I liked having Nira there, but
her presence made it so cold; even with a fire, I was still
freezing. I stared at the box. Of course I wouldn't have seen his
memories with the box. He probably never touched it, but the

notes … he wrote the notes. My heart rate quickened—I couldn't handle his memories.

The door opened and Luca rushed in. He frantically searched the room. "Are you okay?" he said, breathing hard.

"I think so. I touched the box and saw Dorothy's memory," I answered, concerned by how worried he was.

Luca came close to me. "I felt evil. I was afraid something happened to you."

"You held the box and read the notes and you were fine?" I said with confusion.

He leaned his head against a hand, rubbing his head in frustration and still out of breath. "I don't think it's the notes or the box, but I felt evil coming in from every direction, like there was something drawing demons here."

I shivered. "I was afraid I would see his memories, but I didn't. Just Dorothy's, and pretty much only while she was touching the box," I said.

"Was it her box?" he asked.

I nodded. "I think she took it from her parents or something. She was acting like she shouldn't have it. I saw her take it to her room—I guess it was her room. It was the room where they kept the firewood, but there was a mattress and blankets, so I think that must be where she slept. She put some of the notes into the box and hid it behind some firewood."

"So he probably never touched it?" Luca said.

"Probably not," I said.

"But the notes will be different. He wrote those," Luca said.

"Yes, he wrote those," I said, trembling.

"Maybe you shouldn't touch them," he said.

Nira stood and started to pace back and forth.

"Nira doesn't like that idea," I said. "She's pacing in front of us."

Luca slumped back against the couch.

"Did the notes get more evil?" I asked, already knowing they hadn't, or he'd be sick.

Luca raised his head and turned it in multiple directions. "It's in the distance … something is holding it back, but it feels like it did when my mom first started her stuff," he said with a shiver.

I lifted my rosary out of the ceramic bowl next to the box. I wrapped the beads around my right wrist. "I have no interest in knowing anything more than the Lord wants me to know. I do not want to know the future and I don't actually want to know the past," I mumbled. I kissed the crucifix. "Protect me," I whispered, and pried the lid from the box.

"What're you doing?" Luca asked with wide eyes.

"Jumping in," I said.

Twenty-Six

I took the first note from the box.

It was dark and freezing. I could see Dorothy's misty breath as she entered the narrow room where the firewood was stored. It was more open in this memory because there was not as much firewood lining the outside and interior walls. But the wall of firewood that divided her room from the rest of the space was the same. She carried the nub of a candle; it was the only light in the room. She was wrapped in a coat and two scarves. She went around to where her mattress lay and carefully set the candle nub on a piece of firewood that stuck out a little farther than the rest of the stack. It created enough light to see, at least a dim outline of the thin mattress beneath it. When she sat on it, the mattress sunk down to the floor; it was barely thicker than a blanket. She took off her shoes, revealing socks that had been darned in more than one area. She rubbed her feet with her mittened hands. She kept her legs close to her, her long dress and coat covering her legs and most of her feet when she pulled herself into a ball. She lay down and wrapped the wool blankets around her like a cocoon. There was no source of heat in this room. She was freezing. I wondered how she would be able to sleep. No, I wondered how she would be

I released the slip of paper. It fell to the table below.

Luca was beside me, his leg touching mine. His hands held his rosary and his lips moved silently in prayer.

"I saw only her memory," I said with relief.

"Thank you, God. That was my prayer," he said.

"And mine," I said.

"Maybe because she was the last one to touch it?" Luca said.

"I have no idea, but I'm going to expect the others are the same, so hopefully they will be," I said, rubbing my thumb against the crucifix of the rosary wrapped around my wrist.

"She found the note under her pillow, if you can call it a pillow. It was more like rags piled together in a worn piece of fabric, but it served as her pillow."

"That bad, huh?" Luca asked.

"The inn looked nice in the last memory. That was the part the guests saw. Dorothy shared a room with firewood, but she had no heat."

In disbelief, Luca said, "How did she not freeze to death?"

"I don't know," I said sadly. "Her life was so much harder than I imagined, and that was only a few seconds worth of a memory. It was so cold."

"Could you feel the cold?" Luca asked.

I thought back. "No, but it seemed like I could. It was like I experienced it all through her, and she was freezing."

"Did she know who left the note?" Luca asked.

"I don't think so. It scared her, but she was too cold to do much about it. She was just trying to survive the night," I said, starting to reach for the second note.

Luca placed his hand on mine and said, "In case there are any saints around, we'd love for you to be here. St. Michael, St. Benedict, and Padre Pio would be particularly welcome, and St. Catherine of Siena, St. Teresa of Àvila, and St. Thérèse of Lisieux are always invited."

I said, "You're creeping me out."

"Why?" Luca asked innocently.

"You tell me there's evil waiting in the wings and now you invite some of the saints best known for battling demons to come hang out with us," I said.

"That wasn't everyone I invited," he said.

"Right, and the saints my sisters and I are named for. Why not invite Jesus, Mary, and Joseph too," I said sarcastically.

"Yes, you three are invited too," he said, looking around as if he expected them to be floating nearby.

In front of me, Nira started to grin. I turned, expecting to see someone behind me, but did not. Jackson got up from his place beside Nira and went around behind the couch Luca and I were sitting on.

"Is someone there?" Luca asked.

"I can't see anyone," I whispered, "but Nira is very happy."

Luca turned, but saw no one. "Wonderful. Welcome, whoever just arrived."

"You're so weird," I said, still whispering so whatever ghosts or saints or whatever they were wouldn't hear me.

Luca whispered back to me, "They can hear whispers."

In a normal voice, I said, "Fine. You're so weird."

"No offense, but that's kind of the pot calling the kettle black," Luca said, his leg now touching mine.

"What does that expression even mean?" I said.

He thought a moment. "It means you're watching memories hidden in slips of paper and you're calling *me* weird," he said, knocking my leg with his.

"Yeah, I guess, but at least I don't talk to ghosts I can't see," I said.

He chuckled. "That's true. You only talk to those you *can* see."

"Big difference," I said.

He leaned in and kissed me. "I love you."

"Because of or in spite of the weirdness?" I said with a grin.

"Because of … definitely because of."

I leaned my head against his neck. "I love you too."

"Because of or in spite of the weirdness?" he asked, teasing.

I laughed and kissed his cheek. "Definitely because of."

I sat up and pulled the blanket over my shoulders as I reached for the second note.

It was early evening. There was enough light to see, though there was no window in the room. The dim light was coming from the interior of the inn. The wall of firewood between Dorothy's sleeping area and the rest of the room was gone, making the room appear much longer, though it was still far from a large space. Along the outside wall, there was one layer of firewood, rather than two, and it went only halfway up the wall. Dorothy entered the room, her gaunt features clearly visible in the dim light. On the gray pillow was a square of white. She stopped and stared. She turned back toward the main room. No one was there. She went swiftly to the pillow, stuffing the note into the pocket of the apron she wore. She looked back, again expecting someone, but no one came. She stood still, as if listening.

Dorothy waited a few seconds. She took the note from her pocket and read the words: "I hope your day was pleasant." She studied it, examining the handwriting and turning it over, searching for clues. There were none. She faced the open doorway. She hesitated and then retrieved the first crumpled note from the woodpile. She smoothed it out and placed this one on top of it. She slipped them into a crack between two logs that were close to the floor. After gathering some firewood, Dorothy went back to the main room of the inn.

Luca was watching me.

"Still only her memories," I reported, and sighed with relief.

Luca leaned back against the couch. "Thank God."

"This one was on her pillow, not under it. He clearly had access to her room—if you want to call it a room."

"How did she feel when she saw it?" Luca asked.

I thought about it. "Confused. She was trying to figure out who it was from. It wasn't dark out, and she didn't seem as … as isolated," I said, trying to think of the right word.

"Most of the firewood was gone. I think the worst of winter must've been over. It seemed warmer. She seemed afraid, though, like she didn't want anyone seeing the note and she hid this one with the last one. Not in a romantic way, but more because she couldn't think of anything else to do with them."

Luca said, "It would make sense to be afraid. I doubt her parents would be kind if they saw the notes."

"If they don't care enough to let her sleep in front of a fire, they definitely aren't going to believe anything she says. He was seriously putting her at risk," I said.

"I doubt he cared," Luca said.

"But he's leaving her notes," I said. "Shouldn't he at least not want the notes to get her in trouble?"

Luca said, "He isn't leaving the notes for *her*, he's leaving them for himself. It satisfies something in *him* and has nothing to do with her."

I was silent.

"Think about it. If he actually cared about her, would he risk getting her in trouble? Her life is hard enough. Would anyone who cares for her even a little bit, want it to be harder?"

"No," I answered as the truth of his words settled. I stared off toward the fire.

"What else are you thinking about?" Luca asked, his leg tapping mine.

I turned to him. "She was really thin. I mean she was thin in every memory I've seen her in, and in the photograph, but in this one she was scary thin."

"You said she'd been hungry when Nira gave her that food," Luca said.

"This was more than hungry," I said, picturing her prominent cheekbones. "This was near starvation."

"Winter in Maine is a hard time to find food," Luca said.

"They ran an inn. It wasn't like they were living in the wilderness. I mean, they were, but not like that. There was a town nearby. Her parents could've bought food," I said.

"That assumes they had money or they wanted to spend it on food for her," Luca said.

"How do you not feed your own kid?" I said, staring at him. "I mean, I knew she wasn't loved, but I didn't realize she slept without heat or went days without food," I said. "No child should have to live like that."

"A lot do," he said softly.

I leaned against him. His hand held mine. I said, "Her life was so hard."

"Yes, and he made it harder," Luca said.

Twenty-Seven

I was back in the room of firewood. It was dark, like the first time Dorothy found a note, but it was different. Not as dark and not as cold. The wall of firewood had returned, along with the narrow walkway. Firewood was stacked to the ceiling and at least two rows deep along the walls. Dorothy came into the room. She remained dangerously thin, but she wasn't as emaciated and she wasn't freezing. She wore the same dress as before—she had no coat on—and her sleeves were rolled up. She moved slowly through the dark room and around the wall of firewood. She sat on the mattress and unlaced her boots. Tiny groans escaped when she pulled them off. She stretched her toes. The boots were too small; I could feel the ache in my own toes.

When she lay her head back, she heard the crinkle of paper. She sat up and felt for the paper. She hesitated, and then stood and went to where a sliver of moonlight came through the cracks in the slanted edge of the roof. She angled the paper so the words became visible. The words seemed to glow in the silver light of the moon. "You made me smile today." She held the paper, seeming to be lost in thought. She went back to her mattress, still holding the note in her hand. She lay her head sideways and stared at the paper. Her expression was blank. After a few

I placed the slip of paper that bore his words with the other two.

"How did it go?" Luca asked, placing his hand on my back.

"She'd gained some weight. It wasn't winter anymore. The firewood had returned and her sleeves were rolled up. It was spring, at least, maybe summer. I think she figured out the notes were from him."

Luca asked, "How can you tell?"

"Something in her expression shifted. Recognition. But that's all. Not excitement or fear, just a sort of understanding."

"What about him?" Luca asked.

"Still no sign of him. No memories of him writing the note or slipping it onto her bed," I said with relief.

"Maybe his memories aren't the important ones," Luca said thoughtfully.

"They aren't important to me," I said with disdain.

"Probably not to Dorothy either," Luca said. "If you're supposed to help her, then it matters what *she* remembers, not what *he* remembers."

"Whatever the reason, I'm thankful," I said, sucking in air as I reached for the next note. I felt Luca's hand on my back … the world around me dissolved.

Dorothy walked into her room. It was evening, yet plenty bright enough to see. She appeared healthier than she had in the other memories. It must've been late spring or summer; birds were chirping outside. There was a thin layer of sweat on her face and neck. The dress she'd been wearing in the other memories had been replaced by one with short sleeves, made of fabric that didn't appear as heavy. She wore different shoes too. They were boots, like the other ones, but several sizes bigger.

She went swiftly around the wall of firewood and stopped at the sight of the paper on her pillow. She'd expected it to be there. She knelt on the mattress and picked up the paper. It was different from the others: it was not a slip of paper, but a piece of stationery. "I'm glad you figured out I'm your admirer. Though there was some fun in keeping things mysterious. I hope you like the gift." She held the note for several seconds, her expression blank. She ran her fingers along the boots she wore, and her gaze shifted to the interior wall of her tiny room where there was another pair of boots. These were the ones I'd seen her in before: heavily worn and smaller. She refocused on the boots she wore. Her fingers glided across the smooth brown leather. Then she turned to face the woodpile. She carefully removed a few pieces of wood and found the green metal box. She placed the square of paper inside the box with the other notes. She replaced the box and the pieces of wood to hide it. She kept her hand on the firewood for some time and then slowly released it.

I was silent as I reentered my dad's office.

Luca asked, "Did you discover what the gift was?"

"A pair of boots. The others were much smaller," I said, feeling the exhaustion from what I was witnessing.

"What did she think of them?" he asked, watching me for an indication of what was really happening.

"She wore them, but I think she understood …."

"Understood what?" Luca said.

"That he was buying her," I said, feeling the heaviness push against my chest.

"Don't judge her," Luca said softly.

"I'm not," I said, looking him in the eyes. "I love your eyes. I can't remember if I've told you that before, but I do. They remind me of amber, and there is such depth and caring. You think I'm judging her, but I'm not. I understand things more than I did before. The boots she had were far too small. I can't imagine wearing shoes that don't fit."

"It isn't fun." He grimaced.

"At least in Florida you can go shoeless, but up here …."

"Up here, you would lose toes in the winter or maybe a whole foot," he said.

"She didn't have a choice," I acknowledged. "Not accepting the boots would've been foolish."

"I wonder how he gave them to her without her parents noticing?" he said.

I shrugged. "I haven't seen her parents. The memories only last as long as she's near the note. Once she puts it away, the memory fades."

"That's probably a good thing," Luca said.

"Yes," I said, leaning forward, noticing Nira watching me. I'd forgotten for a moment that she was there.

"Her life was hard," I said to Nira, who didn't respond.

"It's the sort of life that makes a person the perfect prey," Luca said.

I shivered at the truth of his words.

Twenty-Eight

I was outside, in the center of the moss-covered boulders. I swirled around and jumped out of the way. Dorothy had surprised me from behind. She didn't see me; she was running full force to the boulder with the flat spot that I was standing beside. On the flat spot was a square of paper hidden under a small moss-covered rock. Yet she'd gone right to it. She expected it to be there. She lifted the rock and retrieved the folded piece of paper. This one, too, was on heavy stationery. I felt it in my hands as she held it in hers. She unfolded it and read the message: "Thank you for showing me this place. You're right, it's beautiful, though not as beautiful as you. Forgive me, that was too forward."

A broad smile formed across her lips. She held the note to her chest and spun around, which caused her dress to flare. She was giddy as a little child who'd been given a favorite toy. Or a young girl ... in love.

In the distance, I heard her name called: "Dorothy, are you here, Dorothy?"

It was Nira calling to her as she was skipping through the forest. Dorothy's expression changed, though she continued to grin despite trying not to. She hurriedly went to the side of the boulder and retrieved the green metal box. She placed the note inside and replaced the box in its hiding place. It was the same hiding place where we had found the box.

Nira was closer. "Dorothy," she called again.

Dorothy hopped up, saying, "Here I am," and ran toward her friend.

Across the table, Nira was watching me.

"You were in that one," I said to Nira. "You were calling to her. Did you know he was leaving her notes?"

Nira didn't answer; I didn't expect her to.

Luca said, "Nira was inside the inn?"

"No. They were in the enchanted forest. Dorothy must've shown him the boulder with the flat spot, the other side of where we found the box. She ran right to the note even though it was hidden under another rock. She must've known it would be there."

I turned over the note and ran my fingers along the slight green marks left from where it had rested against the moss. "She was happy, really happy," I said with despair.

"Someone was giving her attention," Luca said. "That would make her happy."

"It's more than that, Luca. She has feelings for him," I said as I watched her twirling with joy in my mind. "She wore a different dress. It was new—or at least, newer than the other dresses I'd seen her in."

"Another gift?" Luca asked.

"Probably," I said, slumping back against the couch and staring at the fire. "It was so easy for him to buy her."

Luca took my hand in his and said, "He was hunting her and he was good at it."

"She had a choice," I said, hoping somehow I was wrong … but knowing I wasn't.

"Sort of," Luca said thoughtfully.

Nira was watching him intently.

"What do you mean, sort of? She could've ignored the notes or not accepted the gifts. Maybe keep the boots because she needed those, but not the dress," I said.

"Why would she do that? He's supposedly this amazing guy everyone loves. He's even the mayor. He's got a beautiful wife and an adorable little boy. Everyone wants to be his friend, and here he is giving his attention to a scrawny teenage girl who's nearly alone in the world. Why would she turn down gifts that she needed, from someone who was supposedly wonderful?"

My mouth fell open. "Because he was married! He took a vow and he was breaking that vow with my great-grandmother!"

Luca shrugged and said, "How could she care about that? She was a kid who had no example of a true marriage. All she saw was a supposedly amazing guy doting on her. She had no idea who he was. She saw what everyone else saw—the charismatic mayor of her town."

"Are you falling for him too?" I asked sarcastically.

Luca laughed. "No, but I get it. And I'm not angry at Dorothy for falling for the lies. I wish she wouldn't have, but I'm not going to pretend like I would've done any differently if I was her."

I stared at him. "I … I disagree."

"You've never been starving," he said as if that summed it up.

"That isn't fair. My opinion still counts even though I've always had enough food to eat."

"That's true. But it's also true you fell for Thomas," he said in a tone that made me cringe.

"I wish you would stop bringing that up. It was a momentary blip."

"Maybe this was the same," he said, eyeing the stack of notes.

"I doubt it," I grumbled, staring at the next note in the box.

It had not been folded and was easy to read. *"Watching you with my son yesterday brought me both joy and sorrow. If only my wife was as much a woman as you are. You will be an excellent mother."*

I felt my stomach churn. "You can read it the same as I can. That's gross! He's making his kid part of this."

"She was a kid herself," Luca said, shaking his head.

"A kid who should've known better," I said as I reached for the paper.

Dorothy and Nira were coming toward the enchanted forest. Dorothy immediately spotted the note. She started fidgeting with a pleat of her dress, nervously chewing on the inside of her cheeks.

"What's that?" Nira asked as they got closer.

The white paper seemed to glow against the green moss that covered everything in sight. There was a rock on it to hold it in place, but not the one he'd used before. This one was not as large as the last one, making the note plain to see.

"Nothing," Dorothy lied.

Nira looked at her as if sensing the lie. She ran toward the note and grabbed it before Dorothy could get it.

She read the note. "What is this?" she asked, holding the paper with a puzzled expression.

"How would I know?" Dorothy said defensively.

Nira cocked her head and studied Dorothy. "Because you do. I can tell. Is it for you?"

"I'm sure I don't know," Dorothy said, straightening her dress.

"Yes, it is for you, that is clear. Do not lie any longer. Who is it from?" Nira said, sounding hurt.

Dorothy remained silent.

"You were with me yesterday. We went to the beach just beyond the Padgetts' house. Their little boy was there." Nira cupped her hands to her mouth. "Mr. Padgett!

But he watches me. I've told you he watches my house. Even my ma saw him."

"That's a misunderstanding. He's a good man, a man of his word," Dorothy said with an air of an adult talking to a child.

"A good man? Surely, you cannot mean that!" Nira exclaimed. "He makes my skin crawl. He makes your skin crawl—you've told me yourself many times!"

"That was before I got to know him," Dorothy said, swaying so that her new dress twisted this way and that.

"Dorothy, you cannot! I have the worst feeling about him, and he is married. His wife is kind, far too kind for him. He treats her bad. I told you what I've seen."

"You have, and I asked him about that. He said whoever told me that was mistaken, that he has never laid a hand on his wife or his boy," Dorothy said.

"That's not true!" Nira exclaimed, stamping a foot into the earth.

"You're asking me to call him a liar when I know him to be a man of his word," Dorothy said, crossing her arms.

"And what about me? Do you not know me to be a girl of my word?"

"There's a great deal girls don't understand. He has made me understand that," Dorothy said with her hands on her hips.

Nira's mouth fell open as she stared at Dorothy. "You're serious?"

"He has been kind to me, and if you care for me, you will not speak poorly of him," Dorothy said staunchly.

"He has been kind to you? Toward what end?" Nira said, her arms crossed in front of her.

Dorothy exclaimed, "Your mind goes too far!"

"Does it? You're playing a dangerous game. My ma is honest with me and she has explained things. A grown man doesn't show that sort of kindness to a young girl without wanting something in return. Not that sort of man, anyway," Nira said with repulsion.

"You call me a young girl? You're far younger than me. You know nothing of the world," Dorothy shot back.

"I understand more than you think I do. How did he know to leave you a note here?"

Dorothy turned away.

"You brought him here, didn't you! Did you take him to our cave as well?" Nira asked.

"No!" Dorothy shouted. "That is ours. I've never shown that to anyone. I merely walked with him toward his home and we came this way. He liked the moss."

"It's dangerous to walk alone with such a man and to show him our enchanted forest. I never expected something so betraying from you!" Nira said, dropping the note into a bit of mud.

As the note touched the ground, she turned and walked away. Dorothy snatched the note up and carefully *wiped the mud from it. She ran her thumb lovingly across the paper as she read the words.*

Nira was at the trees. She called out, "Mr. Padgett is many things, but he is not a man of his word. You are playing with fire."

"And you are a silly little girl," Dorothy shouted back.

Nira turned and stormed through the trees.

Clenching her left hand into a fist, Dorothy watched her disappear. "She knows nothing, nothing of who he is or who I am," she grumbled to herself.

She was so still, some birds gathered on the boulders, picking through the moss for insects.

A couple minutes later, Dorothy turned and went to the boulder that had held the note. She knelt near the hole in the side and retrieved the box. She carefully opened it, smiling as she reread the other notes. She placed this one on top and put the box back inside the cavity of the boulder.

She stood and straightened her dress before slowly walking back toward the inn.

"You warned her," I said to Nira. "You saw it from the beginning, and she didn't listen. If she would've just listened," I said, biting the inside of my cheeks.

Nira stared up at me; her green eyes with amber flecks seemed to hold the memory within them and at the same time seemed to be begging me to forgive Dorothy.

"That's a lot to forgive," I said in answer to her silent plea.

Luca asked, "What happened?"

I dropped the note on the pile of read ones. "Nira predicted it all."

"She knew he was a serial killer?" Luca said, astonished.

"No, but she said he was a total creep that watched her house and beat his wife and kid. Seems pretty clear to me."

"What did Dorothy say?" Luca asked.

"That he was a man of his word," I said flatly.

"He tricked her," Luca said.

I rubbed my head. "I hear what you're saying. I do … but it was clear who he was. You can compare it to me and Thomas all you want, but Thomas wasn't old or married, and he became possessed, but he wasn't when I thought I liked him. That happened later. Dorothy already knew he watched her best friend and beat his wife. She was choosing to believe him over Nira."

"He must've been very good at convincing her—at convincing everyone, if you think about it. If he was that much of a psychopath and still got elected mayor, he must've been really good at pretending. I bet he was super charming."

"You really don't want her to be the bad guy, do you?" I said.

Luca shook his head, "I truly don't think she was the bad guy."

"You think too highly of her," I said as I leaned forward and reached for the next note in the box.

Twenty-Nine

I was in front of the BayTree. The day was warm, and I heard the sound of gentle waves in the distance. The grounds around the house were artfully manicured. A picket fence with an ornate carving at the top of each post surrounded the front of the house. Its bright whiteness matched the house. A lovely little archway of jasmine complemented the fence. Outside of the fence, tall purple lupins were swaying gently in the breeze. It was the most beautiful summer day. The house and flowers were so vibrant—such a contrast to my own memories of the BayTree and its gravel parking lot.

A side door opened and Dorothy hurried out. I stepped aside as she came toward me. Her long, straight hair was neatly brushed. She was pretty in her new dress and boots. So different from the undernourished child in the memory of the first note. She held a basket that appeared empty except for a gray dish towel. From around the back of the house, a little boy ran toward her.

"Dorothy, wait," he called.

She stopped and waited for him, giving him a tender smile.

"Here," he said, handing her a slip of paper. "This is from my pa."

"Did you read it?" she asked, sounding nervous.

He shook his head. "He told me not to, plus I don't read too good."

"It took me a long time to learn, too."

"How did you learn?" the boy asked.

"A friend"—her voice caught a little—"taught me."

"That's a good friend," he said, kicking a shell across the dirt path.

"Yes, a very good friend," Dorothy said solemnly. "Next time you visit me, we can practice."

"Ma said we won't visit again," the boy said.

"Oh?" She sounded concerned.

The boy said simply, "It wouldn't be good for you."

"It wouldn't be good for me?" Dorothy said, her brows pulled together in confusion.

"That's what Ma said," he replied, bending down and digging at a tiny shell in the dirt.

Crouching down to his level, Dorothy asked, "Why did she say that?"

The boy shrugged in an exaggerated way. "I think it has something to do with Pa."

"Oh," Dorothy said, her voice catching again.

"It don't matter, anyway. Pa says I'm too stupid to learn to read."

"Your pa would never say such a thing," Dorothy said, now kneeling on the ground beside the boy, whose blond curls practically glowed in the sunshine.

"Yeah, he did. He says lots of stuff, but it don't matter." He picked at the shell in the sandy path.

The woman from the photograph called from the porch: "Peter, come inside, please."

How long had she been there?

"See ya," the boy said, and moved toward his mother, who was watching Dorothy.

Dorothy looked back at her for a moment, her hand tightening around the note.

"Take care," the woman said to Dorothy.

She was not angry, but she wasn't a fool, either. Her tone said she understood everything, far more than Dorothy did, and Dorothy seemed to pick up on that.

When the boy reached the steps, he flung his arms around his mother. She kissed the top of his head and tousled his blond curls. They held one another for a moment before going inside.

Dorothy slowly crossed the dirt street and entered the woods. She climbed upwards, the note still held tight in her hand. When she reached the top of the hill, she looked backward. She could see clearly into the BayTree's attic window. There was a telescope and some movement behind it: two people—a tall one and a much shorter one; it was hard to make them out. She stared until the larger figure, a man, turned toward the window. It was Mr. Padgett. He held his arm straight, keeping the other figure from being seen. With his left hand, he waved at Dorothy.

She turned away, her face flushed red. I tried to stay and watch the window, but that part of the memory became blurry as she rushed through the woods.

She soon reached a clearing with a small vegetable garden walled off with rocks and, beyond that, a simple house.

Chickens squawked in protest as Dorothy hurried past them. She went to the house and knocked lightly. The door opened. Nira was there, her arms crossed.

"I'm sorry," Dorothy said. "May I come in? I think he's watching me."

Nira let her in and shut the door.

"I don't think he can see us this time of year when the trees and shrubs are thick. It's in the winter when he watches us the most," Nira said.

Dorothy shuddered. "You were right, Nira. You were right about all of it."

"Why do you now believe me?" Nira said, with her arms crossed.

"I saw it with my own eyes a moment ago. I was there delivering fish from my pa and, in truth, I wanted to go, but when I was there, he was staring at me so. Even with his wife and boy right there, he was staring at me. I was so uncomfortable, and he didn't seem to care. And his boy, Peter ... he's a good boy, and his ma is as good a ma as anyone could ask for—far better than mine. She don't *deserve her husband to be acting like that, not right in front of their boy."*

"Is that another note?" Nira asked, nodding her head toward the scrunched-up paper in Dorothy's hand.

"Peter gave it to me. I haven't read it," she said, dropping the paper onto the wooden table.

Nira unfolded it so that they could both read it.

"How I wish I was with you. You will tell me I shouldn't say such things, but I can't help myself. I am under your spell."

The girls looked at one another. Then Dorothy picked up the note and moved toward the stove.

"No," Nira said, stopping her. "Keep it in case you need it as proof."

"Proof of what? That I put some spell on him?" Dorothy said fearfully.

"No one would believe such a lie. Proof that he's been writing to you all along. You've saved the others, haven't you?"

Dorothy blushed with shame. "Yes."

"Good," Nira said. "They show he was writing to you."

"No one would ever believe me, even with notes," Dorothy said.

"At least they're something in his own writing," Nira said, taking the note from Dorothy and stuffing it under the gray towel in Dorothy's basket. "I'm glad you came here."

"I shouldn't have. He probably knows I'm here. I worry for you and your ma," Dorothy said.

"Don't worry about us. We can take care of ourselves," Nira said, pouring hot water into two cups for tea.

The memory faded.

I held the note, the crucifix from the rosary around my wrist resting against the crumpled paper.

"You were right," I said. "She realized he's awful, and apologized to Nira. That's who lived next to the skating rink. Dorothy went right to her and told her everything."

Luca sat silently watching me.

"Please don't say I told you so," I said.

"I wouldn't, but I did," he said.

"Yes, you did, you saw exactly who he was and who Dorothy was from the beginning, like Nira did," I said.

I turned to Nira. "You were such a good friend to her. It was your idea to save the notes in case she ever needed proof of things."

"And now they're providing you with the memories of things," Luca said. "I doubt she could've predicted that they would be used this way."

"I'm sure not," I said, staying focused on Nira. "He watched your house with a telescope, from the attic window," I said with a shiver.

Nira sat perfectly still, her hands folded in her lap, her head bent down.

"Nice neighbor," Luca said, his tone sarcastic.

"The whole thing is horrible," I said. "He was awful to his wife and son. His son, Peter, told Dorothy his dad says he's too stupid to learn how to read. His wife seemed nice and she loved their little boy so much, and Peter loved her." I stood as tears started to form. "She knew something bad was going on with Dorothy and she told their little boy they weren't going back to the inn because it wouldn't be good for Dorothy. She was trying to protect her, at least a little bit. Why did she stay with him? Why didn't she leave? Maybe they wouldn't have been … maybe they would've lived." I gripped the mantle and sunk down in front of the fireplace, allowing its heat to warm me.

Luca sat beside me. "I doubt she knew he was that bad. Most cheating husbands aren't killers."

"I guess not," I said, running my fingers through my hair.

A memory flashed and I said, "There was someone in the attic with him." I felt my stomach twist. "A child. He'd already kidnapped a child. His wife must've known about that. I only saw them for a second, but there was a small person in the attic with him as he was watching Dorothy."

Luca said, "Maybe it was Peter."

"Peter was outside with Dorothy. I doubt he had time to make it up to the attic."

"Dorothy had time to climb the ridge," he said.

"That's true," I said, trying to remember the figure. "From my angle, I could only see Charles."

"That's probably because that's where Dorothy's focus was. I wonder if she even noticed the other figure," Luca said thoughtfully.

"She didn't mention it to Nira," I said. "But she realized something was very wrong with him."

Luca took my hand in his. "Why don't we stop for today. You've done a lot. It might be good to let your senses rest."

Nira sat taller. The thought of us stopping made her uneasy.

"I'm okay, Luca. I want to finish," I said, pushing myself up from the hearth and going toward the notes. I didn't wait until I sat down. I grabbed the next note as if ripping off a Band-Aid.

Thirty

I was back in the forest. The day was hot; Dorothy's hair was stuck to the back of her neck. She looked very much like the young girl she was. When she saw the note on the boulder, she slowed her pace and cautiously scanned the woods. She was nervous as she went toward the note. She read it quickly: "You're right, it was wrong of me to kiss you. Yes, I'm married, but you're so enchanting. It isn't fair what you do to me. I lose all sense when you're around."

She heaved a great sigh and went to the side of the boulder to place the note inside the box with the others.

"That was fast," Luca said when I laid down the paper.

"It was a short memory. She found the note on the boulder and hid it in the box. She was alone and scared."

I reached for the next slip of paper.

Luca grabbed my wrist. "Are you sure? If he's kissed her, things are progressing," he said, pulling my hand away from the note.

"I want to get this over with," I said, and he released my hand.

"Be careful," he said as I reached for the next note.

It was the middle of the day, and Dorothy moved quickly through the room, toward the wall of firewood that separated where she slept from the rest of the room. She stopped. He was there, leaning over her makeshift bed, note in hand.

He flashed a bright smile. "I didn't realize you saw me come in. I was just leaving this for you," he said, his voice soft and sweet.

Many voices came from the main part of the inn. Dorothy stepped backward so that she was no longer behind the wall. Now she could be seen by anyone who came into the room for firewood, though in the middle of summer, that seemed unlikely.

"You shouldn't be here … you could be seen!" she said in a frail, trembling voice.

"You're good to think like that. I can't. I can think only of you," he said, stepping toward her.

She backed up.

"Why are you moving away from me? Didn't you come here searching for me?" he said, his expression puzzled.

"No-no, I-I came to retrieve something. I didn't realize you were here," Dorothy said.

"Ah, then you've been surprised. A good surprise, I hope," he said, studying her.

"Ye-yes, good. How could it be anything but?" Dorothy said, though she was clearly lying.

He smiled. "It's good you care for me so. I don't know what I would do if you didn't," he said, his eyes holding the danger that she sensed.

Dorothy's eyes became wide with fear and she lowered her gaze.

He tilted his head, studying her expression. "Why do you act so coy with me?" he asked, placing a hand on her left hip. "Is this not what we've talked about? These precious moments that we must take fullest advantage of until we can truly be together."

"But there are guests everywhere. W-we could be caught. It wouldn't be good for either of us."

He stepped closer, taking one of her long braids in his hand and delicately lifting it. "You have such pretty hair."

She stood, too scared to move.

A woman's shrill voice rose above the others: "Dorothy! Where is that wasteful creature?"

At first he didn't move, except to lean in closer to her.

"My mother. She will come here looking for me," Dorothy said, keeping her face turned away from his.

His lips brushed her neck as he let his arm fall, allowing her to move past him.

She grabbed some pieces of firewood and dashed from the room.

"Here, Ma," she called as she hurried toward her mother's voice.

He remained. The hand that had been holding her braid picked at a piece of firewood while his eyes remained trained on where Dorothy had stood.

That memory faded and another appeared.

It was nighttime, and she was making her way through the opening in the firewood. On her pillow was the note he'd left her, along with a purple lupin. She picked up the note, her fingers shaking as she read it in the moonlight. "I wish I could take you away from here. You deserve better, but no one would understand. You're the only one who has ever truly understood me." She held the note as a single tear slipped down her cheek. She hurriedly swiped it away and shoved the note into the woodpile.

She held her knees close to her body, rocking like a young child.

A moment later I was inside the cave. Nira was at the table arranging wild roses in a chipped ceramic vase. A fire burned in the center of the cave.

"He was there," Dorothy said as she pulled the note from her pocket. She sat in one of the chairs, her legs bouncing with nervous energy.

"What do you mean, he was there?" Nira asked with concern.

"In my room. I went there hoping to avoid him, but I hadn't realized he was there. He held me so close. I didn't think he was going to release me, but then my ma called for me."

"He was in your room?" Nira said, eyes wide as she sat across from Dorothy.

Dorothy nodded. "I didn't stop shaking for the rest of the day. Thank goodness the inn is crowded and I had a hundred things to do, with my ma watching me every second."

"You can't hide forever," Nira said.

"What else can I do?" Dorothy said, near tears.

"Me and Ma have been talking."

Dorothy exclaimed, "You told her!"

"No! You know how she is. She'd go right up to him and wouldn't care that he was the mayor and she was a poor, widowed, colored woman. I think she forgets she's not white like my pa was, or maybe she don't care. Anyway, what I told her was I think we should go on to New York like she's been talking about since Pa died. Now that he's gone, his family doesn't have anything to do with us, so it would be nice to be with her family. I met them once when I was little. I remember them being nice to me. Ma's been talking about it since he passed, but neither one of us wanted to leave you or the memories of him here. I told her I thought it was time and I asked if you could go with us."

"What did she say?" Dorothy asked, leaning forward.

"She said she can't go kidnapping a child."

Dorothy's expression fell.

"But then I said, 'What if Dorothy happened to leave the same day we did and happened to go to the same place, and then asked if she could stay with us until she got things figured out?' And she said that might be okay, as long as she wasn't the one taking you away. If you were leaving and we were merely going to the same spot and then we let you stay with us a while. That would only be the right thing to do since you can't go turning a child out on the street," Nira said with a grin.

"I'm fourteen," Dorothy said. "It'll be a few years before I can move out on my own."

"I mentioned that too, and she said, 'Well, folks take different amounts of time to get things figured out,' and she didn't expect you would need to leave until you did," Nira said with a giggle.

Dorothy clapped her hands together. "She truly said that?"

"Of course she did. She loves you," Nira said.

Dorothy started to cry, and used the palms of her hands to push the tears off her cheeks.

"There now, it's good news," Nira said.

"You and your ma, you two are the only ones who ever cared for me. But you can't go uprooting your lives for me. I can't stay here. You're right about that. I can hide for the summer while the tourists are here and the inn is full, but after that … I'll have to go."

"Hopefully, by then we'll all be gone. Ma hates the winter. Plus, that's when he watches our house more, so that makes her hate it all the more. I'll remind her about that, and I bet we'll be moving on before then too," Nira said, taking hold of Dorothy's hand. "Be strong until then."

Dorothy nodded, but she appeared anything but strong. She was staring at the note on the table.

Nira said, "There now, don't think any more about it. I'll go put it away."

"What if he's out there?" Dorothy asked, trembling.

"They had a visitor. Her grandfather was there and you know it's not a short walk. He won't be out here today. But you're right, we should both head back. You stay at the inn. I'll work on Ma and I'll come to you. Don't come out here anymore," Nira said.

Dorothy was in tears as Nira took the note and ran from the cave to hide it. Dorothy fought back tears as sunlight streamed in from the upper slit in the cave wall, landing on the vase of wild roses.

"You were right, Luca, things are spiraling fast," I said, rubbing the rosary in my hand. "He was waiting for her in her room. She barely got away from him. It was horrible. But it's summer and the inn is crowded, so she and Nira think she's safe for now."

"Nira was there?" Luca asked, holding his rosary.

"No, I watched three memories. The first, when he found her alone in her room when he had the note in his hand." I shivered. "Then later that night, when she went to bed and saw the note, and then later, when she took the note to the cave and showed Nira. That's when Nira told Dorothy she was trying to talk her mom into the three of them moving away to New York."

"New York was Nira's idea?" Luca asked.

I nodded. "Her ma's family was there. Nira's pa was dead, and his family here had nothing to do with them, so her ma had been wanting to go to New York since he died. But they didn't want to leave Dorothy. Now Nira was trying to convince her ma to let Dorothy come with them."

Luca grinned.

"What?" I said.

"It's cute hearing you say ma and pa," he said.

"None of this is cute, it's horrible," I said, feeling the weight of what I'd witnessed.

"You're not part of this. All of it, every awful second, happened long before even Gigi was born."

"It feels like it's happening now," I said, fingering the beads in my hand.

He put his arm around me and said, "But it's not. Don't let the pain enter your heart. Nira is safe and that man is long dead."

"What about Dorothy?" I asked.

Luca's expression fell. "You're learning what you can to somehow help her, if that's what she needs. But you getting sucked into the darkness won't help her."

I exhaled and sat taller. "Right. That won't help," I said, reaching for the next note.

Thirty-One

I was back in Dorothy's room. It was the middle of the night. Her boots were muddy and her long braids had twigs stuck in them. She was being as quiet as possible as she entered the room and made her way around the walls of firewood. On the bed was a note; she wasn't surprised to see it. She was clearly exhausted, but she took the time to take the torn piece of paper to the moonlight. It read: "Where are you? It's been days! I'm beside myself with worry. I must see you!" Her face remained blank. This note didn't create any emotion in her, at least none that wasn't there before. She went to the bed and slipped off her boots. She stared for a long time at the mud that had splashed up on them. Finally, she turned around on her thin mattress and shoved the note into the woodpile. She lay her head down on what counted for a pillow, her eyes trained on the muddy boots.

"This one was back in her room. It was the middle of the night and she was filthy. I think maybe she was hiding from him. The note was on her bed, so he must've come to the inn to try and find her, but based on what he wrote, he didn't see her," I said, thinking of the words he had written in the fast, angry scrawl.

Luca said, "What do you mean hiding from him? There were people everywhere, weren't there?"

"I'm not sure, but that's what it seemed like. From the looks of her, she spent the day outside," I said.

"She must've thought he couldn't hurt her if he couldn't find her," Luca said as Nira watched us.

I grimaced. "She thought wrong," I said with a feeling of dread as I picked up the next note.

"You shouldn't have come out here alone!" Dorothy exclaimed when she saw Nira standing in the front room of the inn.

"I'm not alone," Nira said. "My ma came with me. We're selling eggs to your ma, or trying."

The two girls went to talk on the whitewashed porch of the inn. Sweet-smelling roses grew around it.

In a hushed whisper, Dorothy said, "Your ma hates my ma and my ma hates her right back."

"That don't matter," Nira said, grasping her friend's hand. "He came to my house."

Dorothy's eyes grew wide. "To your house?" she said in a whisper.

"Ma was there, thank the heavens. He started out friendly, asking how things were going, but Ma can't stand him, so she knew right away something was off. He asked if we'd seen you. That made Ma ask him why he

was curious about a little girl. It's like she knew exactly what was going on," Nira said.

"You'd told her?" Dorothy asked.

"No, but now I did. I had to. After the way he acted, there was no way to hide it," Nira said. "He got real mad. Maybe he'd been drinking, I don't know, but he wasn't right in the head. He said he'd come out here but you weren't here, and he was worried about you. I said you were busy this time of year. He called me a liar, which made Ma try and kick him out, but he wouldn't go. So she grabbed my pa's gun and finally he left. That's when I told Ma everything. She said she wanted to come out here and lay eyes on you herself. So that's what we did. We found this on the way," Nira said. She took a note from her pocket and read it aloud: 'I understand now, she has poisoned you against me. I'm a gentle man. You know that better than anyone, but I am a man and a man fights for those he loves.' "

"He's blaming you!" Dorothy said with wide, fearful eyes.

"Let him." Nira shrugged, taking the note back and crumpling it.

"He's dangerous," Dorothy said. "I don't want him blaming you or anyone."

"What he thinks, he thinks. I can't change that," Nira said as two guests came out onto the porch.

Dorothy nodded to them, and then led Nira toward the ocean, away from everyone else.

"You have to be careful," Dorothy said. "He's not right in the head—you said it yourself! He came out here looking for me two days ago and he stayed the entire day."

"What did you do?" Nira asked.

"I hid in the woods. There's a spot where I can watch the inn but not be seen, so that's what I did. He didn't leave until long after sunset. When I finally went inside, I found a note on my bed that asked where I was and that he had to see me."

"What did your ma and pa do with you being gone the whole day?" Nira asked, her voice quiet from fear.

"The inn is crowded, so I'm safe for now. But they won't forget. I'll be beat this winter for it, for sure!"

"You won't be here that long. Ma said we can go next week. She said if I'd told her before what was going on, we could've already gone. But she wants to give her family in New York time to prepare for us."

"She really said we can all go?" Dorothy said with caution.

"She did. She said she wished I'd told her sooner," Nira said.

"Did you explain why we didn't tell her? That we didn't want her getting hurt?" Dorothy asked.

"Yes, but she said a girl should tell her ma stuff like this, at least if the ma is good. She doesn't fault you for not telling your ma, of course."

"My ma finding out would make it worse for me," Dorothy said.

A woman was walking toward them. She carried herself with confidence, though her clothes were shabby. The girls became quiet as she approached them.

"Do you girls believe it? That old sourpuss bought our eggs," she said cheerfully. Her skin was dark and her eyes were the same golden color as Luca's. She held her head high and her shoulders back.

"Hello, Ms. Gemma," Dorothy said. "Ma bought your eggs because the eagles got our chickens."

"That's what your ma said. She said your pa shot the eagles right out of their nest as repayment," Gemma said with disgust.

"Yes, ma'am, that's the truth," Dorothy said sadly.

Gemma made a sour expression and said, "I've never understood how two such loathsome creatures created such a good one."

"I'm not so good," Dorothy answered, her head bent low. "I cause a lot of trouble."

Gemma put her fingers under Dorothy's chin and lifted it. "Don't go believing those lies. There's trouble and it's around you, that's true, but you didn't cause it. Maybe soon you can leave the trouble behind. Has Nira told you about New York?"

"Yes, ma'am, but it isn't fair for you to leave your home."

"It hasn't been much of a home since Isaac passed. Half of our hearts went with him. At least in New York we can be with my family who will accept Nira as their own. And they'll accept you too, though you certainly won't fit in," she said with a chuckle.

"I don't suppose I've ever fit in," Dorothy said.

"You fit in with me," Nira said, looping her arm around Dorothy's.

Dorothy grinned and squeezed Nira's arm.

"Dorothy," her mother called from the porch.

Dorothy's expression changed and she released Nira.

Gemma said quickly, "Nira won't be back here—not without me, anyway. Colored children have been going missing up and down the coast."

"Missing?" Dorothy tilted her head.

"Ma says they're being hunted," Nira said solemnly.

"That's exactly what's happening. There's no other explanation," Gemma said, her back as straight and strong as a soldier's.

Dorothy said, "I don't understand."

"No one does, but Nira won't be leaving my sight. We'll get a message to you when it's time," Gemma said.

"You're far too good to me," Dorothy said.

"You're my best friend. How else should we be?" Nira said, hugging Dorothy.

Gemma laughed softly and said, "Go on now, before your ma's face gets stuck like that."

"Be careful," Dorothy said, and turned to see a thin woman with such pale skin it seemed to glow. She was standing on the porch, glaring at them.

Nira and Gemma made their way down the beach. Gemma took Nira's hand in hers.

Gemma said, "I don't like this place."

"Me neither, but I like Dorothy," Nira said as they entered the woods.

"Yes, she's a good one, but the rest of this place isn't right," Gemma said, cautiously watching the trees. The leaves were no longer the bright green of spring and early summer. They were not far from becoming the leaves of autumn.

"I almost never came this far, anyway. We always met in the enchanted forest and it never felt bad. But now that he's been there, it's bad too," Nira said with a feeling of loss.

"I think that's true," Gemma said, holding her daughter's hand. "Has he been to your cave?"

"Lord, I hope not! I do hate to leave it," Nira said lovingly. "There's so much of Pa in it. It's such a nice little home because of him and the furniture he made for us."

For the first time, Gemma's shoulders fell. "It's hard to leave the memories," she said. "They were good memories while Isaac was alive. He was a good man."

Nira said, "Nothing like Mr. Padgett."

"Never compare them. Your pa was so good, and that white trash neighbor of ours so bad, that it's like they aren't even both descended from Adam."

"That's true," Nira said as they neared the boulders. "Should I save this one too?" Nira asked her mother.

"Yes. Like you said, it's good to have it all in his own handwriting, and I certainly don't want such filth in my house," Gemma said, her back straight again.

Nira released her mother's hand and retrieved the box from the boulder as Gemma stood by, alert like a sentry on guard duty.

After storing the box, Nira stood up, and Gemma took her hand, saying, "You don't leave my side, you understand? I don't like the feel of things."

Nira gripped her mother's hand.

I clung to the note, saying, "No. Come back." I squeezed my eyes shut, but nothing more came.

"What is it?" Luca asked with concern, his hand still on my back.

I shook my head. "It's falling apart so fast."

I stared at Nira. Her eyes were lowered, her hands resting delicately in her lap.

"You were such a good friend," I said to her. "You and your ma. Dorothy named Gigi after your ma, didn't she? She must have. She loved you both, and you loved her, and you were going to leave, and—." A sob broke from my throat.

Luca pulled me toward him. I clung to him.

"I'm sorry, Nira," I said, gasping for breath. "I'm sorry he killed you."

I turned my head and saw Nira stand up and come toward me. She looked down at me and, with a beautiful smile, touched my cheek where the tears were dripping.

"You feel real," I said, and sniffed as the touch of ice retreated from my face.

Luca said, "Is she next to you? It's really cold."

"She's right beside us. She looks beautiful, like she did when she was laughing and carefree in the memories she showed me—not like the ones from these notes."

"I think she's telling you she's okay," he said. "She experienced evil while she was alive, but now she's okay."

Nira looked at Luca and grinned even more.

"She agrees with you," I said, sitting taller.

"The smart ones always do." He grinned in Nira's general direction.

Next to us, Jackson whined, his gaze focused on the almost empty box and the stack of papers beside it.

Luca said, "There's only one left."

"Yes," I said.

We sat, unmoving, for what seemed like forever … until Nira left our side and returned to the couch across from us. Her shoulders were tall and strong, like her mother's.

Thirty-Two

People were everywhere. I tried to avoid them, but it was impossible—and unnecessary. They went right through me. I searched frantically for Nira and Dorothy. Finally, I spotted Dorothy. She and her mother were coming toward me. Some of the buildings I recognized, others were different, but it was similar enough to recognize we were in the center of our town … mine and Dorothy's. The leaves on the trees were the same as they were in the last memory. Not much time had passed. Suddenly he was in front of me, seemingly appearing out of nowhere.

Dorothy's mother stopped in front of him. Dorothy lowered her head.

"Good afternoon," he said to Dorothy's mother.

"Good afternoon," she answered.

"Good afternoon to you too, Dorothy."

Dorothy kept her eyes fixed on the dirt at her feet.

"Answer him," her mother said in a scolding tone.

Dorothy remained silent.

"You know how awkward she is," her mother said with great irritation.

"She's shy," he said sweetly. "There's nothing wrong with that. When she says something or graces someone with that tender smile, it means that much more."

"Ha! You flatter her," Dorothy's mother responded.

He bent his head lower in an attempt to make eye contact with the girl. She bent her head even lower, making eye contact virtually impossible, but as they did this he subtly slipped a note into the basket she carried.

His expression shifted to one of frustration over not being able to communicate with her, though he quickly regained his composure. "I've kept you both long enough," he said, and left them.

"Why are you such a despicable child?" her mother said, rounding on her.

Dorothy winced and stepped backward as if expecting to be hit, but her mother simply started walking away.

Seeing her opportunity, Dorothy quickly removed the note from the basket. It read: "I give you my word. No one will get in our way. We will be together—soon!" Dorothy started to shake. Turning her head, she found him almost immediately. He was there on the far edge of the street, watching her.

Her mother called out, "Come on."

Dorothy stuffed the note into the pocket of her dress and ran to catch up. She was trembling as she walked alongside her mother. She turned again. He was gone. She focused on the far end of town. I recognized the direction. Past the houses and woods in view were more woods, and beyond, there was the skating rink—though I doubted *anything was there at the time. Beside that was Nira's house.*

Dorothy chewed on her lip and then said, "I'll meet you at the inn."

A moment later she was sprinting down the street. Her mother pursed her lips. It was clear she wanted to yell at her, but didn't want to make a scene. I was carried along, not far behind Dorothy. I went with the memory contained in the note as we wove first through people, then homes, and, lastly, trees.

Dorothy ran fast while constantly watching over her shoulder. Eventually, the smoke from Nira's chimney could be seen and then her house. Dorothy was breathing hard when she stepped in front of the door. She didn't bother to knock. She threw open the door and ran inside. Nira and her mother were together at the sink.

"Dorothy!" Nira exclaimed, and ran to hug her.

Gemma stood with a hand over her heart. "You gave me a fright."

"I was afraid … afraid he got you," Dorothy said, panting and clinging to her friend.

"I'm all right. No one has gotten me," Nira said, trying to calm her friend.

Dorothy collapsed into a chair and began to sob. "I was so afraid. He'll hurt you, I'm sure of it. He thinks you're what's keeping me from him." She clutched her arms around her chest and started to rock.

"There now, child, calm down," Gemma said, smoothing Dorothy's hair.

"It's all my fault. All of this is my fault," Dorothy said, almost out of her mind in fear.

Nira and Gemma glanced at one another.

Nira knelt down in front of her friend. "I'm safe, and even if I were not, it wouldn't be your fault. What he does is on him, not on you."

"Has something more happened?" Gemma said with concern, her golden eyes going nervously to the unlocked door of their tiny cottage.

Dorothy rubbed her arms and tried to calm down enough to speak. "He handed me this in town," she was finally able to get out.

Gemma took the note from the trembling fingers. She read it and then passed it on to Nira.

Gemma asked, "Did he follow you into town? How did he know you would be there?"

Nira said softly, "It's Wednesday. Her and her ma always go into town on Wednesday to buy supplies for the next round of guests."

"Ah, routine is good," Gemma said, "but not so good when you're being hunted."

Dorothy stared up at her, her dark lashes thickened by the tears. "Hunted?"

Gemma asked, "Did you think it was love?"

"N-no," Dorothy said, though it was clear she had believed it was love or some warped version of it.

"It's good you're here," Nira said, trying to sound cheerful. "It saved us a long walk to the inn."

"Oh, do not go to the inn. Do not go anywhere!" Dorothy exclaimed, clutching her friend.

"I will not, I promise," Nira said, doing what she could to calm her friend.

Gemma said, "Nira's right. We were going to tell you that we received a note from my sister earlier today. They're happy to have us."

"Us and you," Nira said, glowing.

"Really?" Dorothy asked.

"Yes," Gemma said with a gentle smile.

Dorothy looked up at them. "Now? Can we go now? The bus to Portland leaves in a few hours."

"Too many people watching in the middle of the day," Nira said, glancing at her mother.

Gemma said, "Everyone knows your folks don't exactly approve of us, so if you got on a bus with us in the middle of town in the middle of the day, it might make things worse and keep us from being able to leave."

"Especially if he's watching us," Nira said with a shiver.

"The bus Friday morning is at a quiet time. Very few folks around. From there, we'll take the train to New York City."

"Can't we go today? I could get on separately and act like we aren't together," Dorothy said desperately.

"We'll go Friday morning," Gemma said calmly. "It will be better for everyone."

"Including my chickens," Nira said with a grin. "I'm taking them to Mrs. Williams tomorrow. She's always been good to them. And she won't tell no one we're leaving. At least not until after we're gone. Then she'll tell the whole town."

Dorothy nodded, her face troubled.

"A day won't hurt," Nira said.

"I'm not so sure," Dorothy said, "but I was thinking about money."

"What about it?" Nira asked.

"I haven't got any," Dorothy said. "I didn't think about it until now, but a bus and a train aren't free."

"I have enough for the three of us," Gemma said as she took the one photograph in the room off the wall. She placed it near a cloth bag on the bed she and Nira must've shared. The picture was of her in a plain white dress and a handsome white man beside her, wearing a suit and the same loving smile Nira had. The photo was in black-and-white, yet I could tell his eyes were light-colored. That must've been her and Isaac on their wedding day. He looked madly in love. She did too, but she also looked troubled, like she knew life for them would not be easy. I focused on the one-room cottage. It had definitely not been easy, but their love created Nira, and so whatever hardship they faced was worth it.

Dorothy said, "It isn't right. I have no money to get there and no money to live on. It isn't fair to you. I hadn't thought about that. I was so excited to get away, I didn't think about what a burden I would be."

Nira said, "You're not a burden!"

"When we're in New York, you can get a job," Gemma said. "You'll make enough to help a bit with food and you'll save the rest for when you're ready to move out on your own. It'll be tight at first, living with my sister, but I'll start working right away. She said we could stay with her as long as we need to. I expect that won't be more than three or four months."

Dorothy asked, "You truly think I could get a job?"

"Sure you can," Nira said. "I can too, and I'm going to. My aunt wrote Ma that wealthy folks hire girls to help with their children. She thought I might be fair-skinned enough to find a job with folks that aren't that wealthy, but she figured you would get in with a good family."

"You think someone would hire me?" Dorothy said with reserved hope.

"They'd be fools not to," Nira said.

Gemma tsked and said, "Hush, now. We'll worry about all of this in a few days. For now, Dorothy needs to go back to the inn before her ma comes searching for her or gets suspicious of something."

Dorothy went to the door, but turned around. "Promise you'll be careful," she said to Gemma and Nira. "I have an awful feeling."

"Don't you worry, I won't let her out of my sight," Gemma said.

"And I won't let her out of my sight," Nira teased, swishing her pale blue dress side to side.

"All right then," Dorothy said. "I'll be at the bus stop by first light on Friday."

"Be careful," Nira said, wrapping her arms around Dorothy.

Dorothy held on to her as if trying to absorb some of her strength.

"You too," Dorothy said.

She unlatched the door behind her. After one last glance, she shut the door and darted through the woods. I was again dragged along with her. She was careful not to get any closer to the BayTree as she quickly made her way through the woods. It was a long way back to the inn, but not as long through the trees as it was along the roads that I was used to driving. Going in a straight line cut many miles out of the journey. Every time Dorothy heard a noise, we both jumped, but no one ever appeared. When she reached the enchanted forest, she hid the note with the others and began to sprint through the woods, toward the inn. I watched her go as the memory faded and he appeared ….

In my dad's office, I yelled, "No! No, no." I clutched the note and fell to my knees. "He found her ... alone in the woods," I said, frantically trying to bring back the memory. "I don't know what happened." .

Luca said softly, "Maybe it's better you don't."

"They were so close to leaving, so close to safety," I said, beginning to cry.

"You already know how this story ends," Luca said sadly.

"It can't end that way," I said, sobbing. "It can't."

"But it does," Luca said, holding me. "It does."

Thirty-Three

Luca gently petted my hair, holding me, praying for me, protecting me. When I finally opened my eyes, orange coals glowed in the fireplace and Nira was gone.

I whimpered, "She was so close to being free."

"I'm sorry," Luca said.

"They could've gone to New York and been happy together. Dorothy could have had a family that loved her, a real mom and sister."

"And you would've never existed," he whispered. "The life you have would never have been."

"Isn't that okay, if she was okay?" I said, aware that Luca was right. But it wasn't right for my existence to depend on Dorothy's tragedy.

"I, for one, would miss you. But yes, if Dorothy's life had been different and she hadn't worked for a scumbag that got her pregnant, that would be okay. But that's not what happened."

I held my knees and lowered my head onto them. I watched the coals being washed in orange and fading to black, and washed in orange again.

"How does God stand it? He's all good, and yet the people he created are so evil."

"Many people are good—most of them, probably."

"But the bad ones are so bad," I said, lost in grief.

"That's why it's so important for the rest of us to be who he created us to be," Luca said, holding his rosary in his hand.

I turned my head and saw the notes stacked on the coffee table next to the ceramic bowl. I hated them, those memories, the lies Charles had told Dorothy, the fear she felt. I took the notes in my left hand and rocked forward so that I was on my knees in front of the fireplace.

"Wait. What're you doing?" Luca asked.

"Burning the evil," I said, holding my hand above the coals. I released the papers onto the coals.

"But the memories?" Luca said, moving quickly beside me.

The papers began to shrivel.

"I'll never forget them."

A few small flames arose, burning what remained of the notes. When the last of the paper had been turned to floating ash, I sat back.

"What do we do now?" he asked, watching me.

"I have no idea, but I'm leaving this room," I said, pushing myself up onto my feet.

Behind me, Luca grabbed the rusty box from the table.

***

Life felt better, or at least less depressing, as we entered the kitchen. Sam and Avi were there, hovering over a large pot of nearly boiling water, with a box of pasta beside them. Gigi was sitting on a stool at the counter, sipping a mug of tea.

"You two look like you've seen better days," Sam said, studying us as we entered.

"Did you watch the memories?" Avi asked, her large green eyes blinking up at me.

"You really do know everything," I said with exhaustion.

Gigi said, "I told her I gave you the box and not to disturb you."

I wondered when her voice got so frail.

Eagerly, Avi asked, "Can I read the notes?"

"Avila, you have already asked me that question," Gigi said sternly, "and I have given you the answer."

Avi opened her mouth to object, when Luca spoke. "The notes are gone." He opened the box for her to see it was empty.

"Where are they?" Avi asked, wide-eyed.

"I burned them," I answered as Luca threw the box into the trash container.

Gigi inhaled audibly. "That was for the best," she said, recovering quickly.

Avi said in astonishment, "You burned Great-grandmother Dorothy's love letters?"

"Why do you think they're love letters?" Sam asked, holding the wooden spoon over the pot on the stove.

In an exaggerated tone, Avi replied, "Gigi said they were notes from a man to her mother. What other sort of notes would a man write a woman?"

Sam and Gigi exchanged a worried expression.

Gigi said, "She was not a woman, she was a girl the same age as Lisieux. And yes, he was a man. Old enough to be married and have a child."

Avi's face contorted. "Oh! That's creepy."

"That's putting it mildly," I said, and filled a glass with water. I drank deeply.

"Were the notes from who I thought they were from?" Gigi asked. She hunched forward with her cream-colored shawl, that was now stained on one edge with rust, wrapped around her.

Luca waited for me to answer. When I didn't, he said, "Yes, it was the man from the BayTree. Charles is his name."

"The BayTree!" Avi said with a gasp.

"No wonder you look so awful!" Sam said, touching my forehead and cheeks. "Are you okay? I had no idea … is she okay?" she asked Luca.

"She'll be fine, unless you keep pinching her face up all weird," Luca said.

Sam removed her hands from my face and wrapped her arms around me. "I'm so sorry. If I'd realized, I would've barged in and—"

"Done what?" Gigi asked in irritation. "She needed to view them."

Sam asked, "Why did she need to see something so awful?"

"That's not for me to understand, but I feel it," Gigi answered.

Sam slipped her hands around my arm. She wouldn't release me and I didn't want her to.

"But to have her view *those* memories," Sam said.

"Gigi's right," I told her. "I had to do it."

"Why?" Avi asked, settling onto a stool next to Gigi.

I hesitated. In truth, I had no idea. "It helped me understand things."

"What sort of things?" It was Avi who asked, though Sam was just as curious.

"I suppose it was good to learn more about Great-grandmother Dorothy and how loved she was," I answered.

Avi said, "I thought you said they weren't love letters."

I shivered at the thought. "They definitely were not love letters, but she was loved. Not by him, by Nira and her mother, Gemma. They loved her like a sister and a daughter. They tried to protect her."

"Gemma," Gigi said.

I nodded. "Did your mother tell you who you were named after?"

Gigi shook her head. "She never told me I was named after anyone. She never told me anything about either of them."

"Their story with her had a tragic ending. ... I don't suppose she could talk about them, but Gemma was strong, determined, independent, fearless, and she loved Dorothy like her own."

"She sounds like you," Avi said, nestling up to Gigi.

"Yes, they were quite a lot alike," I said. "Gemma did everything she could to protect Dorothy. In a day and a half, they were planning to leave for New York, where Gemma's family lived."

Avi asked, "What happened?"

Sam was watching me as intently as my sister.

"I didn't see the end," I said.

"Thank God," Sam said, and in my heart I agreed.

"The last I saw was Charles finding Dorothy alone in the woods," I said, not looking at anyone as I spoke.

"Did she tell him what they were planning?" Avi asked as the others continued to digest my words.

"I don't know," I said, praying she hadn't.

"My mother would never do that," Gigi said, though I heard the doubt behind her words.

"She was a young girl and she was probably terrified of him," Sam said. "Whatever she did or didn't do was not her fault."

I ran my finger along the rim of the water glass. "She was terrified of him, but I think she would've died before saying a word about Nira." I slumped against the counter. "It didn't matter. He watched Nira's house and knew they were friends."

Gigi asked, "They lived near one another?"

"Nira lived in the woods, next to our skating rink. From his attic window he could use a telescope to watch them … and he did," I said.

"That's so creepy!" Avi exclaimed, shuddering.

"Disgusting," Sam said.

"Did you expect a serial killer to not be disgusting?" Luca said quietly to his aunt.

Sam said. "I thought he would've been more secretive. If he's stalking a teenage girl and using a telescope to watch his neighbor's house, surely there were other warning signs that others saw."

"Someone would need to be paying attention," Luca said. "And be willing to see the truth."

I said, "His wife tried to keep him away from Dorothy."

Sam asked, "She knew?"

"She knew he was too focused on Dorothy. Perhaps she was trying to protect Dorothy, or merely keeping her husband away from a possible rival. Maybe she realized he was totally deranged …" I said, my voice slipping into silence as I remembered the other figure in the attic window and Gemma's warning that children were going missing.

Luca said, "What is it?"

I glanced at Avi. "Nothing. Just thinking through the timing of everything," I mumbled, my stomach churning at the thought of what he must've already done by the time I saw him watching Dorothy.

"I remember going there," Gigi said, interrupting my thoughts.

"To the BayTree?" Avi asked with a gasp.

Gigi shook her head. "To Nira and Gemma's home. I'd forgotten until now, but when my mother and I got off the bus in town, we walked for some time through town and into some woods. Mother was so sick, it took us a long time. It was late in the day and we hadn't eaten. I remember asking her if we were going to the inn. She said we were going somewhere else first. Close to sunset, we reached an old shack. Mother was sliding her hands along the trees as we came toward it, like she wanted to feel them. It was clear the place had been deserted for years. She knocked anyway. I got the feeling she was hoping her eyes were wrong, that someone still lived there amidst the partially collapsed roof. But no one answered. She opened the door and stood in the doorway. It was the only time I ever saw her cry. I asked her again who lived there, but she didn't answer. She dabbed at her eyes, and we started back toward town. Then she stopped and leaned against a tree that had some boards nailed to it. It looked like it could've been a chicken coop. There, she wept. I asked her again who had lived there, and this time she said, 'People I knew once … good people.' We never spoke about it or them again."

We were silent for a long time.

"Nira had chickens," I said, silently wondering if that was how Charles caught her, when she went out to feed her chickens or to take them to Mrs. Williams.

Avi said, "I wonder if your mom was taking you there."

We stared at her.

She said, "Wouldn't that make more sense than leaving you at the inn with her parents, who were awful?"

Wrinkled lips slightly apart, Gigi stared at Avi. Gigi's eyes started to well with tears as her lips pressed together. She tilted her head toward the ceiling and took Avi into her arms.

Thirty-Four

This new understanding and the peace it brought Gigi was enough to make all the horrible memories not as horrible, or at least to lessen how much I hated having them. If I had to experience them to help Gigi better understand her own life, it was worth it. She'd always wondered why her mother brought her back to the parents she had fled from. Now Gigi understood that though her mother did flee from her parents, she was mainly fleeing from their deranged friend, Charles. And with Avi's insights, we understood Dorothy wasn't leading Gigi to her parents, she was leading her to Gemma. It brought a sense of peace to my grandmother and a better understanding of her own mother.

***

"Should we check on them?" Avi asked as she helped Sam dish up the pasta.

"Yes," Sam said, "Lisieux is probably exhausted."

"I'll go. I don't have much of an appetite," I said, and began climbing the stairs.

Lisieux and Jason were lost in a chess match, while my dad lay on his bed with his eyes closed. Though he had showered, the room had a sick, putrid smell to it.

"How is he?" I asked when Lisieux and Jason noticed me.

Not bothering to lower her voice, Lisieux said, "He's been asleep since right after his shower."

I went to my dad. His breathing was shallow and uneven. "Is he okay?" I asked them.

"Withdrawals aren't easy, especially when he won't be honest about what he was taking," Jason said, glancing at my dad with contempt. "My parents were the same. The number of times I watched this …. It isn't fair to you three."

"It's not," Lisieux said, standing abruptly and hurriedly shoveling the pieces back into her chess bag. "I've been his babysitter long enough," she said, and stormed out of the room.

"This is a lot harder on her than she lets on," Jason said as we heard her stomp down the stairs.

"It always is," I said. "She keeps it inside. She has friends, but she'll never tell them about any of this."

"When I was her age, I never told anyone either," Jason said. "It's embarrassing to admit your dad is a drug addict."

"Did she talk to you?" I said.

Jason chuckled. "Naw, me and her—we're the strong, silent type. It's why we get along so well."

"I worry about her," I said, watching my dad's chest move unevenly with his breaths.

"She'll be all right. She'll stomp around and then realize we love her and aren't going anywhere, and she'll open up a bit now and then. She talks sometimes, when we're working in the kitchen."

"That's good. I have a feeling once you move, she's going to be at your house most of the time."

"And Luca will be here," Jason said with a grin. "We'll trade one for the other."

I hoped he was right, at least about Luca. "How do you think Dad is doing, truthfully?"

Jason's grin faded. He focused on my dad. "You want honesty?"

I nodded.

"You're the oldest, so I'll give it to you. It's not good. Whatever he's using, it's a lot, and I have a feeling it's been going on for a few months. Which means he was only sober for a few weeks after the last time. None of that is a good sign. Frankly, it reminds me of my parents. They were never particularly good or honest people, but they weren't always addicts. Once they started using … it's hard to quit and they didn't. It's how they lived the rest of their short lives and how they died."

"And you think Dad is on that path?" I asked, my arms wrapped around my shoulders.

"If I'm being honest, he's in the middle of it. For him to quit will be a miracle. Maybe he could use less, maybe that will keep him functioning okay and decently healthy. My parents sort of had each other, which made it worse. Since he doesn't have someone using with him, maybe things will be better for him."

A cold breeze blew into the room, causing us to shiver. Even Dad reacted, uttering a couple unintelligible syllables.

Jason looked around. "The windows aren't open."

Nira stood on the side of my dad's bed.

"Nira's here," I said, my eyes locked on the partially translucent child.

"What's she doing?" Jason asked, his voice troubled.

"She's kneeling on the floor, next to Dad," I said, confused by what I was seeing. "Her hands are clasped like she's praying."

Nira made the sign of the cross, and then stood and locked eyes with me. I stepped back from the intensity of her expression. She came around the foot of the bed, passing Jason and me. She went slowly toward the door, turned back, and seemed to be waiting for me. At that moment Jackson ran up the stairs and stopped in front of her. She smiled briefly at him before returning an intense gaze at me. Jason was watching me watch her.

"I think I'm supposed to follow her," I said quietly as I started to walk toward Nira, who was slowly moving toward the stairs.

In a worried voice, Jason said, "Okay."

I passed Sam on the stairs. She was carrying a plate of food up to Jason.

"It's freezing up here," she said when Nira passed her.

"It's warmer upstairs," I said, continuing to follow Nira.

In the kitchen, she disappeared. Jackson went to the back door and whined.

"What's with him?" Lisieux said, irritated.

The rest of them were focused on me as I took my coat from the hook.

"Where are you going?" Avi asked, though I could tell she already knew the answer.

Luca shoveled the last bit of food into his mouth and hurriedly put his plate into the sink. "Is Nira here?" he asked.

"She's outside," I said as Nira turned and gazed back at me through the window of the kitchen door.

Outside, Jackson ran around to the side of the house. Nira was there, her bright white dress glowing in the fading daylight. Nira was using her index finger to trace the burned handprint that the ghost boy had left on the side of our house so many months ago. The burned handprint was the concrete sign that the life I'd lived before Luca moved onto our land was over and a new, bizarre one was beginning. Luca had not been lying when he told me he wasn't watching our windows but was watching holy souls enter my yard and ascend, maybe into heaven, while my family was in my dad's office praying. Within a few short days, Thomas entered my life in a way he hadn't been a part of before. He was drawn to the evil of the inn, created decades earlier by Dorothy's mother and my father.

I wondered now if that evil perhaps had at least part of its roots in the horrific things Charles had done to Dorothy … and to Nira. He had killed so many in one way or another. And now Thomas was dead. Was he one more innocent that Charles's evil had somehow killed? I supposed I'd never know who was truly part of Charles's list of victims. I thought of my dad upstairs. His blood had been used to help draw evil to the inn. Evil that led to Thomas's death and to my father's addiction.

A horrible thought entered my mind. Would there be another victim? Would my father die from his addiction like Thomas had died from his fascination with evil? The shadow was still there; Gigi said it was over all of us, but especially my dad. If it took my dad, would it be satisfied or would it continue hunting my sisters and me? Nira was not my child, but would my child someday be hunted, as she was?

"It's all interconnected," I said to Nira.

She placed a hand on the burn mark. The dark edges of the burned stone peeked from the edges of her light-brown skin. She looked up at me.

Luca said, "Everything each of us does affects everyone else. All the good and the bad."

He was right; the sins of those who long ago passed beyond this life were continuing to haunt my family. No doubt, the good of those who went before us was also helping to protect us. My mother was right. I needed to help Dorothy. I needed to help anyone I could … living or dead.

Thirty-Five

Nira stood and moved away from the stone wall of our house. She slowly began making her way down my yard, toward the trailhead. Jackson ran after her, causing the chickens to scatter.

"She wants me to follow her," I told Luca.

Nira passed the chicken coop and stopped, seemingly waiting for me.

Luca slipped on his coat. "Then I'm glad we have our coats. I have a feeling it's going to get colder."

"You're coming with me?" I said.

He grinned. "When have I ever not come with you?"

"Never, but this is getting weirder and weirder," I answered.

"Like I said, it's good we have our coats."

He held a hand out for me, and I took it. We walked down the slope of the yard. We followed Nira, with Jackson right beside her, down the trail.

The night was silent. I wasn't sure if it was the presence of Nira or us and Jackson that kept the animals hidden, but something did.

"How was your dad?" Luca asked as we took the side trail that went to his house.

"Not good," I answered. "He was asleep, but looked horrible. Jason said Dad reminded him of his own parents."

"That's not good."

"It's hard to believe this is my reality. I have a father who's an addict, and I'm following a ghost through the woods after watching horrible memories of a serial killer stalking my great-grandmother."

"Life is tough," Luca said.

"That's all you have to say?"

"What else can I say? If I try to say that isn't so bad, I'd be lying. But I'd also be lying if I said life was always awful, because it's not. There are some really beautiful parts and some really awful parts. It's tough."

Nira veered from the trail and went toward the pond. She was taking us to the enchanted forest.

I swallowed hard, trying to be courageous. "Yeah, life is tough."

Before long, the ground began to shift. There was moss underfoot and along the tree trunks. A little farther up, the edges of boulders came into view. The moss covering them was not the neon-green color I saw during the day. In the light of dusk, it appeared almost brown. If I didn't brush my hands along it to feel that it was still very much alive, I would've thought it had died. I realized how similar this moment was to the last memory I'd witnessed. Dorothy had been coming through these woods at this time of day, though later in the summer. A breeze rustled the branches above. The wind blew at my hair, so I turned my head to keep it from covering my eyes. As I did, I saw *him*.

I gasped and stepped backward.

Luca said, "What is it?"

I couldn't speak. I was too terrified. I shuffled backward, tripping over a moss-covered root. I landed in a soft patch of moss, my back pressed against a boulder.

"Siena, what's wrong?" Luca asked again, kneeling beside me.

I wanted to tell him to run, but couldn't form the words. My heart beat so loud in my ears, I could hear nothing else. Charles was staring at me … a disgusting smirk crossed his lips. I wanted to scream out of fear and anger, but nothing came. I was frozen in fear.

I whimpered. It was the only sound I could make. Jackson came and stood in front of me. Nira was with him. She took note of Charles, but did not respond to him. Instead, she stood between him and me. She was looking directly at me. She held her hand out as if she wanted me to take it. Charles was still behind her, smirking at me with such evil that I wanted to cry. Jackson licked my face; it was enough to make me focus on him. I clung to Jackson. He would protect me. If there was evil, he would bark and Luca would be sick, but neither was reacting.

Why were they not reacting?

Nira knelt in front of me, her eyes even with mine. She wanted me to see her, not Charles; she was trying to block him so I couldn't see him, though I could see through her the same way I could see through him. I whimpered like a child. She touched my knee. It felt like a blast of ice—not solid or wet, but so cold.

"What is it? What do you see?" Luca asked, his arms around me to protect me.

I clung to him and whispered, "Charles."

Luca turned as if searching for him. "I don't feel him," Luca said. "I don't feel anything."

I squeezed my eyes shut, praying the man would be gone when I opened them, but he remained. He was stepping closer and laughing in an awful way.

"Siena, if I don't feel him, then he's not here," Luca said calmly, still holding me.

"You don't feel Nira and she's here," I said, clinging to Luca.

"She isn't evil. This guy is. If he was here, I'm sure I'd feel him and so would Jackson," Luca said softly.

"I'm not lying," I said.

Charles stayed where he was, grinning wickedly.

Luca said, "Of course not, but it must be something else. Maybe a memory. You saw lots of horrible stuff in the memories, and I didn't feel the evil."

"A memory?" I loosened my grip on him the smallest bit.

"Maybe," he said.

"I'm not touching anything other than you," I said, studying the translucent man who had stepped back a little but was again smirking at me.

Luca said, "Maybe some memories are powerful enough that you don't have to touch anything. Maybe being in the area where they happened is enough. Especially now that you watched all the other memories, you're probably more in tune with them."

I studied Charles. The sight of him still made me cringe, but it was like he was on replay; he kept moving in the same way and then would start over. I wondered if Luca was right.

I looked around. "I think this is where the last memory was, when he appeared in front of Dorothy," I said, breathing a little easier.

"That would've been a pretty potent memory," Luca said.

Nira was standing, slowly moving away from me, making her way around the boulders and toward the cliff wall. Jackson was beside her. Both of them paid no attention to the man.

Watching Jackson, Luca said, "Is Nira moving again?"

I nodded.

Luca stood and held out his hand for me to take. I took it, careful not to move any closer to the man or the memory or whatever he was. Luca led me as I walked backward, making sure Charles wasn't following us. But he didn't change his path; it was as if he was on a loop, repeating the same gestures and focused on the same spot.

"He really is just a memory," I said with relief.

"All of this is a memory," Luca said, as if reminding me not to get lost in the past.

"Sort of, but Nira is real—or at least here. But that man, or whatever he was, was on a loop, like an old recording," I said. "It feels like there's so much we don't understand."

"That's because there is so much we don't understand," Luca said, squeezing my hand as we passed the boulders.

"It's getting dark," I said, realizing how much time had passed since we left the safety of my home.

"Yes," Luca said, sounding as uneasy as I felt.

"Most sane people wouldn't walk in ghost-infested woods in the dark," I said.

"No, they wouldn't," he said, no less uneasy.

Charles reappeared in front of us.

"He's back," I said, trembling.

This time Jackson turned and started barking furiously.

The man glared at me. In one hand he held a large rusted knife. He took a step toward us. I clung to Luca. The man was Charles, but his face was more distorted in this memory, as if the darkness of his soul had become more visible.

"Get out of my way, you're dead," I said to the memory in a feeble attempt to be brave.

He didn't care about my words and instead took a step closer. His face grew more contorted as a wicked smirk crossed his lips.

"That's not a ghost, that's a demon," Luca said weakly. "Don't talk to it. If you engage with it, it's allowed to engage with you."

I gagged as the smell of rotten eggs filled my nostrils. My legs became so weak, it was difficult for me to remain standing. Nira came toward us, with Jackson barking angrily as he ran through the demon.

"He ran right through him," I said, my stomach so uneasy I thought I would vomit.

Beside me, Luca did vomit, and the demon man laughed. I started to pray. As I prayed, I moved Luca away from the demon. We did not back up, but moved to the side. The whole time, Nira was standing in front of us, acting as a sort of block. The demon Charles was now smirking at her, much like the memory had smirked at me, though the face of the demon was becoming more and more distorted every second.

We were nearing the cliff wall when more figures started to emerge.

I said, "There's more of them."

"I know," Luca said, leaning heavily against me.

"Can you keep going?" I said as the rotten egg smell caused my throat to spasm and my stomach to heave.

"I'm not sure," he said, and then he vomited again.

I was now supporting almost his entire body weight. I could barely keep us moving.

"Nira's leading us through them, toward the cave entrance," I said as gruesome figures were materializing from every direction and my mind started to throb with pain.

The pain of my own memories, my mother's death and Thomas's, were mixing with the memory of Nira being tortured and drowned, of Dorothy frantically searching for her, of Thomas's bloody hands ripping up floorboards trying to get Luca, of Luca being viciously stuffed under the inn ... of children being murdered.

"Don't give in," Luca said, his words heavy.

He was barely conscious. I hadn't realized I'd stopped moving. I took a step and then another.

In front of me, Jackson was standing at the entrance of the cave, barking furiously at the horde of demons around us. Beside him, Nira stepped through the stone and into the cave.

"She went into the cave," I reported to Luca.

"We need to go with her," he said weakly.

"If we go in there, no one will know where we are," I said, terrified by the images flashing in my mind and of the possibility of more evil within the cave.

"Is your mind filling with horrible images?" he asked, so weak it seemed hard for him to speak.

"Yes," I said, clinging to him as demons encircled us.

"The demons are angry. They're attacking our minds. We have to keep going," he said, turning to the side and retching.

I took another step and then another. More and more horrible memories, memories I didn't have. My mother walking the trash out at the soup kitchen, a man coming behind her, a rusty knife in his hand. The same rusty knife the demons held.

"No!" I shouted. "Get out of my head. I do not give you permission to be in my head!"

My mind became silent.

Luca was leaning hard against the stone wall. The cave opening beside him was so low to the ground, no one would see it if they didn't know where to look.

I said, "We could be lost in there forever."

Before I could stop him, Luca was on the ground, crouching through the narrow entrance.

"Wait," I whispered, too scared to speak any louder.

Jackson remained outside; he was barking and growling. The demons, all in the form of Charles, were moving closer. Out of fear, I fell to the ground and began to scoot backward. This motion took me through the cave.

The night was silent.

Thirty-Six

Inside the cave it was peaceful. Luca was lying beside me, catching his breath.

"I don't see them anymore," I said, shaking.

"I don't feel them anymore," he said, his back against the floor of the cave, a hand over his stomach.

There was barely enough light to make anything out. I reached for my phone. I didn't have it.

"Do you have your phone?" I asked, terrified of the dark.

"No, but I have some matches from your dad's office," he said. He pulled a matchbook from his pants pocket and struck a match.

The cave was empty except for Jackson and Nira, who were facing the back wall. Beside me, Luca hurriedly retrieved some of the dried sticks and makeshift firewood that had been in the cave for decades. He struck another match … the kindling caught quickly.

"It's well aged," he said, and breathed deeply with relief.

"Thank God for that," I said, grateful to no longer be in the pitch-black cave nor be surrounded by demons.

"You can say that again. It was definitely the easiest fire I ever started."

"I guess a few decades of drying out and …"—I moved one of the pieces sitting to the side—"a few decades of rodent poop makes for an easy fire."

I rubbed my hands in front of the flames, the warmth feeling good. Luca added more firewood, causing the cave to become illuminated. I took a moment to catch my breath. Then I stood and went the few steps to the back wall where Nira and Jackson were. Nira was sitting cross-legged like the little girl she was—or had been. Her head was resting on her hands as she and Jackson were watching the wall. In front of them, the wall seemed to move. There was a figure coming out of it.

From his spot near the firewood, Luca said, "I think I found something."

"Me too. Someone else is here, or at least I think someone else is here. I can't quite tell," I said, crouching beside Nira staring at the spot of rock that seemed to be moving.

Luca came toward me. "I think you need to see this," he said, holding something gingerly in his hands.

"If it's a dead baby mouse, please don't show me."

He knelt beside me, his hands cupped together. He looked at me with an expression of loss much deeper than a poor dead rodent would create. "It's a piece of paper."

I shifted backward, falling against the hard dirt floor into a sitting position.

"The writing is faded, but I think it's a note," he said of the worn piece of paper in his hand.

"No," I said, shaking my head, refusing to believe what I was seeing.

"The mice probably dragged it into the woodpile when they made their nest," he said as he carefully unfolded it. He took it over to the fire. "I can't read the first few words, but the end says,"—he held it tilted toward the firelight ....

A thoughtless prayer escaped my soul: *Please let it fall, let it be burned, don't let me touch it.*

" 'My word.' "

"I can't. I can't watch another one," I said with a whimper.

I felt Jackson's cold nose against my arm. Nira had shifted and was now in front of me, her eyes locked on mine. Those green eyes with amber flecks. The ones I was so convinced meant she was my child, mine and Luca's. How wrong I had been. Thank God.

She placed a hand on my bent knee. I gasped.

"What is it?" Luca asked.

"Nira's touching my knee. And it feels warm. What does that mean?"

Luca looked down at the note in his hand and then back at me. He came near me. The three of them were lined up in front of me, with Jackson and Luca on the side and Nira in the middle. Luca held a hand up. Nira was still staring at me. Her eyes were so much like his. It was as if they were each begging me to take it.

Another prayer entered my mind: *God, give me strength.*

I lifted a trembling hand, palm upward. Luca raised his hand above mine and allowed the softened paper to drift from his hand into mine.

Thirty-Seven

I was in the middle of the inn and, based on the sunlight's angle coming in through the windows, it was late in the day. Dorothy was standing, expressionless, beside the check-in desk. Her mother was next to her.

"There you are, all checked in," Dorothy's mother said, her voice sounding syrupy sweet. "Dorothy will help you take your bags to your room. It's our very finest, with the most beautiful view of the ocean you've ever seen."

Without saying anything, Dorothy lifted the two heavy bags and started up the stairs.

"Oh, goodness, she doesn't need to do that," the woman said, tapping the man beside her.

"She's as strong as an ox," Dorothy's mother said, paying no regard to her daughter, who was trying to hide her discomfort.

The man chuckled and took the bags from Dorothy's hands. "That makes two of us," he said as he carried them effortlessly.

"We don't like the guests doing anything other than relaxing while they're here," Dorothy's mother said. "She's more than capable of carrying them." Her tone was still sweet, though I could tell she was somehow blaming Dorothy for the man taking the bags from her.

"As am I. Lead the way, young lady," the man said with a jovial laugh.

Dorothy did as instructed and led the way up the stairs. She took them to the first door on the right, removing a key from the door as she entered. It was a lovely room: simple, clean, and fresh feeling.

The woman gasped, saying, "This view is heavenly!"

Dorothy said, "The cove is pretty, and protected from all but the worst of storms."

"Protected is good in these strange times," the woman said, turning from the window and looking intently at Dorothy.

As she did, I saw that the side of Dorothy's face was red and swollen. I thought back to the last memory of Charles meeting her in the woods. Had he hit her in the face? The rest of her body was covered by clothing except for her forearms. They were bruised in the shape of a hand print. She'd tried to fight him.

"Ye-yes," Dorothy said, clearly uncomfortable by the woman's focus on her.

The woman glanced at her husband. He shrugged.

She took a slight step toward Dorothy. "We met a man in town. He asked us to give this to the girl with long brown hair that worked at the inn," the woman said, removing a slip of paper from her handbag.

Dorothy recoiled at the sight of it.

The woman held it for her. "We have a daughter about your age, so I feel I can tell you this as a mother to a child. That man, whoever he is, is not someone we would ever want around our daughter."

"He's the mayor," Dorothy responded in barely a whisper.

The husband scoffed. He clearly wasn't impressed by the title.

"Yes, he told us that," the woman said kindly. "You remind me so much of our daughter. She has the same beautiful brown eyes. Here's the note and here's your tip for showing us to our room." The woman held out a five-dollar bill.

Dorothy's eyes became wide. "Oh, no, I could never accept so much. Besides, I didn't even carry your bags."

"We want you to have it," the woman said.

"It's too much," Dorothy said, shaking her head.

"It's important for a girl to have her own money," the woman said, still holding out the bill and the note.

The man came up beside his wife. "My wife has a generous heart and she can sense when someone needs a little extra. Take it," he said.

Dorothy hesitated, but then took the note and the five-dollar bill. "Thank you," she said, stuffing them in her pocket.

Her pleasure of receiving the money seemed to be overshadowed by the fear of the note, but she hid it well.

"If you need anything while you're here, please tell me," Dorothy said as she neared the door.

She was leaving the room when the woman spoke. "Thank you, and do be careful. I'm sure it's perfectly safe out here, but we heard in town that a young girl was missing."

"A young girl? Which young girl?"

The husband and wife glanced at one another, trying to remember.

A moment later, the wife spoke. "We should've thought of learning her name. Of course you would want to know. This is a small town. You probably know everyone, though maybe not this girl. Someone mentioned she was part colored."

Dorothy faltered, and the man reached out and caught her.

I heard the woman's muffled words through Dorothy's unsteady mind: "Are you okay?"

Dorothy didn't respond. She righted herself on the doorframe and left the room. She made her way downstairs. Slowly at first, and then faster.

"Where are you going?" her mother called to her, but she didn't turn. These words, too, were muffled, like they were being spoken through a pillow.

Dorothy was now running at full speed across the loose sand. The tide was low. The sun had sunk behind the trees. In the forest, the light became even dimmer, though she could still see.

She reached the boulders and stopped for a moment. She was panting hard.

"Nira?" she said, quietly at first … and then shouted over and over again. She spun around, the world became dizzy, but no one was there.

Dorothy ran to the cave and scrambled into it, her dress becoming filthy as she slid across the entrance. Light streamed through the top crack, allowing her to see everything clearly. No one was there, but on the table where Nira had placed the vase of wild roses, the vase was now filled with purple lupins. At the sight of them, Dorothy stopped. Her hands were shaking as she reached into her pocket. It was as if she'd been reminded of the note. The paper shook as she unfolded the note.

"I'm a man of my word."

Her eyes grew wide, her sobs guttural, as her knees hit the stone floor. For a moment I thought she would pass out, but she pulled herself up with the help of the table and ran from the cave, screaming Nira's name. I tried to follow, but I remained in the empty cave, the slip of paper at my feet.

Thirty-Eight

As my vision shifted and I returned to the present moment, Luca said, "Are you okay?"

"He gave the note to a couple staying at the inn," I said with resignation. "They sensed he was bad and warned her, but it didn't matter. She already knew it. Her face and arms were bruised. Who knows what else he did to her?"

Luca asked softly, "What does the rest of the note say?"

" *'I'm a man of my word,'* " I repeated, trying not to cry.

"He's seriously messing with her head."

"It's over now," I said. "The couple that gave her the note told her a young girl was missing. She knew right away it was Nira. She ran here and found the lupins in the vase. That's when she pulled the note from her pocket and read it. It dropped to the ground as she ran out, screaming Nira's name."

"That's a lot," Luca said, slumping forward.

"Yeah," I said, feeling too numb to say anything else.

In front of me, Nira was kneeling, facing the wall. Jackson was sitting beside her, his head cocked to one side as the figure in the wall sighed a heavy sigh.

"Did you hear that?" I asked Luca.

He shook his head.

At that moment another figure stepped fully from the wall. I pushed backward as a giant man stepped out of the wall. I kept scooting backward until I hit the back of the bench that served as a couch.

Luca was following my gaze. He whispered, "What … is … it?"

I couldn't speak.

Nira raised her head toward the giant and grinned. Jackson wagged his tail, the action sweeping loose pebbles across the dirt floor. The giant pressed his hands together as if in prayer, then released them and strode across the cave, reaching the entrance in a few steps. He stood, his back to us, his body so tall he could see out of the upper window of the cave.

I twisted my body so I could see him.

Luca asked, "Are you okay?"

"The guardian is here," I said, my throat dry from fear.

"The one from your dream?"

"Yeah, I think so. He's so tall, he's looking out the top window."

"I feel goodness … a lot of goodness," Luca said.

Jackson whined. In front of us, the figure in the wall was slowly becoming more human in appearance, and sighed again.

"What's going on now?" Luca asked as Jackson whimpered. His tail was wagging so intensely that his entire back end moved from side to side.

"I'm not sure," I said, still watching the wall as the figure in front of me continued to take shape. I gasped and clutched Luca's arm. "Dorothy's here."

"Good," Luca said enthusiastically.

"Why is that so exciting?" I asked.

"She's the one you're supposed to help, so it's good she's here," Luca said. He made the sign of the cross with the crucifix of the rosary he held.

"You're praying?"

"What else should I do?"

I thought for a moment. "Yes, okay. You should pray and I should ..." I hesitated.

"Talk to Dorothy," he said.

"I can't talk to her, she's a ghost," I said.

"You can talk to Nira," he said.

"But she never talks back."

"That doesn't mean she doesn't hear you," Luca said.

At the wall, Dorothy had continued to become clearer. Her upper body was out of the wall and she stretched her arms. Nira clapped and grinned toward the guardian, who winked at her. Nira carefully reached her hand out to Dorothy, but Dorothy pushed back, causing her left shoulder to return into the stone. Nira fell back. I had the sense that if ghosts could cry, she would. Instead, she sat, her hands folded in her lap, her expression sorrowful. Jackson lay down beside her, looking just as pitiful. At the same time, I felt an oppressive sense of guilt, like everything that had ever gone wrong in the world was my fault. The weight was so physically heavy, it was hard to breathe. It felt as if I was suffocating. I gagged and coughed.

Luca's hand was on me. "Are you okay?"

The weight lifted and I gasped for breath. "The guilt was so intense, I couldn't breathe," I said.

"You felt guilty?"

"It felt like I was the cause of every bad thing that had ever happened, and I couldn't breathe. It was depressing and suffocating."

Nira's gaze shifted between Dorothy and me.

"I wonder if that's what Dorothy feels?" Luca said thoughtfully.

I turned to Dorothy, who was hunched over, only partially out of the wall. "It's like she has the weight of the world on her shoulders. The cave is literally covering her and so was the castle in my dream."

"Tell her it isn't her fault," Luca said.

Nira sat taller. She agreed with Luca and wanted me to talk to Dorothy.

I said, "What if she's a demon and this is a trick?"

"There's nothing evil here, other than the remnants of evil that Charles left a long time ago. Otherwise, it feels pretty good in here. So she's not a demon. I think she's like the holy souls I see. Not exactly the same, because she's stuck. I think that's why she's appearing to you stuck in the wall, to show you she's stuck."

"What do you mean stuck? She's dead," I said.

Luca shrugged. "It's just a guess. Ask her. She's your great-grandmother, and your mom said to help her, so you may as well say hi and ask if you can help her with something."

"You make it sound so simple," I said as a thin layer of sweat covered my body even though the cave was freezing.

"Try it," he said.

I forced myself to swallow, though my throat felt like it had cotton in it.

"Hi, Dorothy," I said.

At my words, she raised her head and locked her eyes on mine. Her gaze was so intense, it caused me to jump back.

"What happened?" Luca asked, his arm going protectively around me.

"She's looking at me," I answered.

"That's good. Keep talking to her."

I forced the words out. "Hi, I'm Siena. You're my great-grandmother. Maybe you already knew that. You're a ghost, so maybe you know everything, but maybe you don't. I have no idea how any of this works."

"I know who you are," Dorothy answered, her voice sounding even younger than I expected.

"You spoke to me?" I said with surprise. "I didn't think you would speak to me. I figured you would listen, maybe, if I was lucky, but you actually spoke to me."

"It's polite to speak when spoken to," Dorothy answered, watching me with curiosity.

"Yes, I suppose it is," I said.

Dorothy was moving a little farther out of the wall so that her shoulders were free.

"I-I've heard a lot about you. Gigi—I mean, your daughter, Gemma—loves you so much. We all do. But we've never met you, so it's different. But your daughter really misses you," I said, unable to keep from babbling.

"She was the bright spot in my life, her and …" Dorothy started to slump in toward the wall.

Nira looked up at me with a panicked expression.

"Her and Nira, your friend. Is that what you were going to say?"

At the mention of Nira's name, Dorothy became so still, I wondered if she'd turned into the stone that encased her.

Nira leaned toward Dorothy, but Dorothy didn't appear to notice.

I said, "Nira's here. Can you see her?"

Dorothy tilted her head, the rest of her body remaining motionless. "She died," she said, her voice sounding far away.

"Yes, she died," I said, "but she's here with us now."

Dorothy's body relaxed a little—at least the part that was out of the stone. She said, "She is dead."

Nira was leaning forward as if trying desperately to get Dorothy to see her.

"It was a very disturbing death," I said, pausing as I tried not to think of the memories. "But she is here, like you are," I said.

"She cannot be here, she is dead," Dorothy said, her voice monotone.

"You are here and you're dead," I said.

Dorothy lifted her face to mine. It was a pretty face. She looked even more like Lisieux here than she did in the memories and much more so than in the picture.

She said, "That is true, I suppose."

"Yes, that's true, so if you are dead and you're here, then can't she be here too?" I said.

Dorothy shook her head. "She is dead. He killed her. He killed her because of me. A few more hours and she would've been safe. He would not have found her in New York. She would have been safe," she said, sinking back into the rock.

Nira reached for her friend to try and pull her back, but it did no good.

"Don't go," I said, also trying to keep her from returning to the rock. "Yes, he killed her, but it wasn't because of you. It isn't your fault what happened to Nira or … or the others. He was evil. He is dead, and he is not here. Nira was good. She loved you. She chose God. She is here."

Dorothy was still slipping into the stone.

My mind was racing. I needed to say more. "I've seen your memories. I know that you cared for him—in the beginning, I mean. He pretended to love you, but he didn't. It was a lie. It was all a lie. A boy lied to me like that once, and he died too. It-it wasn't my fault, just like Nira dying wasn't your fault."

"Thomas," Dorothy said, and came forward a little.

"Yes," I said, feeling the color drain from my face at the mention of his name.

She said glumly, "He did not care for you."

"He didn't. Just as Charles did not care for you," I said.

She sighed. "Charles cared far too much for me. That was the problem. I should've stopped him. If I'd stopped him, things would've been different, but I did not, and so it is my fault. He couldn't help himself. He cared for me too much," she said, shaking her head morosely.

I tilted my head. "Yes, I read that in one of his notes, but you must realize that what he did was not your fault."

"All that he did was because of me," she said.

"Why do you say that?"

"He told me so, and he was a man of his word," she said simply.

"Yes, he did say that quite a lot," I said, shuddering at the memories.

"He said what was true."

"So you believe him to be a good man, someone you could trust?"

"Oh, he was not good. He was quite bad, but he was a man of his word," she said as if on repeat.

I lowered my head in frustration. Nira sat taller, as if encouraging me to keep trying.

I decided to go a different direction. "I saw the bruise on your face. Did he do that to you?"

She stared at me as if confused. "Yes, he did that."

"If my grandfather had done that to Gigi, would you have said it was Gigi's fault?"

"Gemma would never deserve to be treated like that," she said.

"But *you* did?" I asked, making a puzzled face.

"Yes. He told me so."

I asked, "Does his saying something make it true?"

"Oh yes, Charles never lied. He was a man of his word."

I sat back, trying not to be frustrated. "So, he was a man of his word because he said he loved you and he did?"

"Yes, and for many other reasons. But yes, he said he loved me and he did."

"Who did you love most in your life?"

"My Gemma," Dorothy answered quickly.

"That would make sense. And if she needed something and you had it, would you have given it to her?" I asked.

"I would give anything for her. I would still give anything for her," Dorothy said with conviction.

"So, when you love someone, you sacrifice for them, is that right?" I asked.

"You give them everything, even your life, if that is what it takes," she said staunchly.

"Did Charles ever sacrifice for you?" I asked, praying the answer was no.

She tilted her head one way and then the other. My question had confused her. Nira was bouncing on her knees, she was so excited.

After several moments, Dorothy answered, "He gave me things."

"Giving gifts is not the same as a sacrifice," I said. "Did he ever sacrifice what he wanted for your good, like you probably did every day of your life for your daughter?"

She studied me. "He was not capable of that form of sacrifice, not even with his wife and son."

"Can love exist without sacrifice?" I said.

She shook her head slowly, saying, "Love and sacrifice are intertwined."

"So, if he was not capable of sacrifice, was he capable of love?"

Her features were frozen. I held my breath.

"He said he loved me, and he loved me too much," she said, starting to shrink back into the wall.

"Wait," I called. "You look like my sister, Lisieux."

She stopped. "Yes, I have thought that too. She's a very pretty girl. I never thought I was a pretty girl, but she's a pretty girl. You all are. And good girls too. I wish I'd been as good as you."

"Were your parents good?"

Dorothy shook her head. "They were not good people. I saw what my mother did to your father. She caused him such pain, and because of her, my Gemma has been hurt. Her heart has broken a thousand times over, and mine with it."

"You're right, your mother wasn't good, and I am told your father was no different."

"He was worse. He shot eagles in their nest and then forced me to eat them."

I cringed. "I didn't know you ate them."

"He did far worse things, but I do not discuss those," she said.

I pushed away the sadness. "Why did you bring Gemma back here when you were dying? Did you want them to take care of her?"

She did not answer.

"You hoped Nira's mother would be here," I said.

Dorothy nodded. "I didn't think she would be, but I hoped. I'd written her letters. She never answered them. I hoped it was because she was angry with me because it was my fault Nira died. She would've taken care of my Gemma, no matter how mad at me she was. She was a good woman and would never turn her back on a child."

I said, "But she wasn't here."

"She wasn't," Dorothy said sadly. "I found out later she went to New York after … after they found Nira. Once I was in this place, I was able to watch her life there. Several days, we were on the other side of the street from one another. If only she'd looked up. If I'd seen her, I would have been too ashamed to call to her, but if she'd seen me, she would've come to me. Things would have been different. I wouldn't have been alone. She never would have left me alone, not with my Gemma to care for. Gemma's life would've been so much better," she said with regret.

"If Grandmother's life had been different," I said softly, "I may never have existed."

Dorothy beamed. "She and George were created for one another. Not all pairs are, but they were. They would've met no matter what, though it would have been up to them what to make of that meeting. It always is. But you're right, in a way, because her life would have been easier and perhaps easier is not what she needed. Perhaps she needed to go through things at a young age to be able to handle all she would go through later. Still, it wasn't fair to her. She deserved a better life."

"So did you," I said.

"I got what I deserved, but Gemma deserved better."

"And Nira deserved better too," I said, guessing what was in Dorothy's mind.

"She chose the wrong friend," Dorothy said despondently.

I said, "She loves you. She wouldn't be here if she didn't."

Dorothy moved her head slowly from side to side, saying, "She is dead. He killed her. He loved me too much."

"He killed many," I said.

She nodded sadly. "Yes, many more than I realized when I was alive. More than anyone living realized."

I shuddered, thinking of the children in the attic. "Why did you run away?" I asked.

She sighed and said, "It was all my fault, the things he did. I had to run. I would've sacrificed my life if it had saved Nira, but it was too late for her. That was what he meant by the lupins and the note. I never dreamed he'd hurt his boy or his wife. They were good to him. Far too good. He didn't deserve either one. I would've stayed to protect them. I didn't know …."

"You didn't know he was going to kill them?"

"I didn't know about them or about the others. All I knew was Nira was gone and there was nothing I could do to help her, so I ran."

"Because you thought he was going to kill you?"

She looked up for a few moments. "He loved me too much to kill me, but he would've made me go with him, which I think would have been worse than death. Though perhaps that would have been a fitting punishment. In truth, I couldn't think clearly. All I could think was that I had to run away and so I did."

"You believe he would've captured you?" I asked.

She looked up at me. "Yes, that's a good word. He would have captured me."

"If capture is the right word, wouldn't that imply he was hunting you like he did the others he kept in the attic?"

Dorothy looked puzzled. "Yes, he would have captured me, and yes, that is something a hunter does, but I do not believe he was hunting me. He said he loved me and—"

"He was a man of his word," I repeated with frustration.

"You do not believe me?" Dorothy said, frowning.

"I believe you completely, but I do not believe him. I do not believe he loved you or that he was even capable of real love. Lust, yes. Love, no. He was hunting you the same as he hunted the others, and that means none of it was your fault. Not even in the beginning, when you maybe had some feelings for him."

"I never had feelings for him," she said bluntly. "But it was nice to be thought of by someone … especially someone like him."

"This man who is twenty years older than you tells you he loves you so much that he can't help what he does, and then he goes off and becomes a serial killer—or maybe he already was—"

"He already was," Dorothy said glumly.

I cringed. "Okay, he already was. Then he stalks you, and kills your best friend, and you blame yourself?"

"He said he was a man of his word."

"He was a liar," I said, getting up on my knees so that I was eye level with her.

Her face contorted, and an ear-piercing shriek came from somewhere. My mind was crowded with memories, horrific memories I didn't have before. Memories of the horror that had defined her life and his.

I held my hands to my head, and Luca started praying out loud. The words of the Our Father, the Hail Mary, and St. Michael prayer reverberated in my mind, pushing out the memories. My breathing steadied after Dorothy stopped shrieking.

"Why do you allow him so much power over you?" I asked, panting.

"I never gave that to him. He took it," she said, her hands pushing against the stone.

I couldn't tell if she was trying to push out of the stone or deeper into it.

I said, "He took it in life, but you give it in death. He's not here. He is dead. You must allow his memories to die. You must allow them to leave your mind and soul, and you must forgive yourself."

"Nira is dead," Dorothy said, crying out in anguish, her hands pushing hard against the stone.

"Nira is here! She's dead, but she's okay. Just as you're here, except she's not stuck in a wall. She is free." I held my head as more memories flooded my mind, but this time they were not Dorothy's. They were mine.

They were of Luca, passed out on the beach, surrounded by dead fish. Of the ghost children in the attic. Gigi, lying on the beach, her face bloody after the possessed Thomas punched her. Thomas racing up the cliff, and his cries as he fell. My cries when I saw my mother's coffin. My dad, strung out on drugs. My family falling apart. My life falling apart.

I couldn't stop them. All the awful moments of my life rushed into my mind. I couldn't breathe or move. I felt trapped. I felt like I was drowning. Charles was there, his hands around my neck, pushing me under the icy water. I fought, but couldn't escape. Another wave came. Seawater filled my lungs. I was dying. I struggled against his hold, but it was too strong. My mind was drifting and the darkness was taking over. There was no light ... no goodness ... no ... hope.

Warmth. I felt warmth radiate through my body. I gasped.

"Oh my God, Siena," Luca said, kneeling in front of me. I was lying on the hard dirt floor, the rough pebbles pressed against the side of my face.

I didn't understand what was happening. In front of me was a woman.

"Thank you, Siena," the woman said, her hands on my face. She helped guide me into a sitting position.

Luca scooted backward to give me space.

I touched my neck where Charles's hands had been.

"Thank you for fighting for me. His memories can't hurt you anymore. We are both free," she said.

Struggling to form the words, my throat scratched and swollen, I asked, "Who are you?"

"I'm Dorothy," she answered. "The girl you saw was the part of me that died when Nira died. Thank you for helping me forgive that part of myself."

"You're so pretty," I said, wondering why I would say something so silly.

She smiled at me. "This is how I appeared before I died. When I was healthy, anyway. I'd been stuck for so long, I'd almost forgotten who I was, but you helped me remember."

"Nira is here," I said, turning from side to side. "She was the one who led me to you."

"She is the very best of friends, but she has gone now," Dorothy said lovingly.

"Gone where?"

"Back to where she belongs. She was only here to help me. She doesn't belong here anymore, and neither do I."

"Are you going to be with her?"

"Not quite yet. But yes, eventually I will be there with her, when I'm ready."

I said, "I don't understand."

"That doesn't matter," she said, and leaned her head slightly to the side. Then she touched my face and said, "Your mom is so proud of you."

"My mom?" I said, hopeful she would appear. I longed to see her, if only for one more moment.

Dorothy seemed to be glowing as she spoke. "She is not here. She is far beyond where I am, and even beyond where Nira is. She is one of the most radiant. She was never stuck, not in life or death."

"So she is okay?" I asked.

Dorothy touched my face again. "My darling girl, she is far beyond okay. She is with the Church Triumphant, and she loves you and your sisters and your father so much. She is always with you and always interceding for you."

Dorothy started to fade.

I realized Luca was holding my hand.

"What about—" I stopped, remembering I was not supposed to ask questions about the dead, even the dead that Luca loved the most. It was not for the living to know such things.

Dorothy looked lovingly at Luca and said to me, "I am to tell you that Luca's mother is here in the same place I am. She will be here a great deal longer. But she is free from the demons that hunted her. Tell him not to worry, just to pray. She is in need of many prayers. We both are."

"We will pray," I said.

Suddenly, the giant was beside us and Dorothy stood up. He winked at me as they both started to fade.

Dorothy turned back to me and said, "Tell my Gemma I'm okay now. She has been so worried."

"I will," I said.

Thirty-Nine

Moonlight streamed through the upper window of the cave. I felt the softened paper in my hand and stared down at it, studying the weathered writing. I held it carefully as I got up. My legs were unsteady. Luca helped me stand and make my way to the fire, as if he knew exactly what I wanted to do. We both knelt beside the remains of the fire. Jackson whimpered when I released the paper, allowing it to float down onto the coals. Its edges turned up and the fire surged.

"You were not a man of your word," I said as a putrid smell arose from the flames and just as quickly disappeared.

From somewhere far away, I heard two little girls giggling. Then more children's joyful voices joined theirs. Peace washed over me.

"They're going to be okay," I said, speaking to Luca. "They all are. All the ones he hurt are at peace. I can feel it."

"I can feel it too. All the darkness of this place and this land and …"

"My family."

He squeezed my hand. "It's all lifted."

I sat back and gently touched my throat. It felt bruised and swollen.

"What about you? Are you okay?" he asked as I winced while touching my tender neck.

"I think so," I said, and leaned my head against his shoulder.

He said, "That was a lot, and I saw only half of it."

"It was a lot," I said. I began to feel the exhaustion of what I'd been through.

"What happened when you passed out? I felt the evil … it was intense," he said with a shudder.

"One horrific memory after another, and then it was as if Nira and I traded places, and Charles was drowning me. It felt so real," I said, trying not to cry as I felt the swelling of my throat. "Then I felt warmth and Dorothy was there. But she was no longer a child. She'd become the age she was when she died. She said the part that was stuck was the part that died when Nira died."

Luca said, "The demons must've been attacking you to try and get you to stop helping Dorothy."

"She'd been trapped for almost seventy years. She finally realized the truth and it literally set her free."

"The truth will do that," Luca said with the slightest grin.

I nestled into him. "Yeah, I've heard that," I said, too exhausted to laugh.

From beside us, Jackson stretched and meandered out of the cave.

"How can he be so calm?" I asked.

"He must understand things we don't," Luca said. "Are you ready to go?"

"Beyond ready," I said, and he helped me maneuver out of the cave.

The moon was high and full, causing the boulders to cast long shadows in the silver night.

"Are you going to tell your sisters about the cave now?" he asked as we made our way through the enchanted forest.

I thought for a moment. "I think Nira and Dorothy would like them to have it."

"Yes, I would think ghost girls would want to share their cave with actual girls," Luca said with amusement.

"They're very nice ghost girls, like you said."

"I have no doubt," he said, trying to sound happy. Instead, he sounded nervous.

"What is it?" I asked.

"I heard you talk about your mom," he said.

How had I forgotten to tell him? I stopped at the edge of the boulders where the moss was thickest and took both his hands in mine.

"Luca, your mom is there with Dorothy. The place she is now, not the stuck place. Dorothy said your mom would be there for a long time, but she is free of the demons that had been hunting her."

Luca fell onto the soft moss, his knees seeming to collapse. He held his hands to his face and his body started to rock with the torrent of tears.

"It's not bad, where they are," I said, kneeling beside him and holding him. "It's not bad at all. Please don't cry."

After a few moments, he sniffed and wiped his face. "I've been terrified since she died that her soul was lost, she was so messed up at the end," he said. "And then she committed suicide. I was afraid …"

"You were afraid she was in hell, but she's not. She must have cried out to God in the end. Dorothy asked us to pray for both of them. I get the sense they're working through the stuff they need to."

Luca held me and whispered, "Thank you, Jesus."

"Yes, thank you, Jesus," I said as I leaned against his chest.

"What about your mom?" Luca asked as he released me and used the sleeve of his coat to wipe his face.

A broad smile lit up my face. "Dorothy said she was one of the radiant ones, part of the Church Triumphant."

"Your own saint," he said with a grin.

"Yeah," I said, feeling a circle of warmth in my chest. "It feels different now that I've met Dorothy and Nira. I still miss my mom so much it hurts, but now it sort of feels like she's on a super long trip or something, which makes the pain not hurt as much."

Luca swung my hand in his. "I know exactly what you mean."

Jackson trotted slowly in front of us, his head bent low.

"I think he misses Nira," Luca said.

"It's strange, but I miss her too," I said.

We had reached the pond. The full moon reflected in the still water.

Luca chuckled and said, "Ghosts grow on you."

"Maybe not all ghosts," I said, "but at least a cute little girl ghost who was best friends with my great-grandmother."

"Yes, I bet she is especially nice," Luca said.

"She is," I said, knowing I would never see her again, at least not in this life. "Oh, Luca, I should also tell you that Dorothy looked almost exactly like Lisieux—much more than she did in the photograph."

"I heard you say that."

"At the end, I saw her as an adult. She's going to be really, really pretty. You might want to pick a different sister," I said, bumping my hip to his.

He burst into loud laughter. "I think I'll stick with the one I have. We have a lot in common."

I joined the laugher. "We definitely do."

We kissed in the reflection of the full moon.

"Though that is something to think about. She is an excellent cook and I do like chess," Luca said, teasing. "Maybe I should keep my options open."

"Watch it, or I'll push you into this pond. It's a lot deeper than it appears."

He laughed. "Fair enough."

The light from the reflected moon faded when we reached the far end of the pond.

"What's that?" I asked, trying to understand what the red and blue lights were, bouncing off the trees.

Luca said, "I don't know."

We continued forward on the trail that went to both our houses.

Sam and Jason had cleared enough of the woods that my house—or at least its lights—could be seen through the trees. To the side, the red and blue lights flashed.

"It's an ambulance!" I exclaimed, and sprinted around the twisting trail, onto the main trail, and on to my house. Luca and Jackson were starting to overtake me. I ran harder up the hill and around the gazebo as the ambulance was pulling forward.

"No, no," I cried out as tears streamed down my face.

We ran hard, but the ambulance was halfway down the driveway before we reached the garage.

Lisieux was there, watching it leave. I fell into her arms. She clung to me as tightly as I clung to her.

I sobbed, "No, no."

In a trembling voice, Luca said, "Who … who was it?"

"Dad," she said, and my knees buckled.

"But he's okay," she said quickly as I dropped onto the rocky driveway.

I stared up at her.

"He wasn't okay," she said. "We thought he was dying, so we called rescue. They worked on him, but things were only getting worse. Then all of a sudden he was okay. Completely okay. Like never better okay. He's inside, eating dinner."

I lay back, the rough gravel pushing uncomfortably against my back, legs, and head. I started sobbing again, unable to control the flood of emotions breaking against me. Fear, horror, relief, dread, evil, good, heaven, hell, purgatory, gratitude.

"I told you he's okay," she said, bending over me and sounding irritated that I was crying.

"It's been a long night," Luca said to Lisieux as he helped me sit up.

I wiped my face with the palms of my hands. The dust of the gravel smeared my cheeks.

"No joke," Lisieux said.

She and Luca helped me stand.

Lisieux asked in an accusing tone, "Where have you two been, anyway?"

I said, "We were in a haunted cave in the middle of an enchanted forest. Great-grandmother Dorothy's soul was stuck, and we helped free her."

"Huh, sounds like a normal night for you two weirdos," she said without missing a beat.

I threw my arms around her. "I love you. By the way, you're going to be totally gorgeous when you get older."

"I'm already totally gorgeous," she said flatly.

"And super humble," Luca added with a laugh.

Forty

"This place is filthy!" Avi said, making a face at the plume of dust floating up from the table.

"It's a cave that's been deserted for over eighty years," Lisieux said as she swept the floor near the entrance. "It's not supposed to be clean."

Avi covered her nose with her left arm. "This table is covered with dust and mouse poop."

"Over eighty years," Jason said, "it's been untouched for eighty years."

Gigi said, "About eighty-five, if my math is right."

"How on earth did they get this furniture in here?" Sam asked, admiring the table. She was using a rag to dust the rest of it.

"Nira's dad helped them. I think he built it all," I said. "His name was Isaac. I saw a picture of him and Gemma on their wedding day."

Sam said, "Aww, that's romantic."

"He must've been a good dad and carpenter," Jason said. He ran his fingers along the back of one of the chairs. "This stuff is extremely well made."

I said, "I never saw any memories with him, but his wife and daughter were incredible and they adored him, so I'm guessing he was pretty great."

"Poor Gemma," Gigi said of her namesake. "She went through so much, losing her husband and then her daughter."

"It wasn't fair," Sam said.

"Life rarely is," Jason said. "It's either far kinder than we deserve or far harsher."

"Ain't that the truth," his wife said, kissing him lovingly.

"Is this where Dorothy was?" Dad said, touching the back wall exactly where Dorothy had been.

"How did you know?" I asked as Jackson and I went to him.

"That's where I saw her," he said, his hand pressed to the spot of the stone where she'd been stuck.

"When you were dying?" Avi asked in her ominous, creepy tone.

Dad winced. "Why do you do that with your voice?"

"She's working on her creep factor," Lisieux said in an irritated teenage way.

"*Creepyyy*, not creep," Avi said.

"Same thing," Lisieux replied dismissively.

Sam said, "It's really not."

Dad was rubbing his hand along the wall as Gigi came toward us.

"My poor mother … being stuck for all of these years," Gigi said.

I said, "She wouldn't forgive herself."

"I'm glad she let go of the guilt," Dad said. He leaned his forehead against the cool stone. "I needed her to be free."

"Isn't it odd how her freedom released all of us?" Gigi said quietly so only the two of us heard.

Dad leaned his body against the stone where Dorothy had been. He said, "It felt like a rope was around my neck, pulling me under the water. I was drowning and there was nothing I could do. But it's gone now. Staying sober is still going to be a struggle, but now it feels possible."

I felt my own neck. The swelling had gone away after the first two days, but it was still a little raw. "I understand what you mean, at least about the rope around the neck part."

Gigi touched the side of my face and said, "Thank you for helping my mother. There is such a lightness to my soul. Without the shadow around me, it's as if I could float away."

"Things do feel very different," I said, noticing how strong Gigi's voice sounded. She was standing taller too, no longer leaning on her walking stick.

Fingering the chipped ceramic vase on the table, Sam said, "I bet the girls had a lot of fun in here."

The three of us turned toward the rest of our family.

Gigi went to the table. "I saw some beautiful lupins blooming near the trees yesterday when I was mowing the front lawn. I'll bring some down next time I come."

I cringed at the mention of the vase and lupins.

"Maybe that's not a good idea," Sam said with a nod in my direction.

"Wild roses," I said. "Nira put wild roses in it, not lupins … never lupins."

Avi said, "I like wild roses better anyway."

Gigi smiled. "Yes, those would be even lovelier."

"And smell sweet. Maybe even sweet enough to cover the smell of all the mouse poop," Avi said, making a gagging noise.

"I don't get how you're so disgusted by mouse poop when your favorite hobby is feeding worms to chickens," Lisieux said with equal disgust.

Jason laughed and said, "She's got a point there."

I went to the table where my sisters were gathered. I gently touched the vase that Avi held. No memories came.

"Are you okay?" Avi asked, studying me.

I kissed the top of her head. "Your hair smells good."

She grinned up at me. "Dad reminded me to wash it."

I pulled her hair back from around her face and said, "I'm glad."

"Me too," she said, throwing her arms around me and Lisieux. She squeezed us as tight as she could.

Near the entrance, Jackson started to growl. Avi released us and ran to him. Luca and I exchanged worried glances.

Jackson snarled and growled as he bolted outside.

"What is it?" Avi said, wiggling out the entrance.

"No!" I shouted, but she was gone before I could stop her.

"Jackson, no," she said quietly as she held his collar. He continued to growl at a large shadow sweeping over the area.

"What is it?" she asked when the rest of us joined her.

Dad said, "An eagle."

"We don't have eagles here," Gigi said as a second shadow appeared, gliding near the other one, followed by several high-pitched calls.

"They're talking to each other," Lisieux said.

She looked so much like Dorothy, it was startling.

Avi asked, "What're they saying?"

Dad held on to Avi and pointed up at one of the tallest trees on our property, a massive pine not far from where we stood. "I think that one is the female, telling her husband to put the stick he's carrying in that pine tree."

"Oh, you're right. They've started a nest," Avi said, bouncing up and down while holding on to Dad.

"But we've never had eagles here," Gigi said with disbelief.

Jason put an arm around Gigi and said, "I think that's changed, Ms. Gemma."

"A lot has changed," Sam said, wrapping an arm around Gigi's other side.

Avi looped her arm through Dad's and grinned up at me and Lisieux.

"Yes," I said, "a lot has changed." I leaned my head on Lisieux.

"I don't think the eagle is saying where to put the stick. I think it's saying 'happy birthday' to Dorothy," Luca said thoughtfully.

We all were silent, gazing at the eagles circling high overhead.

"Yes," Gigi said, "I think you're right."

I took Luca's hand in mine and felt the goodness of our life together. It was far from a normal life … we were gifted, yet we were also blessed. We were surrounded by those we loved—the living and the dead. Their memories lived in us and would never be forgotten. But the memories that had haunted me no longer had power over me or anyone else. Great-grandmother Dorothy was free and so was my family. The shadow that had covered my family for generations was gone. We were no longer tied to darkness. Evil would always be there … always hunting for more prey. It was no longer tied to us, though. We were free.

The End

Author's Note

I hope you have enjoyed *Haunted* and that it has, in some way or another, made you think more deeply about this life and the next. Below is a list of resources I read/thought through while writing this series.

May your life be filled with the good, the true, and the beautiful.

~Jacqueline

Bible verses referenced in *Haunted*

1 John 4

Isaiah 61

Psalm 146

Matthew 10:26-33

John 8:31-32

John 6:22-59

Books

Amorth, Fr. Gabriele. *An Exorcist Explains the Demonic: The Antics of Satan and His Army of Fallen Angels.*

Blai, Adam C. *Hauntings, Possessions, and Exorcisms.*

Lampert, Fr. Vincent P. *Exorcism: The Battle Against Satan and His Demons.*

Lewis, C. S. *The Great Divorce.*

Saint Catherine of Genoa. *Fire of Love!: Understanding Purgatory.*

Thigpen, Paul. *Manual for Spiritual Warfare.*

Thigpen, Paul. *Saints Who Battled Satan: Seventeen Holy Warriors Who Can Teach You How to Fight the Good Fight and Vanquish Your Ancient Enemy.*

van den Aardweg, Gerard J. M. *Hungry Souls: Supernatural Visits, Messages, and Warnings from Purgatory.*

Podcasts

Jimmy Aiken's Mysterious World – Numerous episodes deal with the topics presented in the Awakening Trilogy.

The Joyful Friar Podcast with Father Nathan Castle, O.P. – This podcast helped inform the interactions between Dorothy and Siena.

Luca and Siena's love for the Eucharist is best explained by John 6:22-59. There are numerous other sources related to their belief in the real presence—far too many to list here.

Also by Jacqueline Brown

The Light, Book One of The Light Series
Through the Ashes, Book Two of The Light Series
From the Shadows, Book Three of The Light Series
Into the Embers, Book Four of The Light Series
Out of the Darkness, Book Five of The Light Series
"Before the Silence," a Light Series Short Story

Awakening, Book One
Gifted, Book Two of the Awakening Series

Altered, Book One

To receive your free copy of "Before the Silence," please
join the mailing list or visit
www.Jacqueline-Brown.com.

If you enjoyed *Haunted*, please consider sharing your copy
with a friend and leaving a review.

www.ingramcontent.com/pod-product-compliance
Lightning Source LLC
Chambersburg PA
CBHW051437190726

48289CB00001B/232